DOWNWIND
FROM DEATH

BOOK 3 I SHERIFF ULYSSES WALKER SERIES

C. R. Koons

CAMEL
PRESS
Kenmore, WA

CAMEL PRESS

Camel Press books published by Epicenter Press

Epicenter Press
6524 NE 181st St. Suite 2
Kenmore, WA 98028.
www.Epicenterpress.com
www.Coffeetownpress.com
www.Camelpress.com

For more information go to: www.Epicenterpress.com
Author's website: www.cedarkoons.com

Downwind from Death
Copyright © 2025 by C. R. Koons

ISBN: 9781684922581 (trade paper)
ISBN: 9781684922598 (ebook)

LOC: 2025937038

Cover photo: Black Mesa and La Capilla de la Familia Sagrada by Edward Scheps

Maps drawn by Linda F. Hube

Dedication

For Ridge Koons and Nash Koons

Acknowledgments

I would like to acknowledge my friends Karen Cohen, Linda Hube, and Chuck Wright for reading my manuscript and giving me corrections, copy edits, advice on plot and character, and support and encouragement. My husband, Edward Scheps, listened to drafts read aloud, gave invaluable feedback, and tolerated the many days when I wasn't available to play because I was writing this book. Many thanks also to my editor at Camel, Jennifer McCord and the line editor, Nathan Chu.

Dear Reader,

This story takes place five years after the conclusion of Book 2, *A Thirst for Murder*. Ulysses Walker is serving his fourth term as Sheriff of Taos County. Nine months before the action begins, during the inauguration of Democratic-Republican President Robert McDade, an assassination attempt resulted in the deaths of the Supreme Court Chief Justice and the First Lady. The defeated candidate of the new Nationalist Party, Johnny "Duke" Hadest of Texas, is suspected of orchestrating the assassination and has escaped to Texas, which has seceded from the Union. New Mexico is also facing turmoil due to the death of its popular re-elected governor, Carlos Santistevan, in a helicopter accident, and the presence of numerous heavily armed militias aligned with the Nationalist Party and its religious faction, The Evangelical Church of the Elect. As the story begins, Taos County and much of northern New Mexico remain largely unaffected by the anarchy and violence in the rest of the state. However, that is about to change dramatically.

I hope you enjoy *Downwind from Death*.

C.R. Koons

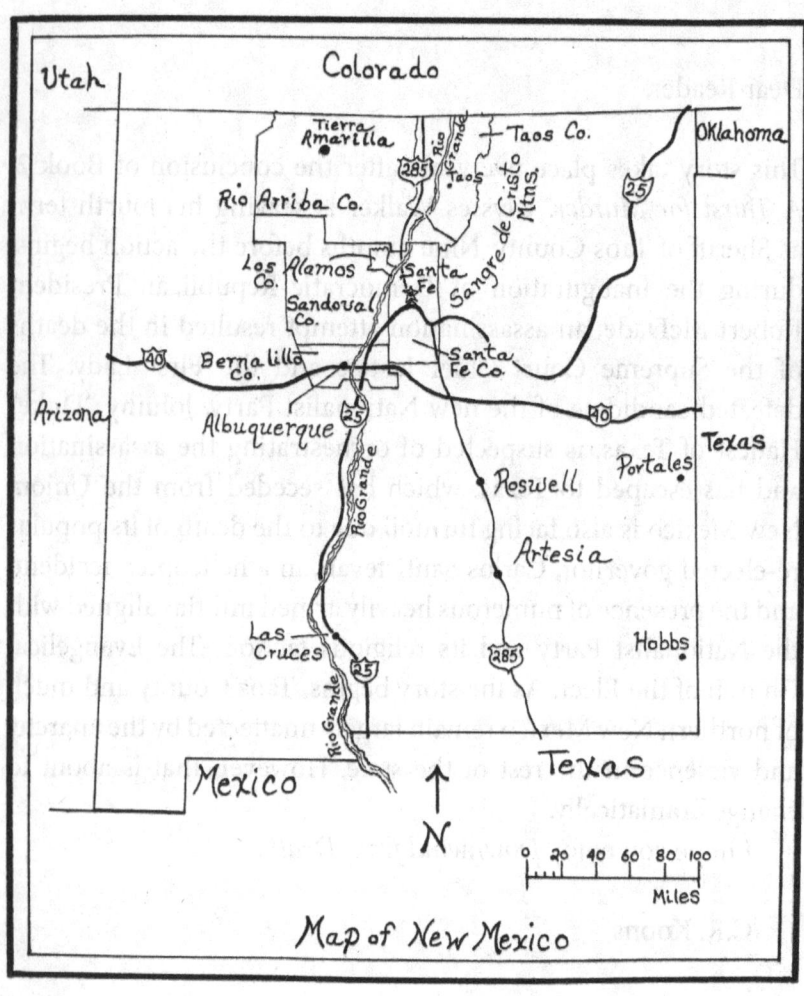

Map of New Mexico

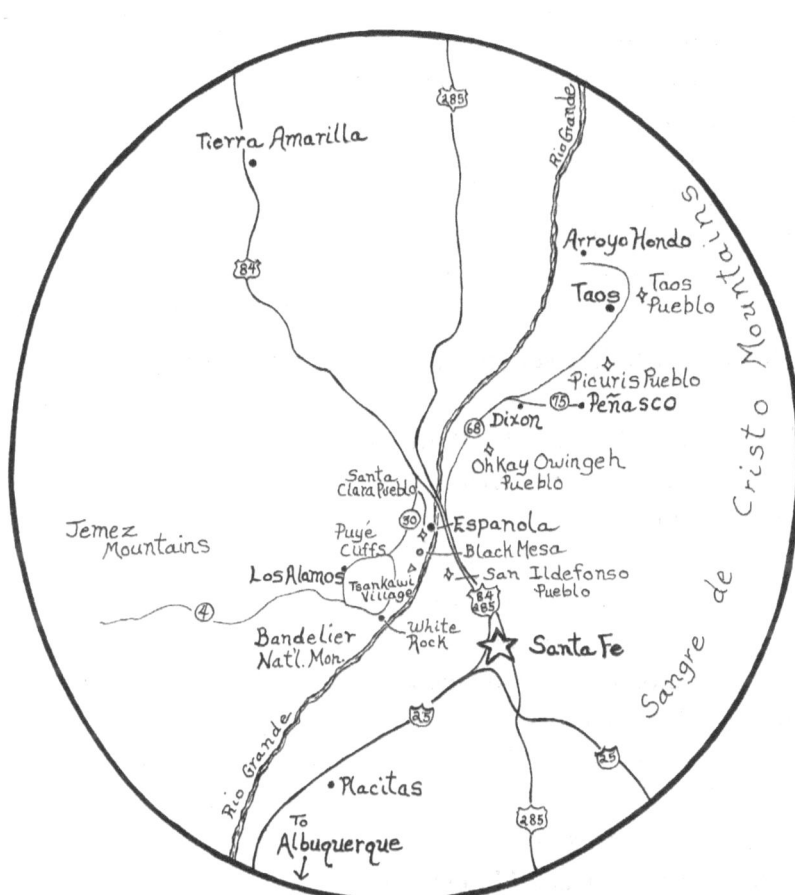

North - Central New Mexico Map Detail

List of Characters

The Walker Family
Sheriff Ulysses Walker of Taos County
Rosemary Walker, his wife
Amelia Walker, daughter, aged 15
Monty Walker, son, aged 13
Frances Walker, daughter, aged 5
Montgomery Walker (also called Monty,) Ulysses' father
    (deceased)
Paloma Walker, Ulysses' sister, immigration lawyer

Taos County Sheriff's Department
Angela Romero, undersheriff
Zach Wright, deputy
Dakota Wilson, 911 supervisor
Michael Jaramillo, 911 operator
Joseph Maes, Taos deputy
Ramona Pino, secretary to Ulysses
Rosie Bischoff, new deputy
Mark Shea (Major Mark), former Taos deputy, now a member of
    the Elect
Marcie Shea, Mark's ex-wife
Patrick Shea, Mark and Marcie's son

FBI Albuquerque Field Office and associates
Nancy Levine, Special Agent in Charge, Albuquerque
Eli Martinez, FBI counter-terrorism cyber expert
LizBeth Tallichet, Deputy Director in charge of northern New
    Mexico
Dawa Tallichet, LizBeth's wife, neurologist
Pema Tallichet, infant daughter of LizBeth and Dawa

Picuris Pueblo
Raymundo Pando, "Ray", Governor of Picuris
Matt Pando, son of Ray, War Chief of Picuris
Sarah Pando, Matt's wife
Micah Pando, their son, aged 7
Billie Arguello, tribal secretary, Picuris Pueblo
Frank and Miguel, War Council members

State Officials
Alfredo Hobbs, Governor of NM
Carlos Santistevan, former Governor of NM (deceased)
Barbara Garcia, Governor taking over from Hobbs
William Gruber, NM National Guard
Sheriff Luis Bustos of Rio Arriba County
Lex Sisneros, NM Attorney General
Acting Sheriff Marjory Blanca of Los Alamos County
Javier Santiago, State Police Chief
Bill Samuelson, Director, Bureau of Alcohol, Tobacco, Firearms
    and Explosives, (ATF)
Sheriff Gary Villalobos of Santa Fe County
Santa Clara Governor Gutierrez
San Ildefonso Governor Montoya
Maurice Baca, Chief of Santa Fe Police
Booth Baca, Chief Baca's nephew

Other Key Characters
Jesse Porter, murder victim
Father Timothy Flynn, parish priest and anti-nuclear activist,
    murder victim
Serena Hurley, activist, and mother
Kaylee Hurley, her daughter, aged 6
Russell Hurley, Serena's husband, aged 78.
Philip Devin, lead engineer at the LANL Pit Production Facility
Monica Lovato, Nuclear Peace and Justice activist
Nick Boyar, LANL Deputy Director

Elena Cadiz Boyar, Nick's wife, and Serena Hurley's mother
Dr. Jonathan Shapiro, LANL Director
Max Castleman, second in command at Elect compound,
Daniel Graves, "the Servant," spiritual leader of the Elect
Isaiah Patterson, an abused boy at the compound
Merrily Patterson, Isaiah's mother
Levi Patterson, teacher, explosives expert and Isaiah's father
David Valdes, an abused boy at the compound
Jacob Graves, son of Daniel Graves and friend of Patrick Shea
Gideon Strum, Elect member and Santa Fe Knights Commander
Pete Dowd, Santa Fe police detective and former partner of
    Ulysses Walker
Cathy Dowd, Pete's ex-wife
Father Dolan, parish priest to the Dowd family
Charlotte Foster, analytic chemist at LANL
Lisa White, social worker, Children, Youth, and Family Department
Johnny "Duke" Hadest, Nationalist Party leader (in Texas, does
    not appear)
Colonel Jack Riggs, commanding officer of Army Rangers
Major Jim Donaldson, second in command of Army Rangers
Katya Sokolova, third wife of Daniel Graves
Lev Kalinin, apprentice assassin

Chapter 1

Father Timothy Flynn said goodnight to his housekeeper and climbed up the dark, varnished staircase to the second floor of his Santa Fe, New Mexico residence. He'd overeaten Josefina's carne adovada and knew the red chile, together with the glass of wine he'd drunk, would likely cause him to have heartburn. Recently, his doctor suggested he lose weight and prescribed blood pressure medication and a statin. *I need to bring down my stress*, he thought, *and overeating won't help.*

Father Tim had struggled to find comfort lately. A persistent fear nagged at him since his old friend and former St. John's College roommate, Philip Devin, had visited. Devin, who had left St. John's their junior year to study at Caltech, worked as the lead engineer on the plutonium pit manufacturing facility at Los Alamos National Laboratory, the weapons facility only forty-five miles from Santa Fe. LANL made triggers for the nation's nuclear arsenal, a process that generated a lot of radioactive waste. Philip told Tim he believed some radioactive materials had disappeared from the production facility, but his bosses wouldn't admit it.

"What is missing?" Tim had asked.

"Stored waste from refurbished plutonium triggers," Philip answered. "Someone could make a radioactive dispersion device with the stuff using the right explosives. A dirty bomb."

"Why are you telling me this?"

"I needed to share this with someone! I can't trust just anyone with this kind of information."

"But what do you want me to do with it?" Tim asked.

"Nothing right now. I wanted you to know in case something happens to me. You have the right connections to get the word out."

"What's going to happen to your job?"

Philip smiled and patted his friend on the back. "You know me, Timmy," he said. "Always on the razor's edge."

"I do know you, Phil. But it's hardly reassuring."

Since the 1990s, Tim had been involved with a nuclear disarmament group called Nuclear Peace and Justice, which monitored activities at LANL. Two years previously, when LANL had broken ground on its 8-billion-dollar trigger facility, demonstrations had erupted in Santa Fe, some of which turned violent, resulting in bloody clashes between protesters and counter-protesters. Concerned about the Church's public relations, Archbishop Guzmán had demanded that Father Tim cease his involvement with the anti-nuclear movement.

Tim had found a way to continue his work secretly, acting mainly as an advisor to the movement. He knew the consequences would be severe if his continued involvement was revealed. "You must focus on tending to your flock, not stirring things up," the archbishop had said. "If I hear you have defied me, you will be transferred and perhaps worse."

After changing out of his cassock and into sweats, Tim walked into his study, a large room at the back of the second floor overlooking a formal garden. Our Lady of Sorrows was a small but elegant stone church built in 1878. The grounds between the rectory and the church included a beautiful heirloom rose garden and a famous labyrinth.

The sun was setting behind the Jemez mountains. The house was quiet, and nothing further was expected of Tim until morning Mass the following day. Usually, this was a relaxing time for him.

Tim closed the door, poured some brandy, sat in his recliner, and turned on the radio. The evening broadcast focused on the news that Oklahoma and Wyoming had seceded from the Union that afternoon, joining Texas. Tim turned off the news, too distressed to listen. National crises have unfolded daily since the last election. He tuned in to the religious station, playing the Taizé music he loved, and increased the volume.

Tim was also troubled by an encounter at Friday night confession the previous week. During the weekly confession period, he usually sat in the priest's booth in the darkened church, waiting for two or, at most, three parishioners to show up, confess their unremarkable sins, and leave with their penance, absolved.

That night, a woman spoke in a whisper in accented English. She did not cry or express remorse. She told Tim she had committed murder and requested to be absolved of her sin. "Absolution requires penance," Father Tim had said, "and your penance is to report your crime to the police. When you have done that, you can come back to me, and I will give you absolution." The woman had left without a further word and hadn't come back. Tim ruminated about the encounter, wondering if he'd done the right thing.

Just before dinner, he'd received an anonymous voicemail. "We know you are still meeting with dangerous leftists," the male caller had said. "We will expose you, and you will be defrocked." Tim couldn't be sure if was the call was related to the woman in the confessional, but his intuition told him the two incidents were connected. The voice on the second call sounded familiar, and he felt sure the man was one of his former parishioners with a foreign-born wife. He couldn't get the thought of this call out of his mind.

The twilight faded into darkness, and the wind started to rattle the house. Tim didn't know whom he could talk to about his fears. Certainly not the Santa Fe Police, whom he'd heard had been infiltrated by a dangerous militia called the Santa Fe Knights. Tim set down his brandy and fingered the rosary in his pocket. Just holding the smooth obsidian beads brought him comfort.

It was chilly in the house. The music on the radio switched to blues guitar. Father Tim turned it off, grabbed a heavy sweater from a hook by the door, and buttoned it over his sweatshirt. The house creaked and groaned when it was windy, but he thought he heard someone downstairs. *It's probably nothing,* he thought. Tim looked at his watch. It was eight-thirty. Josefina had gone home. He went downstairs to make sure she'd locked up.

He came down the steps onto a dark landing. A sodium vapor lamp that lit the parking lot shone through the sheer curtains of the dining room. A shadow flitted across the curtains, and Tim heard the server's door swinging on its hinges. He reached for the light switch at the bottom of the stairs, but before he turned it on, a figure came into the hall, grabbed his wrist, and twisted it behind his body. The priest heard a snapping, electric sound as the man, who wore a hideous rubber mask, pressed something into his chest. Father Tim felt a stabbing pain and fell to the floor, the pressure in his chest becoming unbearable.

He couldn't get his breath.

The deadly instrument continued electrocuting him, and he held his rosary tight until he lost consciousness.

On the same chilly, moonless evening at about eight o'clock, Sheriff Ulysses Walker of Taos County, New Mexico, was almost home when he noticed that the battered car he'd seen on his way to work in the morning was still parked on the shoulder of Highway 522. For a moment, he considered calling a deputy on patrol to check on it. Then he remembered how short-staffed they were since they'd fired Deputy Mark Shea earlier in the week. He couldn't be sure anyone would arrive tonight to register the car, and it shouldn't wait until tomorrow. Resenting another demand at the end of a long and tiring day, Ulysses put on his flashers, turned onto the gravel pull-out, and got out of the cruiser.

A dirty silver Subaru with rust on the wheel wells sat abandoned on the wide shoulder of the rural road. The car had Wyoming plates and an expired registration. One of the back tires was flat, and the vehicle was locked. Ulysses shone his flashlight into the windows. Children's books were littered on the front seat floor beneath a pile of Happy Meal trash. A child's pink hoodie and an empty box of animal crackers rested in the back. Ulysses placed the requisite orange tag on the windshield and returned to the cruiser, where he finished the paperwork.

As he drove, he imagined who had abandoned this car. Most likely, it was a woman without enough money for a tow truck.

Had she called a friend to pick her up? Why hadn't she taken her child's jacket and books? Ulysses mused on the vulnerability of young mothers like the one he pictured. Since the turmoil following the last election and the subsequent economic and social upheaval, he encountered more desperate families who had fallen through the gaps. Some of these people fell prey to proliferating criminal gangs who operated with near impunity in some places. Could that begin to happen here? He didn't think so. This part of Taos County was still relatively safe, unlike Albuquerque and Santa Fe.

In the village of Arroyo Hondo, Ulysses turned onto a gravel road and drove a mile to the driveway of the small ranch his parents had purchased before he was born. A garage, the new pack barn, a goat shed, and a chicken coop came into view before he spotted the silhouette of a two-story house with a gable roof and a wraparound porch that faced the Sangre de Cristo Mountains. He felt the satisfaction he often experienced when arriving home.

The house was mostly dark. His wife Rosemary had probably gone to bed after a busy day selling produce at her Taos Farmer's Market stand.

As he parked in the garage, he noticed a light in his older daughter Amelia's upstairs bedroom. She would turn sixteen just after Christmas and was probably texting with friends. His son Monty's room was dark. At thirteen, he didn't have a bedtime on weekends, yet he still fell asleep early. Puberty didn't seem to have started for him. "I can't smell him yet," Rosemary, his wife and the children's mother, had commented.

Ulysses grabbed his bag and entered the house, locking the door behind him. He removed the clip from his gun and stored them both in the safe. Rosemary had built a fire in the big wood stove, the first of the season, and the house was warm. She'd left dinner on the stove: a hearty vegetable soup and pieces of fresh, homemade sourdough bread. Ulysses, who had already eaten takeout brought in by his new secretary before she left for the day, put the food away, went upstairs, knocked on his daughter's door, and opened it a crack.

"Hi, Daddy," Amelia said, placing her phone face down on her bed. Her face was blotchy from crying. "You're home late. Mama went to bed an hour ago."

"Hi, Bean," Ulysses said, kissing her damp cheek. "What's going on?"

"I'm just texting with Phoebe and Juniper."

"What about?"

"Dad. It's my private business."

"Did something upset you?"

Amelia was used to her father's persistent questioning style, and she answered cagily, "A lot is going on at school."

"Do you want to tell me about it?"

Amelia shook her head and scooted down in the bed, pulling up the covers. "Not really," she said, "I already told Mom. It's okay now."

"Did you get into some kind of trouble?"

Amelia sighed. "I yelled at a boy in my English class. I called him a name. The principal made me apologize, so I did. That's it."

Ulysses took Amelia's hand. He pressed her a little further. "It's good that you apologized. Why were you mad at him?"

"Every day, he interrupts any students he disagrees with to spout his religion. He said a bunch of crap about how girls are supposed to be submissive, so I called him a cult member."

"Oh," Ulysses said, "Is he a member of the Elect?"

"Yes, and he isn't the only one. There are a bunch of them at Taos High, boys and girls. The principal says we should respect their "free speech," but they don't respect us! He called girls 'weaker vessels.' That's when I lost it. I'm only a month into the school year and already hate it."

Ulysses stroked his daughter's shiny, dark hair. "Amelia, I understand that would make you angry. Girls are anything but weak. Still, better not to name-call, right?"

"I know, Daddy," she said. "I won't do it again. But I'm so sick of this."

"Do you want me to talk with the principal?"

"No! Definitely not," Amelia said. She turned off her bedside lamp. "Good night, Dad."

Ulysses kissed her forehead and shut the door. Then, he opened the door to Monty's room. A jumble of clothes, papers, and junk partially cluttered the floor. Monty, wearing only his underwear, lay asleep on top of the covers. Ulysses draped a blanket over him, turned off the light, and headed downstairs.

When he entered the bedroom, Rosemary turned on a low lamp and sat up in bed. She pulled back the covers to reveal Frances on her tummy in the middle, soundly asleep. Frances, five but big for her age, had her own bedroom now, the room that used to hold Rosemary's loom and craft supplies and had once been his sister Paloma's bedroom.

"When did she come in here?" Ulysses asked.

"About two hours after I put her down. She said she had a bad dream. I didn't have the heart to make her return to bed immediately, and we fell asleep."

"You always used to say…" The look on Rosemary's face made him rethink quoting to his wife what she used to say about children always staying in their own beds. "I'll carry her back," he said. "How did the market go?"

"I sold out of everything except turnips. It was probably my best day of the season. They are calling for frost. I had to cover the tomatoes and lettuces when I got home."

"You must be exhausted," Ulysses said.

"I am. You must be, too. I've hardly seen you all week."

"Yeah. Did I tell you I fired Deputy Mark yesterday?"

Rosemary sighed. "I knew it was coming. You've given him three warnings, right?"

"I did everything by the book: warnings, improvement plans, the works. And I documented it to death. But he's still likely to file a complaint, maybe even a lawsuit."

"You can't afford to have a deputy who won't follow the chain of command," Rosemary said. "That's common sense. It would make everyone unsafe. Poor Angela. She deserves a lot of kudos for how she handled him."

"She does. She tried her best, but Mark was so bullheaded nothing would make him budge. In addition to refusing to be supervised by her because she's female, he needled Deputy Zach about eating pork and Dakota in dispatch over wearing a sleeveless top. Once he joined the Elect, it was impossible to work with him."

"Well, Mark wasn't a charmer even before he joined the Elect," Rosemary said. "Amelia had a run-in with an Elect boy at school. She was sent to the principal's office."

"I know," Ulysses said. "I spoke with her about it. He called women 'weaker vessels.' Is that in the Bible?"

"It's in the Epistle of Peter, but it's often misinterpreted," Rosemary said. "Besides, the Elect don't seem to care about the Bible, as far as I can tell. They only care about what 'The Servant' says." Rosemary made quote signs with her fingers. "They never discuss Jesus's teachings, at least not that I've heard. Amelia's new school seems overrun with this bunch."

Ulysses scooped up Frances, who was deeply asleep and limp as a rag doll, carried her to her room and tucked her in. Then he undressed and climbed into bed with Rosemary. Rosemary turned out the light.

"What did Frances dream?" Ulysses asked.

Rosemary sighed. "Bad Rabbit again. This time, he stole her pink hoodie sweatshirt."

"Does she have a pink hoodie?" Ulysses asked, recalling the one on the seat of the abandoned car.

"No. I'm not sure where she got that from."

Undersheriff Angela Romero came into headquarters early on Monday to redo the duty roster for the upcoming week. As supervisor of the six other deputies, Angela oversaw re-assigning former deputy Mark Shea's shifts and recruiting his replacement. She wanted to hire someone to manage the IT upgrade initiated by former deputy Eli Martinez, who was brilliant with tech. Angela thought the sheriff would support paying more for a deputy with the right skills.

Angela had to admit she had never liked Deputy Mark Shea. His interpersonal skills were generally poor, and he tended to blame others for his mistakes. His ongoing conflict with his ex-wife over the care of their teenage son was irritating, and Angela sympathized with Marcie, his ex-wife.

But the real rub for Angela was Mark's disdain toward Eli when they worked together. Eli was a transgender man and a Taos Pueblo tribal member. Angela and Eli had been romantically involved before he left New Mexico for FBI training and duty in Washington, D.C. Once Mark became a follower of the Elect, he began criticizing Angela's "unnatural relationship" with Eli.

"My private life is none of your business," Angela had told him. Just the thought of these encounters could put Angela in a terrible mood, so she pushed those thoughts away.

Ramona Pino, the department secretary, arrived at seven-thirty, bringing cinnamon rolls and a new carton of half-and-half for their coffee. The secretary, talking nonstop to Angela, set about cleaning out Mark's desk, a job he'd failed to do on his last day. In her fifties and married with grown children, Ramona had been assistant to the tribal secretary at Picuris Pueblo for fifteen years and brought skills and good humor to the job. *But her constant talking is driving me crazy,* Angela thought, trying to focus on her work.

Mark's larger cubicle had been assigned to Deputy Zach Wright, who'd joined the Taos County Sheriff's Department simultaneously with Angela. Deputy Zack and Undersheriff Angela got along well. The other staff, except one deputy, Joseph, and the 911 dispatch leaders, Dakota and Michael, were new and green and mostly assigned to traffic accidents and domestic incidents.

As Angela worked on the revised schedule, she struggled not to ruminate about her recent breakup with Eli. Once Eli joined the FBI and moved across the country, seeing each other became difficult. Angela had become concerned as their relationship devolved into texting late at night. Eli worked at FBI headquarters on cyber security and domestic terrorism. He was keeping hours longer than Angela's.

Angela was frustrated when Eli told her he wouldn't take an available FBI job investigating burgeoning criminal gangs in Albuquerque. The pay was the same as he was making in Washington, but Eli had said no. Angela felt he wasn't prioritizing their relationship.

"If you took that job, you could still advance in your career," Angela had said. "And we could be together."

"Angela," Eli had said, "I love what I'm doing now. It's what I've always wanted to do. Can you be patient with me until something better is available nearby? I want to come home, too!" He'd tried to talk her out of an out-and-out breakup. As a compromise, they'd agreed to take a break until after the New Year. But Angela felt the relationship was doomed. It was easier for her to be angry than sad.

Angela had just finished the week's schedule when Sheriff Walker arrived in the office. Instead of his usual pattern of coming into her cubicle to say good morning, he went directly to his office and closed his door.

"What's up with him?" Ramona asked. "He didn't even get coffee or a roll. No good morning?"

"He's just preoccupied," Angela said. "Don't worry, we'll hear about it soon enough."

Ramona answered a ringing phone and sent the call to the Sheriff's private office. "That was a call from the Sheriff in Laramie County, Wyoming," she said. "I wonder what they want."

"Sheriff, this is Deputy Elaine Turpin from Laramie County, Wyoming, calling about an abortion fugitive named, um," she paused, and Ulysses could hear her rifling through papers, "Serena Hurley. She fled the state last Thursday, and we think she was headed your way."

"What do you expect me to do about this, Deputy Turpin?" Ulysses asked.

"Sheriff, we are pursuing her extradition. She left without her husband's consent, and we believe she intends to abort her unborn child. Her husband mentioned that she is eight weeks pregnant."

"Abortion is legal in New Mexico," Ulysses said.

"Be that as it may, Sheriff Walker, in Wyoming, it's forbidden to cross state lines for one. It's punishable by six months in jail and a $10,000 fine."

"Deputy, your travel ban does not bind us here. Until our governor revises his orders, my hands are tied." Ulysses was careful to keep his voice matter of fact. He'd had practice dealing with deputies in Texas who tried to enforce laws that conflicted with the laws of New Mexico. Patience, calm, and firmness had worked so far, and New Mexico hadn't had any armed standoffs as had happened elsewhere.

"So, sir, are you acknowledging that you will not extradite Ms. Hurley to Wyoming?"

"Yes, Deputy, I am."

"Okay, if that's the way you want it. I'll file a report with our Attorney General. Mind if I give her husband your number?"

"Go ahead," Ulysses said, "I'm willing to speak with him." *Maybe I can head off him coming here to harass his wife,* he thought.

"She is traveling with their six-year-old daughter, Kaylee, and the husband is very concerned about the child. He has reason to believe his wife is committing adultery and plans to leave him." Ulysses flashed on the abandoned car.

"Adultery is not a crime in New Mexico, ma'am. But have him call me if he wants." Ulysses had just hung up the phone when Angela knocked on his door.

"Good morning, Sheriff. Did you have a good weekend?"

"I did," Ulysses said, looking at Angela. *She looks stressed out,* he thought. "We took a picnic up to the mountains to see the aspens. They're peaking at the high elevations. Frances loved the grey jays up there. They fly in as soon as the picnic basket opens. One perched on my finger while the children fed it peanuts. How about you?"

"I caught up on rest and ran errands. I came in yesterday to do desk work and supervise the phones. I have to get the ads out for Mark's replacement this morning. What did the deputy from Wyoming want?"

"I received another call regarding a woman potentially crossing state lines for an abortion. I explained our extradition policy, and that was pretty much the whole conversation."

"Anything you want me to attend to this morning, Sheriff?"

"There's a car out on 522 at mile marker 21 that should be towed," Sheriff said, again picturing the old Subaru. "It has Wyoming tags, so it may belong to the woman the deputy called about who was traveling with a six-year-old. There were indications of a child in that car. Can you see what you can find about it, please?"

"Sure, I'll get right on it. I'll arrange to tow the car to our lot today."

"The woman's husband is probably going to call me."

"That should be fun," Angela said.

"I can hardly wait," Ulysses said. Just then, the phone on his desk buzzed. "I bet that's him."

He picked up the phone and pressed the blinking line.

"Sheriff Ulysses Walker," he said. Angela left the room, closing his door.

"Sheriff, my name is Russell Hurley, and I'm calling from Cheyenne, Wyoming." The man sounded older than Ulysses expected. A television played in the background.

"Hello, Mr. Hurley. What can I do for you?"

"Sheriff, I need help locating my wife and daughter. I'm worried about them. Serena's not answering her cellphone, and that's not like her."

"What made you think she was coming to Taos County, Mr. Hurley? The deputy in Wyoming called her an 'abortion fugitive.'"

Hurley coughed. "I'm sure sorry about that, Sheriff. I needed some help finding her, so I told them that. It's all they care about these days."

"So, she's not pregnant?"

"Serena had her tubes tied years ago."

"What kind of car is she driving?"

"1998 Subaru Outback with Wyoming plates."

Ulysses paused. *That's the one we tagged.* "What does she look like?"

"She's short and slender with black hair and eyes, and my daughter looks just like her. Both are real pretty and smart but have no common sense."

"What made you think she came here? Does she have family here?"

"She grew up in Santa Fe. Her mother and stepfather live there, but they've been estranged since before Kaylee was born. Recently, she was in touch with a man named Jesse, who lives in Taos. I think she went down there to meet him. I'm not sure what kind of relationship they have."

The television grew louder as people on the show he was watching began shouting at each other. "Mr. Hurley, can you turn that down?" The volume lowered a bit. "Sir, you can go to court to secure your parental rights regarding your daughter, but you can't control your wife's activities without a court order."

"I know that, Sheriff," Hurley said gruffly. "It ain't right, but that's how it is, and I accept it. I'm too sick to come down there right now and look for her; plus, I'm seventy-eight years old. I only want to know she's safe. I love her, and I love our little girl."

Ulysses softened toward the older man but knew there was very little he could do.

"Sir, I have no current information on your wife's whereabouts. If I hear from her, I will ask her to call you, but I can't compel her to do anything unless she breaks the law. But call me with any information you have, including any contact numbers or an email address for the man you referred to that she's visiting. And you might also call her parents. What are their names?"

"Elena and Nick Boyar. Nick Boyar is her stepfather. But I wouldn't want to call them, Sheriff, unless I must. Serena would be upset if I did that without a good reason."

"Okay, give me Serena's cell phone number, date of birth, and the parents' phone numbers."

Hurley gave Sheriff Walker the information and said, "Find her for me, will you? I'm worried she's fallen in with some bad people."

"What makes you think that Mr. Hurley?"

"It's just a feeling I have. She has not been herself. She's changed. She seems afraid all the time."

"Try not to worry, Mr. Hurley. Be in touch if you find out anything, and I will, too."

Ulysses hung up the phone and mused about the conversation. Serena Hurley was thirty-four years old and married to an almost eighty-year-old. She had been acting strangely and then had run away and might be having an affair. The car would give them some information, but it sounded more like his wife was having an affair than that she had gone missing.

Angela knocked on his door. "Sir, the car is registered to Russell Hurley of Cheyenne, Wyoming. Do you want me to have it towed?"

"Yes, have it towed here," Ulysses said as his phone rang again. It was his old partner from the Santa Fe Police, Pete Dowd.

"Got a minute, Ulys?" Pete asked.

"Sure, what's up, Pete?"

"We had a suspicious death last night, the priest at Our Lady of Sorrows."

"That priest we interviewed a few years back?"

"Yeah, Father Timothy Flynn. It looks like he was home alone, and someone broke in. His housekeeper found him this morning. She swears she locked up, but the door was open. Flynn was found at the foot of the steps. He was killed around nine o'clock that night."

"Anything missing?" Ulysses asked.

"His phone and computer. His wallet was in his pocket with forty dollars in it."

"How'd he die?"

"Not sure, but there were burn marks on his sweater."

"Hmm."

"The body is with the medical examiners in Albuquerque now, and we expect to hear from them soon. Listen, I'm calling because I want to talk about something."

"What is it?" Ulysses asked.

"Ulys, not over the phone. I'm willing to drive up there tomorrow."

"Okay. When do you want to meet?"

"Why don't I come to your office about lunchtime?"

Ulysses tried to remember when he'd last seen Pete. He figured it was five years ago, the time when Dowd, a Santa Fe homicide detective, entered alcohol rehab in Taos. His former partner, a man he'd once liked and trusted, was two days into detox, unshaven and wearing pajamas in a room the size of a cell. He'd asked Ulysses to get him some cigarettes and socks but hadn't had much else to say.

Chapter 2

Ray Pando, Governor of Picuris Pueblo, walked back to his truck parked on NM 75 above the Rio Embudo Box, his favorite fishing spot. He was a little out of breath from his climb out of the canyon but was thoroughly enjoying his day. He had also succeeded in prioritizing what he most loved in life: being outdoors alone with no agenda. He'd just caught and dressed a fair-sized trout. Ray was thinking of going home and having the trout for lunch, followed by a nap.

New Mexico's azure sky spread its beauty before him. A few white billowy clouds peeped from behind the mountains where Jicarita, a high and rounded peak, wore a cap of fresh snow. The air was remarkably clear, even for a place famous for clean air and dramatic vistas. Ray put his rod and tackle in the back of the pickup and scanned the western horizon, his eyes resting on Chicoma Peak, sacred to Puebloan peoples for thousands of years. To its right was Pedernales, a perfect mesa silhouette near Abiquiu, about 40 miles away as the crow flies. Ray relished these views, which he could now see once again with the vision of his youth since his cataract surgery.

Ray believed that having his eyes focused on the horizon was good for his mood. He let the distant blues, browns, and golds sink into his soul. He had been grieving for three years since his wife Clarice had died after a brief but intense bout with cancer. It was only recently that he'd started to have more good days like this one.

Ray's cell phone rang. It was his son, Matt, War Chief of the tribe and father of his grandson, Micah.

"Dad, where are you?"

"I'm on New Mexico 75, near the old mine," Ray said. "I just came up from the Embudo Box. Why?"

"I want you to come take a look at something. Can you meet me at home in about ten minutes?"

"Sure, but what is it?"

"I want you to see it first."

Ray went home and put his fish in the refrigerator. "*I guess you'll be my dinner,*" he thought. When Matt arrived on his ATV, Ray climbed on the back, and they set off up an arroyo leading toward the National Forest boundary.

The trail steadily climbed through piñon and juniper until it reached a hogback, from which people could look down on the pueblo, its plaza, San Lorenzo Church, the old adobe homes, and the new gym, which had opened on the day Clarice was diagnosed.

"How much farther is it?" Ray asked.

"About two miles," Matt said. "We'll cross onto BLM land and then cut back onto ours."

Ray turned up the collar on his jean jacket and pulled his ball cap down on his forehead. They passed the turnoff to a BLM dispersed-camping area and curved around the base of Lizard Head, a prominent cliff face at the end of a long, sinuous hill. On the other side of that cliff was land that had once been a Benedictine monastery and then a Zen Center and had recently changed hands again. Matt began to speed up a series of rocky switchbacks, stopping before descending to a large creek. He turned off the engine. "Now we walk," he said. "Are you doing okay?"

"Fine," he said. Since Clarice died, Matt, an only child, had become very solicitous of his father, but Ray disliked being cared for as if he were frail.

"Follow me," Matt said, "The Rio is kind of deep over there where we're going."

The younger man, four inches taller than Ray and fit from his mountain biking hobby, said, "Be careful, Dad. This is an easy place to fall."

"I know, son," Ray said.

Ray was careful on the loose rocks of the sandy trail, which went downhill at a steep angle. They stopped in the shade, and Matt drank from his canteen and offered water to his father. Then they walked on, crossing the Rio Pueblo on large rocks and arriving at a meadow surrounded by forest where there used to be yurts for cross-country skiers. The yurts had since been moved to higher elevations where there was more likely to be snow enough to ski between them. The meadow was now full of flowering purple aster and gold chamisa. Dozens of piñon jays flew overhead, making their plaintive cries. Ray drew a sharp breath when he saw a twelve-foot-high fence, chain link with privacy slats, at the far edge of the meadow. It stretched away in both directions, tall and formidable.

"What the hell is that?" Ray asked.

"That's what I wanted to show you," Matt said. "When I was up here after Labor Day, none of this was here." They walked through blue grama grass toward a large ponderosa pine that Ray identified as the northeast corner of Pueblo land. A GSPS marker stood at its base, establishing the official boundary. "What does this look like to you?"

"It looks like they've put their fence on our side of the boundary," Ray said. "Wonder why they'd do that?"

Matt nodded. "That's what it looks like to me, too. They built, I'm guessing, about three hundred feet of fence a few feet onto our land. Do you think it was intentional?"

"I doubt it, but hell, who knows? Either way, they are going to have to move it."

"What should we do?" Matt asked.

Ray thought for a moment. "Technically, we are supposed to call the Feds, the FBI. We get them out here and see what they have to say."

"Will we have to go to court?" Matt asked.

"Possibly. Let's call Agent LizBeth Tallichet. She's very familiar with this area. She and I worked a crime here about ten years ago when she was new to New Mexico. Now she's deputy FBI Bureau Chief for northern New Mexico."

"I remember her," Matt said. "I'll call her. I just wanted to show you first and get your advice on how to proceed."

"Thanks, son," Ray said. "That's the protocol."

"Dad, do you want to come over for dinner later? Sarah's making her meatloaf, and you love that."

"I've got a big trout and a cold beer waiting for me in the fridge. Plus, some brownies from The Double Rainbow."

"Okay, well, don't cry lonely to me," Matt said.

"When have I ever cried lonely?"

Matt laughed, "I'm teasing, Dad."

When he arrived home, Ray took a shower and changed clothes, thinking about what he had seen on the mountain. He was troubled by the big ugly fence, let alone that it was on Pueblo land. *What kind of neighbor trespasses with a fence like this? Why would they build it here, in the middle of undisturbed land? What are they hiding?*

Turning away in his thoughts, Ray considered what to cook with his trout. He had some spinach he could steam and an easy cornbread mix, so he decided to pan-fry the fish. None of that would take long. He opened a beer and turned on some jazz. Clarice hated jazz, and Ray didn't like country music, so the couple rarely listened to music together other than the Sunday "native jam" on KUNM.

Cooking had always been Clarice's domain; she was a good cook, though not a particularly creative one. Every night of their marriage, she set dinner on the table: meat, a starch, a green vegetable, or the occasional cheesy casserole, followed by dessert. Not long after her diagnosis of multiple myeloma, she stopped cooking. "I've lost interest," was all she would say. Instead, Clarice stocked their freezer with frozen dinners.

When they'd eaten all the freezer meals, Ray found himself wandering the grocery aisles at Sid's in Taos, curious about foods he'd never tried, like microgreens and pomegranate seeds. He started watching the cooking channels and looking at recipes online. He discovered he enjoyed planning and preparing meals for Clarice even though she was sometimes too fatigued or had little appetite. Ray became interested in traditional Southern cooking and found he could tempt her with spoon bread, okra and tomatoes, flakey biscuits with gravy, fried chicken, and collard greens with ham hocks. He even learned to bake decent apple and pumpkin pies.

Clarice would sit with him in the kitchen while he cooked and take a plate of food to pick at. They'd talk, laugh, or watch television while they ate. Dinner became the event that gave meaning to their days. Then, when Clarice was gone and there was no one to cook for, he lost interest in food for a while too.

Ray wanted to invite a woman to eat with him, but he felt shy. Who would he ask? Would a woman think an invitation to his home for dinner was indecent? Would they expect him to make some move? He wasn't ready for that, and as tribal governor, he had to be careful about his behavior.

Ray had just taken the cornbread out of the oven when Billie Arguello, the tribal secretary, knocked on his screen door with some papers for him to sign.

Ray had known Billie, a widow his age, his whole life. Their children had grown up together, worked together, and he had been friends with her deceased husband. Billie and Clarice had been good friends, and she had often come by to check on them while Clarice was sick. Billie's easy, friendly way put Ray at ease. She had a good sense of humor and an infectious laugh. But she was so much like a sister Ray hadn't ever thought about romance.

He held open the screen door so the stout, smiling woman could enter. Ray tried looking at her with new eyes. She was very tall and broad, with barely any gray in her hair, which she wore in a neat bun. She wore a white blouse, a denim skirt, coral and turquoise earrings, and new sneakers. *She looks pretty good,* Ray thought. *She looks healthy.*

"What you got for me to sign today?" Ray asked,

"The deed to your house. You're signing it over to me," she said, chuckling as she handed him a clipboard and a pen. "It's the grant application for the pickleball court, remember? What are you cooking? It smells good."

"Cornbread. I caught a big trout this morning and planned to fry it with greens." Ray signed the forms and handed them back to Billie, who was admiring the trout, which was lightly floured and ready to be fried.

"You hungry?" Ray asked.

Billie looked up from the documents. "I am," she said.

"Well, set yourself a place at the table," Ray said, turning on the burner under a cast iron skillet. "I'll be just a minute frying up the fish."

While enjoying their meal, Billie and Ray caught up on news and gossip. Billie discussed her daughter Felicia's struggle with infertility treatment, and Ray tried not to mention Clarice, focusing instead on his daughter-in-law Sarah's recent promotion in public relations at LANL. Billie was complimentary of Ray's cooking and said she'd have him over to reciprocate.

"It gets old, cooking for one," Billie said. "I'm used to it, but I don't like it. How've you been doing by yourself?"

"Oh, you know how it is," Ray said. "Today was a good day." He changed the subject. "Matt showed me something this afternoon up on our boundary with BLM. A big, ugly new fence. Some of it trespasses onto our land."

Billie wiped her hands on her napkin. "Tell me about it."

"It's twelve to fourteen feet high, chain link with wooden privacy slats. It must have cost a fortune. It's up there where we have about 500 feet of boundary with the old monastery property."

Billie was quiet for a moment. "Why would they go to the expense to build such a big fence? What do they plan to do up there?"

"I have no earthly idea," Ray said. "I guess they don't want anyone to know about whatever it is, though."

"Does the fence go around that hillside that has the cliff face? You know where I mean?"

"I think it does. We didn't walk that far."

"What are you going to do?"

"I'll call LizBeth Tallichet at the FBI and ask her to come to see it. I hope we won't have to go to court over it."

Billie stood up and started to clear the table.

Ray said, "You don't have to do that."

"It's only fair since you cooked." She knew her way around Clarice's kitchen well enough to put away the clean dishes on the rack and start washing up. "Have you seen any people up at that property?"

"The old monastery property? No. I've not seen anyone there," Ray said. "But Matt says it's owned by something called Western States Resource Group. The Bureau of Land Management is their main neighbor, so why do they need so much "privacy?"

"God knows," Billie said, drying her hands on a dishtowel. "That property has had some strange doings since the Benedictines left. First the Archdiocese with all those so-called "troubled priests" and then that bunch from California, the Sleeping Tiger folks."

"They weren't bad people, really, the Tiger people. Buddhists."

"Well, they sure caused a ruckus though, remember?"

"Yes, I remember," Ray said. "I should talk with Ulys about this, too. I'd like to know what he thinks about it." Ray and Sheriff Walker of Taos County had been good friends and had worked together on several high-profile cases over the years.

"Find out who these people are, Ray. Western States Resource Group sounds like a shell company. And find out what they are planning to do up there."

Ray didn't answer. He thought how nice it was to have a woman in his house. Billie was cleaning the placemats. He never did that.

"Thanks for dinner," she said. "I have an altar society meeting at the church in a few minutes. Maybe we can do this again sometime?"

Ray let Billie out and turned on the television to see if he could find a show to distract himself from his thoughts, as had long been his habit after dinner. Instead, he turned the television off and walked onto his porch to watch the sunset. Ray had already started thinking about Billie. *Would she be interested in him? Was he interested in her?* He had to admit he was, at least a little bit.

Ulysses washed the dishes while Rosemary put Frances to bed, and Amelia and Monty did their homework. The landline rang, and Ulysses answered, surprised to hear the Taos city police dispatcher. "Sheriff Walker," she said, "I'm sorry if I'm not doing this right, but I think I'm supposed to call you if there is a police matter on the Plaza."

"That's right," Ulysses said, "Taos Plaza is under county jurisdiction now. What's up?"

"Sir, a man has been found dead in the rooms above Yosemite Sam's, the tattoo parlor," the policewoman said. "Will you send someone to investigate?"

"Is that the little place that used to be a candy store?" Ulysses asked.

"Yes, the shop is below, and the stairs on the side lead to a small apartment upstairs. That's where the body is."

"Can you tell me any more about it?"

"It's a young man in his early 30s with no visible wounds, lying prone on the rug at the foot of his bed. It appears to have been a break-in, and there are signs of a struggle."

"I'll be there shortly," Ulysses said. He dried the counters and hung up the dishtowel. He then called Undersheriff Angela, who lived five minutes from Taos Plaza, asking her to meet him there. After that, he informed Rosemary of his destination and stepped out into the starry darkness. A fingernail moon was visible near the western horizon, and the night felt frosty.

When Ulysses pulled into the parking lot behind the narrow two-story frame building just behind the central Plaza, Angela had sent the Taos policewoman home and was dictating into her cellphone. Together, they climbed the outdoor stairs to the second story, where the door hung off its hinges. They put on gloves and went inside.

Ulysses looked around the front room and saw a bed covered with a sleeping bag, clothes hanging on a makeshift rack, a tattered, overstuffed chair, and a bookshelf overflowing with paperbacks. Off that room was a galley kitchen with a hotplate and a tiny bathroom.

An overhead light fixture cast harsh shadows on the scene. Shattered glass littered the floor from an overturned lamp, and a white curtain for the room's one window had been pulled down and lay on the floor beside a body.

A young Black man, about five foot eight and slender, lay face down on a shag rug. He wore blue jeans, a grey tee shirt and socks, and a wedding ring on his left hand. His eyes and mouth were closed. His body was still warm, and his muscles were flaccid. He almost looked like he was asleep, apart from the slight blueish cast to his brown skin. Ulysses knelt by the corpse and felt for a moment that he might throw up. *You look like such a sweet young man,* he thought after the nausea passed. *Why did someone kill you?*

Angela watched her boss. She was used to his intense reactions to murder victims. This evening, he seemed calmer than usual. She began taking pictures of the scene and looking around for identifying information among the deceased man's few possessions.

They searched the room but found no phone, wallet, car keys, or laptop, and nothing identifying among the junk mail in the kitchen trash. A laminated sheet provided directions for accessing the Wi-Fi. Above the sink in the bathroom was a medicine cabinet stocked with aspirin, laxatives, antiseptic cream, and band-aids. There was a box of tampons on the back of the toilet. "Do you think a woman lived here too?" Angela asked.

"Maybe," Ulysses said. "But the place feels like an Airbnb -- stocked and move-in ready." He opened the kitchen cupboards, and in addition to plates, cups, and glasses, he discovered a box of breakfast cereal, cans of soup, tuna, baked beans, ramen noodle packets, and jars of peanut butter, jam, and honey. In the miniature fridge, he found a loaf of bread, some tortillas, ground beef patties, a carton of lactose-free milk, oranges, apples, and a bag of ground coffee.

They perused the bookshelf and discovered a Spanish dictionary, cookbooks, road atlases, and several popular novels. Another shelf contained a variety of books, including *Tribes of New*

Mexico, Back Country Cabins, Desert Survival Techniques, First Aid Basics, Surviving the Apocalypse, The Art of War, Principles of Nonviolence, and *How to Disappear.* "Angela," he said, "take a look at these." He selected a few books from the shelf and placed them on the table. "What do you think?"

Angela looked puzzled. "It's not your typical Airbnb library," she answered.

"Did you see a chess set?" Ulysses asked

"No," Angela said, "why?"

"I found this on the bookshelf." He showed her a black rook from a fancy chess set.

"Looks like onyx," Angela said. "It's nicely carved."

"Bag it," Ulysses said, handing her an evidence bag. "I wonder if this apartment serves as a transit house for people coming in to organize?"

"I've heard these folks are around. Are you thinking like anti-nationalists?"

"Maybe. It seems too nice to belong to some random guy. I wonder if the victim was staying here while doing activist work. Based on the books here, I think that's a possibility."

Angela looked under the bed and pulled out a large, battered suitcase with no identification. She opened it up, finding the bag empty except for a leaflet tucked in one of the pockets. "Looks like you may be onto something, Sheriff." She handed him a trifold brochure entitled "Why We Fight/How We Fight," which included manifestos on the environment, racial justice, nonviolence, and the evils of nuclear weapons. The leaflets were unsigned, but an email address was provided: democracyforever@yahoo.com.

Flashing red lights filled the room. "The FDMI's have arrived," Angela said. "I'll go speak with them." The Field Deputy Medical Investigators examined all suspicious death scenes and transported bodies to Albuquerque.

Ulysses returned to the body. He patted down the back, arms, and legs but felt nothing suspicious. He heard people coming up the stairs with a gurney.

"Hello," Ulysses said, introducing himself to the two men.

"Before we go, I'd like to look at the victim's chest."

The men carefully turned the body to face up. There was no blood, but under his shirt, his chest and neck showed burns. There were ligature marks on his neck. Ulysses saw the whole assault as if in a movie, the killer kicking down the door, careening into the victim, and knocking him to the floor as he toppled a lamp and grasped the curtain in desperate fear. The crackle of the taser, the victim crying out for help, and the killer using a wire to strangle him. Ulysses stood up, disgust and anger subsiding into an unfamiliar sadness.

Chapter 3

FBI agent LizBeth Tallichet had just finished a forty-minute treadmill run and was lifting weights when her phone rang. It was her wife, Dawa, with their infant daughter crying in the background.

"Hi, D, what's up?" LizBeth dried her brow and belly with a towel.

"When are you coming home?" Dawa asked.

"Twenty minutes?"

"Can you pick up some takeout?" Dawa tried to quiet the baby's frantic crying.

"I thought you were going to cook," LizBeth said.

"I am losing my mind over here, Liz. Just get some food. I'm starving."

"Okay, I'm coming right away."

When LizBeth arrived home with Indian take-out, Pema, just three-month-old, had nursed to sleep and was lying on her back in her crib in their bedroom. Dawa came out of the shower in her bathrobe and started putting food on a plate.

"Tough day, eh?" LizBeth said.

"Terrible," Dawa said, pouring herself some water. She sat down to eat. "I hope you don't mind if I go ahead," she said. "I want to get some food in me in case she wakes up again."

"Eat, Sugar," LizBeth said, taking a bite of garlic naan. "Mind if I have a beer first?"

"Not at all," Dawa said. "This morning was fine. I took her out in the carriage, and we walked three miles. It was a glorious day. But she's been a little terror since then. I've got nothing whatsoever done on that damn consultation. I should never have taken that on during my maternity leave." Dawa was a neurologist and faculty member at UNM Medical School.

I tried to tell you not to, LizBeth thought. She poured herself a beer, took another piece of garlic nan, and sat across from her wife.

"I had quite the day also," LizBeth said. "This job is one tense, contentious meeting after another. But I'm going to Picuris after my big meeting in Santa Fe tomorrow."

"That's good, sweetheart," Dawa said, shoveling in saag paneer, aloo gobi, and chicken vindaloo and looking calmer by the moment. It took a lot of calories to make enough milk for their infant daughter, who already weighed fourteen pounds. "What were your meetings about?"

"Take a guess—the breakdown of the federal system, as usual. States won't enforce each other's laws, and the FBI is in the middle. Every policy meeting turns into a battle over ideology. I miss basic law enforcement." She took a sip of her beer. "I hope the food isn't too spicy for Pema. I asked for mild."

"It's all mild except the eggplant, which I won't take a risk on. It would most likely make Pema colicky. Any new developments you can share with me?"

LizBeth reviewed the Director's confidential report regarding the rise of heavily armed militia groups establishing themselves in New Mexico, stretching from Artesia to Hobbs. A raid was planned at the Nationalist Party state headquarters in Portales to search for ghost guns. LizBeth couldn't inform Dawa about any of this, as it was classified and would only upset her. The Nationalists were openly hostile towards families like theirs.

"Ray Pando, you remember him. He's the Picuris governor now. He asked me to talk with him about a problem with a neighbor who has built a fence on Pueblo land."

"Are you worried about the meeting?" Dawa asked, getting seconds.

"Just a little curious about what I'll find," she said. "It's usually pretty peaceful up there." LizBeth prepared herself a plate and sat down to eat. Dawa finished her meal, rinsed her plate, and placed it in the dishwasher.

"Do you want me to put away the leftovers?" Dawa asked LizBeth.

"No, but you could sit with me while I eat."

Dawa refilled her water glass and sat back down. LizBeth's job involved so much that they couldn't discuss. Dawa had learned not to ask questions. LizBeth worried that the secrecy created distance in their relationship. They sat in unusual silence while LizBeth ate. She finished her food just before Pema woke up and started to cry. "I'll get her," LizBeth said, picking up a pacifier and a light blanket. She went into their bedroom and scooped up their daughter just as she was crying hard. When Pema saw LizBeth, she widened her eyes, looked surprised, took a big, ragged breath, and smiled. *I love this little girl,* LizBeth thought—*more than I can imagine loving anyone other than Dawa.*

LizBeth wrapped the baby tightly in her blanket, popped the pacifier into her mouth, and rocked her back to sleep.

LizBeth left the house the next day before Dawa and Pema woke up. The morning was chilly and overcast, and it grew colder as she climbed to the capital city's higher altitudes. Snow capped the Jemez Mountains to the west and the taller Sangre de Cristo range to the north, but the aspens remained bright gold. As she drove, LizBeth drank coffee and ate a sausage biscuit while thinking about her work.

LizBeth had served as the deputy director of the FBI field office in Albuquerque for the last four years. She managed the northern part of the state, which included cities like Santa Fe and Taos, as well as small towns, Indian pueblos, reservations, and vast federal lands, including national forests and monuments. She had been promoted after her investigative efforts resulted in a successful RICO prosecution against high-level government and corporate criminals who conspired to illegally acquire water rights, effectively stealing from the region's residents. The case had caused her former boss, who had connections to the criminals, to leave the state in disgrace. LizBeth's new boss, Nancy Levine, was considered intelligent, capable, and fearless. Levine was a strong contender to succeed as FBI Director in Washington once the president resolved the ongoing post-election crisis, which was now in its ninth month.

The crisis began when a failed assassination attempt during President McDade's inauguration resulted in the deaths of the Chief Justice and the First Lady. The mastermind behind the attempt was defeated Nationalist Party candidate Johnny "Duke" Hadest—a billionaire oil refinery owner and two-term Senator. Hadest was widely believed to be hiding in Texas, which had large militias and had recently seceded from the Union. New Mexico remained loyal to the Union.

LizBeth arrived in Santa Fe and parked at the New Mexico Capitol building. Two uniformed state police officers approached her car. They reviewed her credentials, checked her car for explosives, and escorted her into the empty building, which had been closed to the public since the legislature's session had concluded. The officers walked LizBeth down a long hallway with cream-colored walls and a polished marble floor, took her cell phone, and admitted her to the Governor's SCIF, a secure room to discuss classified information.

The SCIF featured a gleaming dark wood table that seated around twenty and included a large interactive screen. LizBeth scanned the room to ensure everything she had ordered was in place before sitting down to review her notes prior to the attendees' arrival. LizBeth's goal was to encourage collaboration among the participants to address the threats posed by Nationalist militias in the northern part of the state.

Most of those invited to the meeting were from law enforcement, government, or the military, including the State Attorney General, Lex Sisneros; State Police Chief, Javier Santiago; Adjutant General of the New Mexico National Guard, William Gruber; and special agent Bill Samuelson of the Bureau of Alcohol, Tobacco, Firearms, and Explosives. The sheriffs of nearby counties, including Santa Fe, Los Alamos, and Rio Arriba, were also invited. The governor was expected.

People began to arrive and take their seats, talking quietly among themselves. LizBeth recognized Dr. Nick Boyar, head of the plutonium pit facility at LANL, chatting with Bill Samuelson of the ATF. Most attendees knew each other, and although many were political adversaries, the atmosphere was studiously polite.

The Governor was late. Governor Hobbs had only been in office for six months, having taken over when the previous governor, Carlos Santistevan, was killed in a freak helicopter accident.

Finally, Governor Hobbs came in and quietly took his seat with his chief of staff. Alfredo Hobbs, a former Los Alamos National Laboratory physicist in his fifties, was a relative newcomer to politics. LizBeth did not know Governor Hobbs well. Her boss had said he was shrewd, secretive, and ambitious.

LizBeth stood up. "Hi, everyone. I appreciate you being here," LizBeth smiled at the polite applause and opened her slide set on the big screen.

"I will talk today about militia activity in the counties we consider northern New Mexico." She brought up a map of the northern counties in the state. "My team and I have traveled to each county to investigate the region's militia activity level. Some of you may have attended Director Levine's briefing last week in Albuquerque, where she focused on the considerable activity in the counties of southern New Mexico, so I won't repeat what she had to say about activity down south.

"Let's start with Santa Fe County. A large militia, the Santa Fe Knights, took root here five years ago during the anti-nuclear protests before the pit production facility was opened at LANL. The Knights meet regularly at their armory and are aligned with the Nationalist Party. We think there may be about two hundred members.

"Militia members also attend a church south of Santa Fe called Flags of our Fathers, which is aligned with the Elect, the religious wing of the Nationalist Party." LizBeth clicked through pictures of the pit production facility at LANL, the Elect megachurch, and several photos of large demonstrations in Santa Fe.

"Members of the Knights have been arrested during gay pride parades, where they sometimes skirmish with marchers. Their leader is named Gideon Strum, a Marine veteran who has served time in federal prison for arson and is originally from Oklahoma. We consider the Knights an incipient terrorist group, one of the most potentially dangerous in the state." Gideon Strum's tattooed face appeared on the screen.

"Santa Fe County also has a Nuclear Peace and Justice contingent. This group, which has chapters nationwide, is estimated in New Mexico to have about three hundred members, mostly in Albuquerque and about one hundred in Santa Fe County. They turn out in force at demonstrations and heckle speakers they disagree with. Some have been arrested for blocking public roadways, violating curfew, or similar crimes. Anything to add, Sheriff Villalobos?"

The short, elderly sheriff with a handlebar mustache who had served Santa Fe County for twenty-five years said, "Nothing about Peace and Justice, Agent Tallichet. The group is mainly a pain in the neck, if you know what I mean. They provoke violence but don't typically carry it out. Most of them are unarmed. However, we must protect them from themselves, which requires manpower. On the other hand, the Knights are large, well-organized, and have infiltrated other state law enforcement agencies."

"Is there an arsenal at the Flags of our Fathers Church?"

"Yes, ma'am."

"How coordinated is the church with the militia?"

"Hand in glove. Church services at Flags double as rallies and information sessions."

"What can you tell us about the militia's illegal activities?" LizBeth asked.

"The street fighting started during the anti-plutonium pit production actions. Last year, we had three fatalities in as many months, plus a lot of injuries. The casualties were all anti-nuclear protestors. We apprehended four militiamen and charged them, but two skipped bail and fled to Texas. The other two are awaiting trial on manslaughter charges."

"Six months of curfews and limits on open carry have not settled things down, am I correct, Sheriff?"

"Well... no. Things haven't calmed down yet, anyway. Limiting civil liberties in the name of public safety gives extremists a reason to argue that the government is tyrannical." A few people laughed. "And they deal in ghost guns as you Feds well know."

LizBeth asked Sheriff Luis Bustos of Rio Arriba County to report on the situation there. Bustos, tall and heavy-set, had a long beard and wore a white cowboy hat.

"Ma'am, as you know, we are a large county with a small population. We have a militia based in Tierra Amarilla that's been around since before the 1967 takeover of the County Courthouse. It's called Los Soldados de la Raza. They seem to care more about local issues than national ones. The members are people whose families have been in El Norte for hundreds of years. I'm not aware of any church involvement. Most militia members are Catholics. La Raza is well-armed these days, but it's more of a Hispano Elks Club." LizBeth clicked through pictures of the historic takeover of the Tierra Amarilla Courthouse in 1967.

"Tell me about the militia in your county's largest town."

"Española's group is known as La Militia. It is like the organization in Tierra Amarilla, primarily focused on cultural issues but a tad more militant. A few years ago, protests erupted over the removal of a statue of Juan de Oñate at a cultural center, during which an Indian man was shot. Española borders Ohkay Owingeh Pueblo, and there are differing opinions about Oñate, a well-known conquistador who was not particularly kind to Indigenous people. However, there has been no recent violence." LizBeth displayed images of the Oñate statue and a clipping from the *Rio Grande Sun* newspaper.

"What about ties to the Nationalists, Sheriff?"

"La Militia has links with the Elect and the Knights in Santa Fe. There is an Elect fortress south of town. It used to be a big, popular evangelical church but became officially part of the Elect after the election."

"What kind of weapons does the militia have?"

"Oh, you know, the usual: ARs, large-capacity magazines, bump stocks, and the like. Some are former members of the Banditos motorcycle gang, and many are ex-military. They all wear sidearms and fly the Gadsden flag. But it's all bluster and mostly harmless." He placed a toothpick in his mouth and sat down.

It doesn't sound harmless to me, LizBeth thought. Moving on, LizBeth looked at her notes. She called on the ATF agent, a Black man LizBeth had previously worked with. "Bill," LizBeth said, "do you have any information on the weapons we are dealing with in Santa Fe and Rio Arriba Counties?"

"El Norte is awash in guns of all kinds," Bill Samuelson answered, "has been for decades. But now, the militias have more military material than you would expect, assault rifles and grenades, even drones. We are closely monitoring the ghost guns operation and have made arrests. Our efforts have been delayed due to the slowdown in the courts."

LizBeth asked William Gruber, National Guard Adjutant General, if he had anything to say, and he shook his head. "Not really, ma'am."

"General Gruber, have you taken steps to assure the loyalty of the Guard?"

"We haven't yet administered loyalty oaths to our troops if that's what you are referring to, ma'am. As you can imagine, it's very controversial right now."

Lex Sisneros, the Attorney General, spoke up. "Why is it controversial? If you are deploying troops to quell civil unrest, don't you want to ensure they are loyal to the Constitution? President McDade has been very vocal about the need to reaffirm oaths."

Governor Hobbs cleared his throat. "Gentlemen," he said, "Let's not argue among ourselves."

LizBeth shifted in her seat. She knew this meeting could devolve into partisan bickering. Too much was at stake to let that happen. Underneath her suit jacket, LizBeth could feel herself break a sweat. "Let's set aside the question of loyalty oaths for now, folks. We'll come back to it."

"This meeting aims to promote coordination for public safety, civil order, and the rule of law. The courts have upheld some limits on civil liberties during civil unrest, including curfews and gun restrictions. It will be our job to enforce them, whether we like them or not. I want us to understand that during this crisis more such limits might be coming. Remember that Abraham Lincoln suspended *habeas corpus* during the Civil War, and the President has the authority to invoke the Insurrection Act." LizBeth cleared her throat, took a sip of water, and changed her slide.

"Due to threats from the Nationalist Party to use radioactive material for domestic terrorism, Congress has allocated funds for enhanced security at our nation's nuclear laboratories, although we have not yet received the money. I will discuss this now."

"What I am about to tell you is top secret and strictly privileged. Classified information is being shared with you because of your law enforcement role in the region around LANL." She read from her slide. "You are strictly forbidden, under pain of federal statute and explicitly under the President's Executive Order, to reveal this information *to anyone for any reason*. Failing to comply with the top-secret nature of this information will cause you to be arrested, held without bail, and tried by a military tribunal." She paused for a moment to let this sink in.

Lex Sisneros raised his hand. "Why isn't Los Alamos Sheriff Marjory Blanca here?"

"Sheriff Blanca was invited to this meeting. Los Alamos Sheriff's Department has remained dangerously understaffed due to the federal indictments of her predecessor. This represents a security weakness in the county that houses LANL."

"It worries me that she isn't here today," Sisneros said. "What about Sheriff Ulysses Walker of Taos? Why isn't he here? Perhaps you are trying to keep this group small for security reasons, but I worked closely with Walker when I was Taos County Attorney, and I know he's very competent. Was he invited?"

"You are correct that I want to keep the initial meetings limited to officials dealing with dangerous militia activity. I have also worked closely with Walker. I'll make note of your interest in including him in these meetings. Mr. Attorney General, I'll continue now.

"As many of you know, building and staffing LANL's nuclear pit production facility brought many new hires to the facility, including technicians, skilled tradesmen, and laborers. Many came from outside New Mexico, with most hired from California, Oklahoma, Wyoming, and Texas. We believe that most new hires, including laborers and skilled tradespeople, came to LANL due to layoffs in the oil and gas sector. Dr. Boyar, Deputy Director at LANL, would you please say more about this?"

In his fifties, Boyar had thinning dark hair, black glasses, and prominent eyebrows. He wore an expensive suit and exuded confidence and composure. "Thank you, Agent Tallichet," he began. "Technical workers have been drawn to us because we offer high wages and relocation subsidies. Many have come to escape the economic turmoil in private high-tech companies that began after the Chinese cyber-attacks three years ago. While new hires undergo background checks and appropriate levels of security clearance, the sheer volume of new employees has increased the risk of infiltration. We are eager to receive government funds allocated to enhance security, and we have already interviewed for twenty-two new security positions.

LizBeth continued, "Thank you, Dr. Boyar. Two weeks ago, using signals intelligence, we determined that domestic terrorists have a foothold in the pit production facility, possibly securing materials that might be converted into a radiological dispersal device, RDD, commonly called a dirty bomb."

Governor Hobbs, showing irritation on his pale, fleshy face, said, "Perhaps, Liz, you could inform everyone that the risk is mostly contained now that we have a suspect, and there's no need for alarm?"

"Of course, Governor," LizBeth replied, "but I must point out that while we've apprehended a suspect, we have not recovered the missing materials or identified additional suspects. That is why Dr. Boyar shut down the pit facility last week—not due to a supply chain problem, as reported in the news media. I'm afraid there is still a significant amount of risk."

"Can you tell us more about the missing material?" Bill Samuelson, the ATF agent, asked.

"What is missing is a large quantity of high-level waste from pit production," LizBeth replied. "It was stolen from a truck on the way to the Waste Isolation Pilot Program in Carlsbad. The material taken is highly radioactive. All that is needed is enough dynamite to disperse it. While we have restrictions on the sale of dynamite, there are stockpiles throughout the state."

The AFT agent nodded in agreement. Murmurs passed through the group.

"What is the latest intelligence about where this material might be?" asked General Gruber. "Do you think dirty bombs might be detonated here in New Mexico?"

"We have some information about where the material might be, but that intel is closely held for obvious reasons. And yes, we believe that New Mexico could provide several prime targets."

The State Police Chief, Javier Santiago, a white-haired man in uniform, spoke up for the first time. "Agent Tallichet, from a law enforcement perspective, could you discuss the main features of a dirty bomb event?"

"Chief," LizBeth replied, "if an RDD is deployed, the Governor will take command and control unless the President federalizes the effort. The National Guard, under the Governor's direction, is responsible for evacuation, establishing emergency shelters for those displaced, maintaining civil order, and coordinating with state, county, and local law enforcement agencies, as well as the Attorney General's office. If the operation is federalized, the White House assumes command and control and deploys the Guard or federal forces for operations."

"Who are your suspects in the theft of the radioactive waste?" Lex Sisneros, asked.

"The suspect in custody is not a new hire. She has been employed at LANL for four years and holds a top-secret security clearance. Her connection to the Nationalists seemed well-established at first, but we now have reason to question some aspects of her history. The investigation is still in its early stages, and we do not yet have an indictment." LizBeth looked at Dr. Boyar, who was already aware of all this information. Boyar remained silent, his face relaxed.

Governor Hobbs looked at his watch, whispered to his chief of staff, and stood up. "Ms. Tallichet, I am expected elsewhere," Hobbs said. LizBeth, surprised at the Governor's departure, asked, "Are there any questions before the governor departs?" No hands were raised, and Hobbs and his chief of staff were let out of the room.

LizBeth continued. "The President has directed me to establish a rapid response team that will meet weekly through a secure platform to receive updates, coordinate efforts, and engage in strategic planning. Experts from Homeland Security, the NSA, and others in Washington may occasionally join these calls. If an emergency arises, the response team will be based at a secure location to assist with command and control. I'm sure I don't need to remind you that, until further notice, monitoring domestic terrorism in your area will be your top priority. Within twenty-four hours, you will receive additional information about connecting with the online team."

"Unless you have further questions," LizBeth said, "we will adjourn. Thank you all for coming and be safe until we meet again."

People began collecting their things and speaking to one another in low voices. A few approached to ask questions, but most left quickly.

Once the room was empty, Lex Sisneros approached LizBeth and shook her hand.

"That was a useful presentation, Agent Tallichet. Naturally, as is often the case, it raised as many questions as it answered. How well do you know the Governor?"

"Not well enough for him to call me Liz," she laughed.

"I am always aware," Lex said in a low voice, "that Mr. Hobbs ran for Lieutenant Governor as a Nationalist and was most likely elected because a third-party candidate took votes away from his Democratic-Republican opponent. Of course, that was before the assassination attempt against President McDade that outlawed the Nationalists. Then we had the helicopter accident that killed Governor Carlos Santistevan three months later." Sisneros looked intently at LizBeth. "Conspiracy theories abound."

"Yes," LizBeth said. "The public is still in shock about Santistevan's death. People are afraid. Social media is full of rumors. When will the inquest turn in their report on the crash?"

"Very soon, I think," Sisneros answered. "It could produce a bombshell."

"Like Santistevan's death wasn't an accident?"

"Exactly," Sisneros said.

"What do you think of the two sheriffs on our team?" LizBeth asked.

"Mixed," the Attorney General replied. "I think Bustos is probably on board with the Nationalists. You know the Party has promised to allow New Mexico to become its own country, not part of the 'New Confederacy.' Villalobos is trustworthy. He has a strong reputation and has been elected six times. But he's seventy and has health issues. He may be unable to keep up with the significant militia in his county."

"His undersheriff is a woman named Ronda Eustace," LizBeth said. "I put her husband in prison for racketeering."

"What's the story with Sheriff Blanca not showing up?" Sisneros asked

"I don't know," LizBeth said. "She was supposed to come, but she's on the outs with Boyar because she got some facts wrong about the suspect we detained for the theft of the nuclear waste. The investigation embarrassed Boyar, and he's turned against her."

"We've been looking into the arrest of the suspect, too," Attorney General Sisneros said. "She's an analytic chemist who is crucial to producing the new plutonium triggers. A few years ago, she was also a whistleblower about safety violations at the facility and is probably on Boyar's enemies list, but they've been unable to find anything implicating her, so she's about to be released, which has made Boyar furious. Sheriff Blanca is probably lying low."

"Do you think Boyar himself may have had a hand in stealing the nuclear waste?" LizBeth asked.

"I couldn't say, even if I knew, which I don't. He's rumored to have ties with the Elect. That's all I know about that."

"Okay, thanks. Good to talk with you, Lex," LizBeth said.

"You too, LizBeth. We should discuss our mutual concerns when we have more time."

Chapter 4

Sheriff Ulysses Walker arrived at the office early the morning after the murder at the Plaza. Undersheriff Angela Romero had already met with the police officer who had discovered the young man's body.

"The city police detective said the gallery owner across the alley heard loud noises in the apartment above Yosemite Sam's, including glass breaking and men shouting, around 7:30 pm. Then he saw a man run down the steps. He wore an over-the-head type mask," Angela reported, "and was wearing all black clothes. Of course, it *was* dark." She laughed. "Anyway, the gallery owner quickly locked his doors and called the police."

"Did he see a car?"

"No. But he said that the man ran west, away from the Plaza."

"Anything on who our victim is?" Ulysses asked.

"The witness didn't know him. I called the owner of Yosemite Sam's, who also owns the apartment upstairs. He said his renter was a woman named Monica Lovato, whom he had never seen. He mentioned that Lovato had someone rent on her behalf: Philip Devin, who claimed to be her uncle. Devin lives in White Rock and works at LANL. The owner was unaware of the victim living there. I called Devin's cell phone, but he didn't answer. I left a call back number and found an address for him."

"Good job, Angela," Ulysses said. "Have they called from the medical examiners?"

"Not yet. I did ask them to let us know when to expect the postmortem. It makes you kind of nostalgic for the old days with Dr. Vigil, doesn't it?"

"It does," Ulysses said. "I knew when he retired, they'd put us into that system. They say it's more efficient, but it's also slower."

"That's for sure," Angela said. "They probably won't have the report until next week. Anyway, I searched through the trash and found a few things." She held up an empty animal cracker box. "There was one just like it at the back of that Subaru."

"There are millions of those. What else did you find?"

Angela held up pieces of a torn postcard. "This is pretty interesting." She handed a piece to Ulysses, which read, "Dear Jesse" in black ink.

"Jesse was the name of the man Serena Hurley was coming to see." Ulysses said. "Do you think that's our victim?"

"Could be," Angela said. "The postcard, together with the animal crackers, got my attention. I'll interview Philip Devin in White Rock and see what I can find."

"That's good," Ulysses said. "Are you hopeful about any of the deputy job candidates you're meeting with today?"

"They aren't Eli," Angela said, frowning. "But they say they have computer skills. We'll see."

"Have you heard anything about this murdered priest in Santa Fe?"

"Just what I read in *The New Mexican*," Angela answered. "Father Timothy Flynn."

"I'm about to get a visit from my former partner at the Santa Fe Police Department. He wants to talk something over with me about the Flynn murder."

"Were the two of you close, sir?"

"He mentored me when I was first made detective. But after the Johnny Catron incident, you know when I killed…"

"That gangbanger?" Angela said.

Ulysses said nothing, momentarily seeing Catron's wide eyes just before Ulysses had shot him. "Right. Well, anyway, after that, Pete and I drifted apart. Then I came up here, and we lost touch."

"Wasn't he in alcohol rehab up here?"

"He was. I visited him, but I don't know if he remembers. He was starting detox."

"I'm surprised they took him back on the force. It must have a strong union."

Ulysses kept his thoughts about Pete to himself. Pete had begun associating with cops who accepted bribes to shield the rich and powerful, which made him hesitant to serve as a character witness for Ulysses during the internal affairs investigation following Ulysses' shooting of Catron. Johnny Catron, the man Ulysses shot in self-defense, was linked to a gang, but his family was affluent and influential. His great-grandfather played a significant role in the Santa Fe Ring.

"Have you found anything further on the young woman who left her car on 522?"

"Serena Hurley? Nothing except an employment record. She had a security clearance job at Warren Air Force Base in Cheyenne, Wyoming until September 29, when she left without notice."

"What did she do there?"

"Secretary to a general. Is that where they house the new nukes?"

"Yes," Ulysses said. "Since Wyoming seceded, everything has gone dark up there. Call Serena's husband and see if he can find any more information about the man Hurley thought his wife was coming to see in Taos. And we should probably try to contact her parents."

"Okay," Angela. "Her father is Nick Boyar, the big wig up at the LANL."

"That's her stepfather, I believe," Ulysses said.

Pete Dowd was still two years away from retirement, but Ulysses was taken aback by how old he appeared when he arrived at the office with a cup of black coffee and a bag of French fries. He was stooped and sallow, with thin arms and legs and a prominent abdomen. He reeked of cigarettes. The two men shook hands, and Pete sat on the couch while Ulysses rolled the chair out from behind his desk. He remembered how Pete had seemed when he first met him: ruddy, robust, and funny. He had been a family man back then, raising two sons. *Once Cathy divorced Pete, it was all downhill,* Ulysses thought.

"How are you doing, Pete?"

"What you see is what you get, bro."

"What does that mean?"

"Not great. But that's not why I'm here."

"Okay. What can I do for you?"

"I need your help, Ulys," Pete said, "I've got a big problem."

Ulysses took a deep breath. "Tell me about it."

"It's our high-profile murder. Turns out Father Timothy Flynn was tasered into that massive heart attack."

"I thought as much when I heard about the burns on his chest."

"So, my taser is missing, and my supervisor is up my ass about it."

"When did you have it last?"

"The day of the murder. It's a high-voltage model I've kept for protection since I first got sick. I put it back in my equipment locker at work before going home."

"How is your locker secured?"

"A combination lock. You know me, Ulys, I'm old school. And the lock is intact. I put it back where it belonged, and now it's gone."

"Hmm. Does anyone know that combination?"

"No way."

"Have you looked for prints?"

"The room is on restricted access. They are fucking with me, Ulys."

"Would anyone think you were on the outs with Flynn?"

"I liked the guy. I went to his church. But once, I called him a Blue Pill. It's a Matrix thing for someone who doesn't see reality. A lot of people heard me say that. Remember when we questioned Flynn?"

"Yeah, I remember. I thought he was a nice guy."

"I can't even remember why we questioned him," Pete said.

"A man accused Flynn of pushing him at an anti-nuclear protest. There was a stampede, and the man fell and broke his tibia. I didn't believe the guy, but you did, so we called on Father Flynn at the rectory."

"Yeah, now I remember. I got irritated with his politics. The guy was a serious lefty. I said a few things. But he didn't go for the bait. That was just before Cathy left."

"Yeah," Ulysses replied. "It was three years before I came up here. So, what are your politics these days, Pete?"

Pete shook his head. "I haven't thought about politics since well before the election. I was diagnosed with liver cancer a year ago last week."

"Does anyone know about your health situation?"

"Yeah, some do. Some of the old gang."

Your dirty cop friends, Ulysses thought.

"What do you know about Flynn's political involvement?"

"I think the archbishop put the kibosh on his anti-nuke stuff several years ago. But I've learned that he was secretly serving as an advisor to Nuclear Peace and Justice all along."

"How did you find that out?"

"He had a bunch of names in a notebook in his desk drawer and notes on recent conversations."

"What did he advise them about?" Ulysses asked.

"He was helping them find housing and support for the activists they brought into town and training them for community organizing. Most were your typical peaceniks, but some are considered more radical, like the members of the Malcolm X Brigade. You know, 'by any means necessary.'"

Ulysses thought of the young man whose body he'd found the night before.

Pete paused a moment. He pulled out a cigarette, looked at it, and put it behind his ear. "The force is riddled with Nationalists and Knights, and Flynn was working with Nuclear Peace and Justice. That's approaching motive, right?"

"Isn't it illegal for police to be in a militia?" Ulysses asked.

"Nobody enforces it. Hell, our chief is a Knights commander."

"Baca is openly in a militia?"

"Hell, yes. I used to be, too, but I choked on the religion part. I'm an old-fashioned Catholic. I don't like all that Elect crap."

"Did you part with the Knights on good terms?"

"So far as I know."

"So, they think a high-voltage model killed Flynn?" Ulysses asked.

"That's what they are saying."

"Okay, but Pete, what does this have to do with me?"

"Ulys, I'm being framed. I just needed to talk to someone who knows I'm not that kind of cop." Pete leaned his head against the couch cushions. "I can't handle the stress of this situation."

"Who could be setting you up?"

Pete sighed deeply. "You know, Ulys, my workplace is full of bad cops. It could be anyone. If they'd kill a priest like Father Tim, they'd do anything. You know what I'm saying?"

Ulysses stood up and began to pace behind his desk. "Why would somebody kill Father Tim, do you think?" he asked. "Just because of his anti-nuclear stance?"

"To send a message? Like, don't resist us? Or maybe he knew something?"

"Does anyone have a grudge against you? A score to settle?"

"Not really. I go along to get along. But maybe they need a scapegoat. And now that I'm sick…" His voice faded, and he looked scared. "I have to find out how they got into my equipment locker."

Ulysses sat back down. "I wish I could be more help, Pete. I'll keep my ear to the ground for anything. But you should get a lawyer. See if you can access your locker. Look for prints. And keep me posted, okay?"

"Thanks for the support, Ulys," Pete said. "You've got a nice scene up here. I thought you were crazy to move back here and run for sheriff, but it's worked out good for you." He rose to his feet. "I appreciate you listening to me. I'll let you get on with your work now." Pete left Ulysses' office, waving goodbye and leaving his meal trash on the floor by the couch.

Ulysses threw the trash in the covered can and opened his south-facing window to let in some sun and fresh air. The visit with Pete made him sad. *There is hardly anything more depressing than burned-out law enforcement,* he thought. *I hope I get out of this profession before it hollows me out like him.*

Ulysses ate the lunch Rosemary had packed, then closed his door and stretched out on the couch for his daily power nap.

He started counting his breath and quickly drifted off to sleep. Ulysses began to dream.

Ulysses had been having disturbing and significant dreams for years. He'd tried ignoring them, hypnosis, and psychotherapy; he even put a rose quartz crystal under his pillow, but nothing had worked. The last method he'd learned about involved trying to recall every aspect of a dream he could, writing it down in detail, and then waiting for it to reveal its meaning. He took his dream journal out of his desk drawer and began writing about his dream.

It is midday, and the UV rays are intense. I am with my father, but he looks different -- younger and thinner than I remember. He appears irritated with me, or perhaps he is terrified. We are searching for someone on a high mesa with Anasazi ruins. A hot, dry wind blows around us. Overhead, a helicopter circles, and someone shoots at us. My father transforms into Pete and yells, "I told you these people would kill us." Then, a huge fire erupts around us, and I wake up.

He put his journal back in the desk drawer and locked it. He reflected on the connection between his father and Pete Dowd. Pete had been a mentor who ultimately let him down. He became a drunk and a liar, failing to stand up for Ulysses when he needed it. Did *Dad let me down?* Ulysses wondered, recalling how, in Monty's final years, Parkinson's had diminished his already fragile grip on a bad temper. He remembered his father hitting him in the face once when he was a teenager. Ulysses had forgiven his father, but he had been disappointed by him countless times.

"He was always hard on you," Rosemary often said. Ulysses couldn't make sense of anything else about the dream other than it being one of his warning dreams.

Ulysses stepped into his bathroom, splashed cold water on his face, checked his teeth, and dusted crumbs off his shirt. He recalled the high mesa from his dream and knew he'd been there before, maybe in childhood.

As Ulysses stepped out of his bathroom, a knock sounded at his office door. He was surprised to see LizBeth Tallichet, an old friend he had worked with on a few cases but hadn't encountered in several years.

"Howdy, Stranger," LizBeth said. "Got a minute?" Ulysses noted crows-feet around her blue eyes and a hint of grey in her blonde hair. She came in. "It's been too long," she said.

Ulysses hugged her, and the two briefly discussed family news. LizBeth showed him pictures of Pema on her phone, and Ulysses shared news of Frances, who was a toddler when they last visited.

"What brings you to Taos?"

"I was just up at Picuris and thought I'd drop in on you before heading home."

"What's going on at the pueblo?"

"Ray and Matt Pando asked me to look at an encroachment on one of the reservation's borders. You know Ray is tribal governor now."

"Yeah, I know. Matt's been War Chief for several years. What kind of encroachment is it?"

"They have new neighbors at the old Sleeping Tiger property. Western States Resource Group, an LLC from Portales, New Mexico, purchased it two years ago, and they've been on a construction spree. Recently, Matt noticed that they had erected a twelve-foot-tall chain-link fence with razor wire and privacy slats. The issue is that about 300 feet of the fence is situated on Picuris land."

"Hmm," Ulysses said, "who are these people?"

"A shell company, I think. The name is associated with an oil and gas outfit in southeastern New Mexico and west Texas."

"Do you think the fence was just a stupid mistake or what?"

"Could be. The ground is steep and rocky on their property line, and maybe they thought it would be easier to trespass a bit and erect a fence on Indian land."

Ulysses laughed. "Yeah, that's always a good idea. So, what are you going to do?"

"I've scheduled a meeting with their administrator," LizBeth said, glancing at her phone. A man named Max Castleman. I'm meeting with him tomorrow, along with Matt and Ray. Would you be able to attend?"

"Why do you want me there?" Ulysses asked.

"A shell company building over the Picuris boundary is worrisome enough. Seeing their massive fence made me wonder what they might be hiding." LizBeth said.

"This morning, I convened a meeting at the Roundhouse about Nationalist activity here in the north. A lot is going on, Ulys. I need your insights. If you come with me, Ray, and Matt tomorrow, we can meet this man and get more information."

"Okay, you got it. What time?"

"Eleven o'clock. Let's meet at the Double Rainbow."

"What was this meeting about militias all about? Who was there?"

"I'll have to read you in to talk more about it. After we look at this Resource Group bunch, I'll do that. But for now, let's say that the post-election chaos has come to El Norte in a big way."

Ulysses thought about the young Black man whose body was still warm when he found it. "Yeah, I'm starting to realize that, too," he said.

Chapter 5

White Rock, a bedroom community for Los Alamos National Laboratory, stood above the Rio Grande gorge in Los Alamos County, southwest of Taos. Angela was out of the Taos County jurisdiction, but she'd informed Acting Sheriff Marjory Blanca of her plans to come to question Philip Devin. She'd heard nothing back from Blanca, who had the reputation of being out of her depth in her new role.

Angela discovered Devin's address on a cul-de-sac and pulled into the driveway of a passive solar house that was set back on a large lot surrounded by native shrubs and grasses. A for-sale sign and a POD moving and storage unit stood out front. Parked in the driveway was a black Tesla with tinted windows. Angela exited her official car and stretched, admiring the mountain view. She approached the front porch, where an expensive mountain bike was locked on a rack. Angela rang the doorbell.

A white man with a trimmed beard and light blue eyes opened the door and looked at her uniform, badge, and the deputy's cruiser parked in his driveway.

"Are you Philip Devin?" she asked. The room behind him was minimally furnished and held stacks of moving boxes. Soft flute music was playing on a sound system.

"I am," said Devin. He was about fifty and wore yoga pants and a sleeveless shirt that accentuated his muscular arms. His thick grey hair was pulled back into a ponytail, and his feet were bare.

"May I come in and ask you a few questions?"

"What is this about?" Devin asked.

"It's about an apartment you rented for someone named Monica Lovato."

Devin held the door open for Angela as she followed him into the living room, where he had been packing books from a shelf. A wood fire crackled in the fireplace, and on the mantle sat a statue of a fierce-looking, many-armed Indian god. Devin turned off the music and offered Angela a seat on the leather couch while he took a seat in a swivel chair. A jar of cannabis and a clay pipe rested on the coffee table next to a French press filled with coffee and two mugs. *Was someone else here?*

"Six months ago, you rented an apartment for a Monica Lovato above the tattoo parlor Yosemite Sam's. Is that correct?"

"Yes."

"You told the landlord she is your niece. Is that correct?"

Devin smiled briefly. "Guilty. No, she isn't my niece. She is just a friend."

"Why did you rent an apartment for her, Mr. Devin?"

"I did it as a favor. She travels a lot for work. This apartment would get snapped up before she could get home to secure it."

"What is her employment?"

"She's a consultant."

"Who does she consult to?" Angela asked.

"Different folks," Devin answered, crossing his legs.

"Could one be 'Nuclear Peace and Justice'?"

"Maybe. She's a lefty."

"Mr. Devin, a man was murdered in that apartment last night. A young Black man named Jesse. Did you know him?"

Devin scratched his chin and then shook his head. "No. I've never met any of the activists who use the apartment."

"Do you know the names of any of her political associates?"

"Not really."

"Do you know where she might have gone?"

"Monica has connections all over the Southwest," Devin said. "Much of her work used to be in Texas, but she doesn't go there anymore. She may be in California."

"How can I get in touch with her?"

"She's asked me not to give anyone her number," Devin said.

"When you talk with her next, will you ask her to call me?" Angela gave Devin her card.

"Of course. She's not a suspect, is she?"

"No, she's not a suspect. But I'd like to talk with her. Do the two of you talk frequently?"

"Now and then," Devin said nonchalantly. *Is Devin her friend? Or are they political colleagues? Or are they lovers?* His hooded blue eyes revealed nothing.

"Please ask her to call me," Angela said, standing. She looked around the empty room. "Are you moving?"

"I just sold this house," Devin answered.

"What do you do at LANL?" Angela asked. "Just curious."

"It's classified," Devin said. He smiled.

"Why aren't you at work?"

"I'm on leave right now. I'll return to work in a week or so."

As she walked to her car, Angela felt chagrined that she had not extracted more information from Devin. In the car, she listened to a voicemail from Taos Deputy Zach Wright: "Sheriff wants you to call on Elena and Nick Boyar down in Santa Fe, at 900 Tano Road. They are expecting you."

On the drive to Santa Fe, Angela thought about her encounter with Philip Devin. With his yoga attire, flute music, and cannabis pipe, he didn't seem like the typical buttoned-up LANL engineer.

Was someone else there at the house, and if so, who? Devin had shown no surprise about a murder at Lovato's apartment, leading Angela to believe he already knew about it. He was very cagey about Ms. Lovato and Angela and mused about what the two might have in common. *It's probably sex,* she thought.

The Boyar residence was an Italianate villa on Santa Fe's north side. It was high on a ridge with spectacular views, landscaped gardens, and two attached garages built to look like stables.

I bet it gets windy up here, she thought as she parked and climbed the steps to a sheltered portico where one of the enormous front doors was already open. A man wearing a fitted shirt, black pants, and an embroidered vest stood in the doorway waiting for her. *The butler,* Angela thought, noting with annoyance that the man was Hispanic, probably Mexican. *Why do these Anglos always have brown servants,* she wondered. Then she paused. *I'm starting to sound like my father.*

Angela's father, who came from an old, well-off Hispanic family, despised Anglos. Her mother, who grew up relatively poor in Mora County, had no prejudices Angela knew about, but Catalina Romero, her mother, had disappeared when Angela was twelve.

"Good afternoon, Deputy," said the man with a slight bow. "Señora Boyar will greet you in the salon."

"Thank you. Is Mr. Boyar at home?"

"He will join you when his meeting ends," the butler said. He led the way into a large conservatory that rose two stories surrounded by a balcony walkway. The conservatory was full of potted orange, lemon, and palm trees. An ornate staircase led to the second story. Behind the stairs, west-facing windows filled the rooms below with light.

Angela was struck with the elegance of the space, especially a dripping marble fountain surrounded by flowering gardenias that looked like it could have come from a plaza in Seville. A long salon and a massive carved travertine fireplace were on the other side of the fountain. A petite, slender woman in a white cashmere dress was waiting for her.

"Hello, Undersheriff Romero. Thank you for coming so quickly. I am Elena Cadiz Boyar," she said with a slight Spanish accent. "Please come in and be seated." She indicated a fawn suede couch with multiple colorful pillows. Mrs. Boyar sat on an identical couch opposite Angela, a low coffee table between them. An antique Art Deco silver service and a plate of tea sandwiches stood waiting on the table. Mrs. Boyar seemed anxious.

"I know you have probably missed your lunch, Undersheriff. I asked Enrique to have Cook prepare some sandwiches and tea." The butler appeared and poured two cups before Angela could catch her breath. *Daddy would have loved this place,* she thought. On the other hand, Angela tended to be suspicious of the very rich.

"You shouldn't have gone to so much trouble," Angela said.

"But thank you; I did miss lunch!" She placed a couple of small triangular sandwiches on a plate.

"Please, please eat," Mrs. Boyar said. "I will tell you why I called you."

Angela sipped her tea and regarded the woman across from her. She was of indeterminate age and stunningly pretty, with jet-black hair in a perfect chignon, an aquiline nose, and full lips.

"I'm sorry Mr. Boyar isn't here yet. He had to be on a conference call. He is in management at LANL. There is always something urgent up there that takes him away! But he wants me to go ahead without him." You see, Undersheriff, we heard last night from my daughter's husband," Mrs. Boyar said. "Serena and my granddaughter are somewhere here in New Mexico. Perhaps you know this? Mr. Hurley worries she may have taken up with another man. I haven't seen my daughter in some years and, of course, I've never met her husband, who is quite elderly. I have never even seen their child, my granddaughter." Mrs. Boyar took a sip of tea.

"May I call you Angela?" she asked.

"I prefer Undersheriff Romero," Angela said, wiping her hands on a napkin.

Ms. Boyar nodded, clasping her hands tightly. "Ms. Romero, we know the sheriff is aware Serena is missing. We don't understand why he never contacted us."

"Ma'am, her husband said you were estranged."

"Estranged? Is that what he called it? Are you not concerned that she abandoned her car and hasn't been seen since?"

"Your daughter has privacy rights, and we cannot reveal anything about her to others without her consent. Her car was abandoned late on Friday, and we had it towed to our lot on Monday. Today is Wednesday."

"It's too long. Anything could have happened by now! I am so apprehensive about her and my grandchild." Mrs. Boyar offered the plate of sandwiches again. "Please," she said, "don't go hungry."

Angela, feeling sheepish, took two more of the delicious little sandwiches while Mrs. Boyar poured them more tea.

"Serena," Mrs. Boyar said, "is a reckless girl. I'm not sure she can care for herself or a child. And my husband thinks she has fallen in with the wrong crowd."

"When did you last see your daughter?"

"Seven years ago." Her eyes filled with tears.

"What caused the two of you to fall out?" Angela asked.

"Serena was always troubled. My first husband and I fled Venezuela during the Chávez regime. Serena was an infant. Rafael died suddenly when Serena was only six years old. She was very close to her papa and never recovered from his death. She refused to accept my new husband when I remarried. Nicholas, Mr. Boyar, treated her like a princess, but she wasn't satisfied. She hated him! I'm told this is not uncommon. She dropped out of high school and ran away at sixteen."

"What caused her to run away?" Angela asked.

"An older boy she met in town. They went to Wyoming, where the boy found a job in the oil fields. Of course, the romance didn't last, so she took herself to Chicago, where I think she lived on the streets. We weren't in touch until my mother died. Serena loved her abuelita, so she came home for the funeral. But after that brief visit, we haven't spoken again."

"How old was Serena when you last saw her?"

"Twenty-one. At the funeral, she was pregnant. Her child is now almost seven. My only grandchild." Mrs. Boyar dabbed at her eyes with a tissue.

A uniformed maid picked up the teacups as Nick Boyar entered the room, shook hands with Angela, and sat on the couch next to his wife.

"I'm sorry I couldn't join you earlier," Boyar said. "Something urgent came up at work. Has my wife told you about Serena?" He took his wife's hand and caressed it.

"A little, Mr. Boyar," Angela said. "It sounds like you and Serena didn't get along?"

Elena pulled her hand away from her husband. He leaned

back on the couch and crossed his legs. "Serena was a challenging girl at times," he said, "but I loved her. I still do. We want to find her and reconcile, right, darling?"

Elena nodded.

"We are also concerned about our granddaughter," Boyar said.

"What do you know about her current situation?" Angela asked.

"Serena's husband says she quit her job without notice," Boyar said. "He was quite concerned, the poor man. He also mentioned that she took their child out of daycare and drove down here alone to meet a man named Jesse, who is likely one of those leftist agitators we seem to attract around here."

"Has Serena always been political?" Angela asked.

"She was always suggestible, but I never knew her to be an activist," Boyar said. "Did you, darling?"

Mrs. Boyar shook her head no but again said nothing.

"But she was promiscuous, sadly," Boyar continued. She showed poor judgment with boys and later with men. She is probably traumatized from her time in Chicago in her late teens. We believe she engaged in sex work there."

Mrs. Boyar wiped away the tears. "I want to help her," she said. "I want us to go to therapy."

Her husband nodded sympathetically, reaching toward his wife, who gently scooted away from him. "Will you try to find her?" Boyar asked. "I don't want her to fall into the wrong hands again."

"We are looking into it, Mr. and Mrs. Boyar. But I can't promise you anything."

"Gracias, Ms. Romero," Elena Boyar said. "If you can locate her and let us know, I'll be very grateful."

Angela walked out to the cruiser and began the drive toward Taos.

She wondered about Elena Boyar's motives for finding her daughter. A confusing mix of regret and fear seemed to pull at Mrs. Boyar, causing her to withdraw from her husband. What did Boyar mean about Serena falling into the wrong hands again? *I have a lot of research to do,* Angela thought, feeling sad that her former boyfriend Eli wasn't around to help.

When Angela returned, she met with Ulysses to tell him what she'd learned from her two interviews.

"Philip Devin sounds like an interesting character. He works at LANL but smokes pot and has a statue of Shiva on his mantle. Let's get more intel on him. You had a hunch there might be something between him and Monica Lovato?" Ulysses asked.

"It was only a hunch," Angela said. "He is very attractive."

"What was your impression of the Boyars?"

"Mrs. Boyar appears emotionally wrought up. She is clearly pampered, but she seemed to shrink when her husband joined us. He was attentive to her, yet their relationship felt conflicted to me."

"Have you received anything from the medical examiner on Jesse Porter's cause of death?"

"Not yet."

"How are the job interviews going?"

"I've found someone I'll probably hire," Angela said. "Her name is Rosie Bischoff, and she's been a deputy in Santa Fe for three years, primarily dealing with minor crimes. She holds a computer science degree from UNM and wants to relocate here to be closer to her family. She's 26, and her references check out."

Ramona knocked on his door. "Sheriff," she said, "there is a man here to see you. He says he drove here from Wyoming. His name is Russell Hurley. Can you speak with him?"

"Okay, send him in," Ulysses said, giving up on his plan to make it home before dark.

Russell Hurley was tall and broad, with a square, ruddy face and thick white hair. He wore a baseball cap that read "Vietnam Veteran" and carried a battered briefcase. He sat in a straight-backed chair that creaked under his weight. Angela introduced herself, and he stood up politely to offer her a handshake.

"Thank you for meeting with me, Sheriff, and Ms. Romero," he said. "I'm staying in town tonight, so if you'd rather I came back in the morning, I will."

"No, this time is good. What can I do for you?"

"Well, Sheriff, I came to pick up my car for one thing. I just turned in my rental car, so I need it."

"We can take care of that, Mr. Hurley. I'll get my deputy to show you to our lot. I'm not sure the car is operational."

"Thank you, kindly," Hurley said. "I can at least have it towed to a garage."

"What else do you need?"

"I want you to help me find my wife. I did a little research and have some information. I brought you this." He opened the briefcase and placed a laptop computer on Ulysses' desk.

"This is Serena's," he said. "I didn't even know she had it. But I found it in a box of things she must have forgotten to put in her car. She left in an all-fired hurry. "I used to be an independent insurance adjuster and have some investigative skills. However, I'm not very good with electronics, so I had a former employee, a man I trust, check the computer for me."

Hurley opened the laptop and typed in a code. The opening screen showed a picture of Hurley, his arm around a beautiful young woman holding a pretty child, both with black hair and eyes and dimpled smiles.

"That's my family," Hurley said. "The code is Kaylee's birthday plus our wedding anniversary."

"You have a very nice family, Mr. Hurley. Tell me what you found, sir." Ulysses thought of his father, who would be about Hurley's age were he alive.

"The man Serena was corresponding with belonged to a group called Nuclear Peace and Justice," Hurley said. "A bunch of radicals. His name is Jesse Porter, and he's from Austin, Texas. Seems like a professional agitator to me."

Ulysses asked, "Do you have an address for Mr. Porter?"

"Just an email address, but I think he must live in town, not far from the Plaza, based on directions he gave Serena."

"Was this a romantic relationship?"

"I can't say it was, Sheriff, but I don't know. It seemed like she had reached out to him first. She told him she wanted to meet with him."

"What about?" Ulysses asked.

"Serena worked for the chief of staff at Warren Air Force Base. Her boss, General Baynes, manages the nukes over there."

Ulysses sat back in his chair. "Is something going on at Warren? Wyoming has seceded from the Union."

"Serena didn't trust her boss, Sheriff. He was overseeing some upgrades to the missiles at Warren. Serena thought he intended to give dangerous material to the Nationalists."

"What kind of material?"

"I don't know, honestly. I told her to stay out of trouble, but she didn't listen. I can see from her emails that she found this fellow, Jesse Porter. It seems like he wanted to help her."

"What did she say to him in her emails?"

"Not as much as she had told me. She just said she needed to meet him to share important information about nukes in Wyoming, and they arranged for her to come to Taos. Then, not long before she left Cheyenne, she sent an email saying someone was following her and she needed to disappear. That was the word she used."

"Why do you think she brought Kaylee with her?" Ulysses asked.

"She was always protective of our daughter, Sheriff. But like I said, Serena doesn't always think straight. Smart as a whip and plenty organized but emotional and impulsive. Maybe she thought Kaylee was in danger, too."

The older man took out a handkerchief and wiped his brow. "I just wish she had told me about it. I would have come with her. Even though we don't see eye to eye about the election and politics, I'd do anything for her and my baby girl."

Angela spoke up. "Mr. Hurley, I met with Serena's mother, Mrs. Boyar. She said you had called them to say Serena was in town. Why did you call them?"

"I shouldn't have called, Ms. Romero. But I've been so worried about Serena and Kaylee that I went against my better judgment. I understand why Serena doesn't trust them."

"Can you tell me more about why Serena is estranged from family?"

Hurley considered for a few moments. "I guess I can tell you now, given everything happening. Serena's stepfather, Nick Boyar, sexually abused her for years. Her mother knew about it and didn't do anything. Her stepfather is a powerful man who wouldn't want this to come out."

"Thank you for that information," Angela said, "Her mother says she wants to reconcile with her daughter, but I understand why Serena might not want that."

"Mr. Hurley," Ulysses said, "a man we believe was working as a political activist was found murdered in an apartment near the Taos Plaza last night. We think it was Jesse Porter."

Russell Hurley's face turned ashen. "My God," he said. "Are Serena and Kaylee okay?"

"As far as we know, though we don't have any information on their whereabouts. Don't try to find them on your own, understand? It wouldn't be safe for you. Here's my card and cellphone number. Give me yours so we can stay in touch. Undersheriff, can you arrange for a deputy to take Mr. Hurley to the car lot?"

On the way home, Ulysses called LizBeth to tell her about Jesse Porter's murder, Serena Hurley's disappearance, and his interview with Russell Hurley.

"Are you saying that Serena Hurley believed her boss might be ready to hand out nuclear material to unauthorized persons?" LizBeth asked.

"That's what he said. And he also said Serena was afraid for her life. And the man she turned to for help is now dead."

"I will share the information you obtained from Mr. Hurley up the chain of command. And I will update you tomorrow on everything you need to know. Matt and Ray will be joining us. Get some rest, Ulys. Who knows what we are heading into?"

Ulysses arrived home after his family had eaten dinner. His two older children were upstairs doing homework, and Rosemary was reading a bedtime story to Frances. Ulysses served himself some green chile stew and warm tortillas and poured himself a beer. He was halfway through his meal when

Rosemary came into the kitchen and put on the teakettle. She took three teaspoons of her homegrown chamomile tea and put it in a teapot.

"How was your day?" Rosemary asked, touching his shoulder.

"Very strange," Ulysses said, wiping his mouth. He decided not to tell her about Pete Dowd's visit. "I saw LizBeth this morning, and she's coming back tomorrow, too."

"What is she doing in Taos?" Rosemary asked.

"Investigating an infringement at Picuris by one of their neighbors. I'm going out there tomorrow to check on it with her. How was your day?"

"I met with Monty's teacher this afternoon. She wants to have him tested for learning disabilities."

"What kind of disabilities?" Ulysses asked.

"Maybe a language processing problem. She said he might have ADHD. He's been checked out in class, and she's worried about him."

"What do you think, Rosemary?"

"I've also been a little worried about him," Rosemary answered. "Something is bothering him, but he won't tell me anything. You should talk with him, Ulys."

"I will. Do you think it can wait until the weekend?"

"Yes, but don't forget. I know you have a lot on your mind."

"It's true, Honey. I have a missing person and a murder, and they look to be connected. But I won't forget about Monty. How is Frances?"

"Rambunctious and pushing every limit," Rosemary said. "Today, she told me Bad Rabbit was setting fires on a mesa. God knows where she gets this stuff."

Ulysses recalled his dream from that afternoon. "I had a dream about a fire on a mesa this afternoon."

"One of *those* dreams?" Rosemary asked.

"Yeah. Dad was in it, but he turned into Pete Dowd."

"Well, it looks like our daughter has your dreaming thing. When she woke up from her nap, she said we needed to catch Bad Rabbit before he blew us all up."

"Holy shit," Ulysses said. "Who is Bad Rabbit, do you think?"

"I asked Frances, and she said, 'Mom, I don't know. That's just his name.'"

"Are you worried about her?" Ulysses asked.

"No. Other than these dreams, she seems right as can be. Kind of like you," Rosemary said, carrying his dishes to the sink. "Want some tea?"

"I'd love some." Ulysses poured the rest of his beer down the sink. "How was Amelia today?"

"She was in a mood when she got off the bus. She had another run-in with some Elect kids. One of them was Mark Shea's son, Patrick. This time, she didn't get into trouble. But Patrick was suspended."

"What did he do?"

"He threatened one of her friends, a kid named Juniper, and they went to the principal."

"It's getting crazy around here," Ulysses said, hugging Rosemary. "And it could get a whole lot worse."

"Are you thinking of how close we are to LANL?" Rosemary asked.

Ulysses was surprised at her question. "Well, it is just across that mesa," Ulysses said, pointing to the southwest.

"I've been praying about it," Rosemary said.

"That's good, I guess. Let's go to bed," Ulysses said.

Chapter 6

It was a windy, frosty night on Blueberry Hill, a community of handmade houses, geodesic domes, old adobes, and vintage trailers that spread over a rolling llano facing the Sangre de Cristo Mountains north of Taos. In a snail-shaped spray foam house down a long, rutted drive, two young women sat near a warm wood cookstove while a child slept on a double bed covered by a quilt. A kerosene lamp, the only light in the room, burned on a trestle table.

"That was my contact on the phone," Monica Lovato said. "He mentioned that a sheriff's deputy was searching for me."

Serena Hurley sat cross-legged on the bed, her hands clasped in her lap. She looked at her daughter, Kaylee, who stirred in her sleep. "Why?" she asked.

"Most likely about Jesse. By the way, my contact is coming by tonight to pick up the thing you brought from Wyoming," Monica said.

"The toolbox? How come?" Serena asked.

"Leadership prefers it to be securely stored in a safe location. We will also be relocating you and Kaylee to a different site soon."

"I'm not sure I want to move." *I want to get away from these people,* Serena thought.

"We relocate all our guests, particularly when the law is searching for them," Monica stated. "Who other than Jesse knows you are in Taos?"

"My husband may know by now."

"Can he be trusted?" Monica asked. "What are his politics?"

"I trust him. He loves me and Kaylee. But he's very old school. He's not a Nationalist, but he will probably go to the sheriff. He's just like that."

"Is he Kaylee's father?"

"Yes. He's a good man. He took me in when I needed someone."

"What is he likely to say to law enforcement?" Monica asked, putting on her coat and gathering her things to leave.

"He'll just be focused on trying to find me. He knows only a little about the intel I've been gathering and nothing about the toolbox. He might try to get in touch with my mother."

"What would that mean?"

"I've told him not to contact her. She's married to Nick Boyar."

"From LANL?" Monica asked. "Oh, my God!"

"I've been estranged from them for over ten years."

"Nick Boyar is an enemy! He's connected to the Elect!"

Serena said nothing for a moment. "Look, Monica, I told my husband never to contact my parents for any reason. He knows how they've treated me, and he gets it."

"You should have told me this before now," Monica said. "My boss is going to be very unhappy."

"Where will Kaylee and I go next?"

"My contact didn't tell me."

Serena had initially liked and trusted Monica, a biracial woman around her age with years of experience as an anti-nuclear activist. However, she no longer felt safe with Monica and suspected that the sentiment was mutual.

Ever since Jesse's murder, Serena had felt anxious and sick to her stomach. She wished she were back home with Russell and had never fled to New Mexico with her intel and the toolbox that held a small but significant amount of weapons-grade plutonium. She especially wished she hadn't brought Kaylee.

"Okay," she said at last, "but I don't want anyone else to get hurt because of me. I feel so bad about Jesse. I liked him from the moment he picked me up on the side of the road."

"Why did he come to get you?"

"I had problems with my fuel pump. The car stalled north of Taos, and I then noticed my tire was going flat. I called Jesse, and he came right away. He thought someone was following him. In our hurry to leave, we left some things in the car. We brought the toolbox, of course. At least I didn't have my computer; Jesse had told me not to bring it to New Mexico."

"Tell me again what you heard and saw the night he was murdered."

Serena swallowed hard and fought back tears. "I'd been staying with him four days. He didn't think Kaylee and I were safe there, but he'd been told another place wasn't available yet. Anyway, it was late. Kaylee was already asleep. He told me a contact was finally coming to move Kaylee and me to another location. I woke her up, and Jesse led us down the stairs and hid us in the shed under them to wait for the contact to come. I had my backpack, Kaylee's things, and the toolbox. Jesse said goodbye and told Kaylee to be a good girl and stay quiet. Then he closed the door and went back upstairs. A few minutes later, a truck pulled up and parked. I thought it was my contact and looked out the door."

"Did you open the door?" Monica asked.

"I could see through the slats. It was a tan truck, a Toyota, with Arizona plates. I had been told to expect a Honda sedan with New Mexico plates. A man got out of the truck wearing a rubber Guy Fawkes mask, and the truck took off. I felt paralyzed. The man ran up the stairs and kicked in the apartment door. I heard a lot of yelling and fighting. Kaylee and I ran as fast as we could to the public bathrooms about two blocks away. I wanted to hide us in the women's bathroom, but it was locked, so we went to La Fonda and hid there. After about an hour, I went to the front desk, and the man there called the number I had for my contact. He came right away, an older guy who said his name was Steve. He must have been nearby. He brought me here. That's when I realized I didn't have my cell phone. I must not have put it in my backpack." Serena began to cry.

"What did you see of the man who killed Jesse?"

"He was about six feet tall, wearing a black sweatshirt, pants, and running shoes. And the mask, the kind you pull over your head. I didn't see much else." Serena wiped her eyes. "I'm so sorry about Jesse. He was a good guy. He didn't deserve what happened to him."

"Look, Serena, this is a war. Jesse was a good soldier. He did his duty to the movement. You've brought us something good, and we'll ensure it gets into the right hands. Please let go of worrying about Jesse. Just thank him in your heart and move on. You need your wits about you to keep yourself and your daughter safe."

Serena nodded and stood up. "I'm going to wash the dishes," she said. She filled a kettle, placed it on the wood stove, and began stacking the plates and utensils.

"Do you have a warm jacket and enough underwear?" Monica asked.

Serena nodded.

"Here is some cash and a burner phone. My contact is bringing a gun for you." Monica placed a paper bag on the trestle table.

"Are you leaving?" Serena asked.

"I have to go to Albuquerque tonight," she said. "We've had two murders now in the northern unit, and leadership wants to talk with me," Monica said.

"I don't feel good about this," Serena said. "It's like you are abandoning me and Kaylee."

"Listen, Serena, I'm sorry I have to go. But remember what I said and be a good soldier. And thanks for bringing the toolbox. We'll take it from here." She patted Serena on the shoulder.

Monica's words sent a chill through Serena. Outside, the wind blew as though a front were moving in. Serena washed and rinsed the dinner dishes, placing them on the sideboard. An engine roared, and both women stood still to listen. A car approached the driveway with its lights off. Monica pulled a gun from her coat pocket and extinguished the kerosene lamp. She lifted the curtain and peered out through a window, then sighed and said, "It's my contact. Don't be afraid. You won't be alone for long. Someone will come for you, maybe tomorrow." She slung her backpack over her shoulder and walked out into the darkness. A few minutes later, Serena heard Monica talking to a man about where the toolbox was hidden. Then, the man entered the house, shining a flashlight into Serena's startled face.

"So, you are Serena Boyar?" he asked.

"My name is Hurley," Serena said.

"Why did you lie to us about your stepfather?" the man asked. "You could get all of us killed, do you know that?"

"I didn't lie to anyone, "Serena said. "I have nothing to do with Nick Boyar." She couldn't see the man's lower face, which was covered by a bandana. He wore a down coat and a wool hat over shoulder-length gray hair.

The man placed a duffle bag on the table and said, "There is a handgun in the bag and some ammo. The gun is loaded, but the safety is on. Lock this door, and don't let anyone in here unless they give the password 'Roadrunner.'" Then they were gone, and Serena and her daughter were alone.

Kaylee sat up and asked, "Mama, when can we go home?"

Ulysses awoke to Amelia and Monty arguing about whose turn it was to do the breakfast dishes. "I can help," Frances said. Ulysses heard something shatter on the brick floor. He got out of bed and pulled on his pajama bottoms.

"Hi, Daddy!" Frances said with her usual enthusiasm. Then, looking at the cereal bowl in pieces at her feet, she said, "I'm sorry!" Neither Amelia nor Monty said anything, and neither was dressed for school. It was seven o'clock, and they had to be at the bus stop in thirty minutes.

"I'll clean this up," Ulysses said. "Frances, go get the dustpan and a rag. Don't step toward the glass! You two, get dressed for school. Where is your mother?"

"Either milking or checking on the garden," Amelia said, "It frosted last night." Monty and Amelia took their dishes to the sink and ran upstairs to get dressed. Ulysses heard Rosemary come in the front door and into the kitchen. She set a basket full of her produce on the floor.

"Those kids roped you into cleaning up for them?"

"I volunteered. How bad was the frost?"

"The tomatoes are officially done," she said. "As well as the zinnias and marigolds. But I got 16 eggs, and the girls gave almost a gallon of milk altogether."

"Will you make cheese?" Frances asked. "Can I help?"

"You most certainly can," Rosemary answered, ruffling her baby's red hair. "Want some hot cereal, Ulys?"

"I'd love some." He finished the dishes, cleaned the counters, and tucked into Rosemary's homemade seven-grain cereal with goat yogurt and honey. Frances left the table and went into her room.

"What do you have going on today?" Ulysses asked.

"I'll be home with Frances. We'll pull up the tomato vines and other frosted things and shred them for the compost, and then she'll help me make cheese. She's a good help, especially for a five-year-old! What is your day like?"

"Not too bad. I want to be home for dinner but don't count on me. There are so many loose ends I can't keep track of them right now."

"Are you meeting with LizBeth first thing?"

"No, not until 11. Angela has a new hire for me to meet."

"Is it Mark she wants to replace or Eli?"

"It's Eli who needs replacing. That's why it's taking so long. Not that many people have skills remotely like his."

"Anything else I should know about?"

Ulysses thought for a moment. "LizBeth wants to read me in on something high-level involving militias and potential civil unrest. I know I won't be able to give you details, but at least you'll know the big picture."

"Thanks for that, Ulys. I hope you'll tell me as much as you can. I must keep myself and the children safe when you aren't here. I hear things, you know, all the time. People are anxious about what's happening in the country now."

"I know, Rosemary. It sounds like you are anxious, too."

"I am, Ulys," she said, "especially about the security rumors at LANL. It's only about 50 miles from here as the crow flies."

"I know. Short of telling you stuff that's classified, I will keep you posted."

"And you know, I'm also hearing that the Nationalists have infiltrated the Governor's office and the National Guard. Could this be true?"

"Where did you hear that?"

"On the radio. Taos Solar News. They have a regular show by a journalist, Ray's friend, Rita Wainwright. I trust her reporting."

"Honey, I need to get going. We can discuss this more later. I'm not saying you're wrong; you're anything but that. But I don't want you to worry."

"I'm just trying to get prepared," Rosemary said. She hugged him and went to check on Amelia and Monty.

After meeting with the 911 staff about an increase in call volume, Ulysses met Rosie Bischoff, Angela's new hire, who said Sheriff Villalobos in Santa Fe had permitted her to start immediately. *That's quick,* Ulysses thought. *I hope Villalobos isn't glad to be getting rid of her.*

Ulysses drove to the Double Rainbow to meet LizBeth, Matt Pando, and Ray Pando. The neighborhood's favorite restaurant had started closing after lunch since proprietor Ernest Charley's wife died several years ago, and business had declined.

LizBeth was waiting for Ulysses in the parking lot, and Ray and Matt had taken a table inside. The day was sunny and cool, with a light breeze making the golden aspen leaves tremble. The place was empty except for Ray and Matt, who were seated in a red leatherette booth, drinking coffee and eating apple rhubarb pie. Lizbeth ordered a macha tea latte, and Ulysses had ginger lemonade. Ulysses and LizBeth agreed to split a piece of carrot cake, the house specialty. As they waited, they caught up on personal and family news.

When their orders arrived, LizBeth took charge of the meeting. "We'll be met at the gate by the vice president of the Western Resource Group, Max Castleman. He is a member of the so-called Council of the Elected Wise."

"Who, of course, are not elected at all," Ray interrupted, taking a sip of coffee. "Maybe not all that wise, either."

LizBeth smiled at Ray. "Correct. We are unlikely to meet the man they call 'The Servant,' Daniel Graves. I'm told that Graves is in residence but on a silent retreat. He's not a big talker on any given day. Graves is the head of the Church of the Elect. He is a close advisor to Duke Hadest, the Nationalist leader in Texas.

"The Church purchased the former Sleeping Tiger Zen Center property three years ago as a 'sanctuary' for the church hierarchy. They refurbished existing structures and quietly built new ones. They run a church school and a training camp for young men, so they have a lot of minors on the property. I'm hoping we'll see some of what they've built. I don't have a search warrant, so today is focused on the boundary violation."

"Who lives there?" Ulysses asked.

"My intel is that about one hundred adults and fifty children are in residence, including the Servant's three wives and seven children, and about thirty men and boys are undergoing religious training. Plus, full-time administrative staff, cooks, maids, and others who live on the property. And there is security, maintenance, and IT. Most live in communal housing, except for Castleman and Graves."

"How did this go under the radar for so long?" Matt asked.

"Because they are a church, they don't have to answer for much of what they do. We checked on their permits, and while they are all in order, it appears that no on-site inspection was ever performed during two years of building. Their property is isolated and in a low-density area, and they have allies in the local community."

"Really?" Ray asked. "Who are their allies?"

"They are aligned with the Sisneros family, who have been influential in Taos politics since territorial days. The Elect have supported some of their pet projects for years, including contributing to Lex Sisneros's run for Attorney General." LizBeth finished her carrot cake and wiped her mouth.

"I thought Lex Sisneros was on our side," Ray said. "Isn't he a friend of yours, Ulys?"

"He is a friendly acquaintance. I've known him since college, but we've never been close. Lex is a man who always hedges his bets. That is the family way, and they've remained so powerful for many years. Hey, don't we have a meeting to get to?"

LizBeth looked at the time on her phone. "We sure do. Today, we'll focus on getting them to move their fence while also keeping eyes and ears open."

Ulysses was surprised at the enormous iron gate installed at the entrance to the property that had once been Sleeping Tiger Zen Center and, before that, a rehabilitation center for troubled priests owned by the archdiocese. LizBeth drove up first, and a man wearing a side arm typed in a code to open the ornate gate on one side, allowing them to enter the property. They parked in front of a modern concrete building with long, narrow windows. A sign above the double doors read "Church of the Elect Welcome Center." LizBeth led the way toward the opened doors. A middle-aged man with an athletic build and dark hair flecked with grey approached Ulysses.

"I'm Max Castleman," he said, neither smiling nor extending his hand. "Please come in." Ulysses thought he noticed a slight accent in his speech. Castleman ignored LizBeth, Ray, and Matt. They walked inside the Welcome Center's reception room, where several young men looked at computers behind a partition. A man sat at a desk in front of a bank of CCTVs.

Castleman led them into a conference room with a rectangular table and sat at the head next to a stack of papers. Behind him were numerous portraits of someone Ulysses guessed was the Servant, Daniel Graves, along with various leaders, including Nationalist Leader Duke Hadest and New Mexico Governor Alfredo Hobbs. Castleman was also in most of the pictures, standing just behind Graves.

Ulysses sat across from LizBeth, with Ray and Matt on either side. The windowless room was stuffy and smelled of its new wall-to-wall carpet. A surveillance camera hung in the back corner near a door to an inner office. A large cross was centered on the back wall, flanked by flagpoles.

"What brings you here today, Sheriff Walker?" Castleman

asked after an awkward silence. Ulysses noticed that one of his hazel eyes wandered.

"Mr. Castleman, I am LizBeth Tallichet, of the FBI. The gentleman to my right is Picuris Governor Ray Pando, and to my left is Matt Pando, Picuris War Chief."

"Yes, we know who you are. What do you need from us?" he asked Ulysses, who gazed steadfastly at LizBeth and said nothing. Ulysses was aware of the Elect custom of not speaking directly to women who were not family members.

"Mr. Castleman," she said. "You have erected a large fence on property you do not own. Here is a survey that shows your fence is improperly placed on Picuris land in violation of federal law."

Castleman picked up the survey, glanced at it, and put it down. "I also have a survey," Castleman said. He unfolded a yellowed document dated 1938 and showed his property when it was a Benedictine monastery before it was surveyed to reflect the actual size of Picuris territory. "As you can see, the boundary on my survey is different."

"Our survey is from four years ago, not 1938," Ray said. "Didn't you get a survey when you bought the property?"

Castleman's cell phone buzzed. "Excuse me, I have to take this call."

Castleman put the phone to his ear and walked through to the inner office.

"What the hell?" Ray said. "He's bound to have a more recent survey than 1938. Is he going to contest this?"

"Dad, you know how these land controversies go. We'll be in court for years sorting this out."

"No, you won't," LizBeth said. "Your survey will stand. Don't worry." Matt shook his head and said nothing.

The man from the security desk abruptly entered the room. "Mr. Castleman has been called away and has asked for your forbearance. He will contact you soon to set up another meeting."

"What in hell is going on?" Ray asked.

"Please proceed toward your vehicles immediately," the security man said. Ulysses looked at LizBeth, who shrugged and stood up. Matt and Ray also stood, looking angry. Ulysses followed them out of the building.

As they headed for their cars, Ulysses heard yelling from the hill behind the Welcome Center. An armed guard approached them, his arms outstretched to herd them away. "You need to leave now," he said.

"Just a minute," Ulysses said. "I am Sheriff of this county; what is happening?"

"Sheriff, this is an internal matter. You don't need to be concerned." A teenage boy ran into the parking area, pursued by other boys in uniforms.

At that point, the boy yelled, "Help me! They are going to hurt me!" Castleman came out behind the building and said, "Sheriff, this boy is having a mental health crisis. He is receiving care here. If you doubt me, call Children, Youth and Families Department. They have already investigated."

"I want to speak with the boy," Ulysses said. "Right now."

"You have no right to intervene," Castleman said. "This is a matter for the boy's family. "Isaiah," he said to the crying boy, "tell the sheriff you are okay, please."

Isaiah nodded, sobbing, but said nothing.

"I will make a further investigation," Ulysses said. "You had better not punish this boy until the investigation is complete. And give me the name of his psychiatrist."

"He is under the care of Daniel Graves," Max said. "The Servant is on a silent retreat."

"Who are Isaiah's parents?" Ulysses asked.

Castleman said, "His father is Levi Patterson, one of my best men."

Ulysses gave Max his card. "Have Mr. Graves call me today," he said. "Do you understand? Today."

As they walked toward their cars, LizBeth said, "I need to make a phone call, but I'd like to meet with the three of you to fill you in on some security matters. Can we meet at your house, Ulys, at about 7:30 this evening?"

Ulysses, LizBeth, Matt, and Ray sat in the Walker's living room where a small fire burned in a kiva fireplace. The room was hushed except for the occasional sound of children's voices in other parts of the house. LizBeth explained in detail the current threats from militias identified by the FBI and the missing material from the plutonium pit facility at LANL. She told them that the suspect at LANL, Dr. Charlotte Foster, had just been released for lack of evidence. Ray and Matt sat in stunned silence, occasionally exchanging shocked looks.

"Agent Tallichet, shouldn't you search the Elect compound?" Matt asked. "Infrastructure there could be hiding weapons."

"It's complicated, Matt. They are a church, and while there's no right to sanctuary in the United States, it is considered a bad move from a public relations perspective to barge right into one. My boss says we don't have probable cause to justify a search for suspects or weapons."

"But we do have a child safety concern that will get us on the property," Ulysses said. "A lot of children live there, not just that boy. I can bypass Children, Youth and Families Department, which would only slow us down. And Daniel Graves has not yet called me as I demanded."

"We have to be careful about civil liberties, Ulys," LizBeth said. "We can't afford to be heavy-handed."

"What do you mean heavy-handed? For God's sake, LizBeth, they could have radioactive material on our land! Shouldn't you send in a team?" Ray asked.

"Do you mean going outside the law?" LizBeth asked.

Ray laughed. "Well, I'm pissed. These people have installed a fence on our property and may pose an existential threat to Picuris. You are talking about public relations and civil liberties?' What about a sovereign nation's right to defend itself?"

No one said anything for a few moments. The fire popped. Ray and Matt glared at LizBeth. Ulysses sighed.

"Ray's right, LizBeth. I'm going to get a search warrant first thing tomorrow," Ulysses said, "based on child endangerment.

I want to see their school, their dormitories, and interview personnel. And I want to talk with Isaiah."

"That's not enough," Ray said, standing up.

"Are you considering informing the other pueblos?" Matt asked LizBeth. "San Ildefonso and Santa Clara are closer to LANL than we are. Or are you just going to leave them in harm's way?"

"I've received permission to tell the governors of the closest pueblos. But the more people we tell, the more we risk political unrest, conspiracy theories, and worse. A widespread release of information could hinder our investigations and lead to a public panic."

Matt and Ray exchanged a look. Matt stood and prepared to leave.

"I will seek a court order to remove the fence on Picuris land," LizBeth said at last. "And permission to conduct a thorough search."

"Okay, see that you do," Ray said. "And we'll consider our options. We're going home now."

Chapter 7

Ulysses and Angela arrived at the Elect compound at eleven o'clock and presented their warrant to the armed security, which met them at the gate. After fifteen minutes, Castleman arrived, looked at the warrant, and took them to the Welcome Center conference room. Ulysses and Angela were not greeted or invited to take a seat. Castleman stood texting on his phone and said nothing.

A young woman wearing a white headscarf entered. She lowered her eyes and carried a tray of glasses and a water pitcher, which she placed on the table. Behind her came a man wheeling a white upholstered chair on a dolly. When the chair was placed at the head of the table, he left again. After a few more minutes, the door opened again, and a man wearing religious garb came in with another man, possibly a lawyer. The man in religious garb had a narrow face, an untrimmed grey beard, and light brown, almost golden eyes. He was introduced by Castleman as "Our Holy Servant, Daniel Graves." He sat on the white chair at the head of the table and gestured to Castleman to sit to his right. The lawyer sat to his left.

"Sheriff, you may be seated," Castleman said. Ulysses and Angela took places at the table.

"Hello, Reverend Graves. I am Sheriff Ulysses Walker of Taos County, and this is Angela Romero, Undersheriff." Graves nodded but said nothing. "We have come to inspect your premises for the evidence of child endangerment." Ulysses handed his search warrant across the table toward Graves, but the man to his left took it and began to read it. Graves clasped his bony hands. He

76

wore a mushroom-like clerical hat with a veil of a style Ulysses had not seen before. A heavy gold crucifix hung from a chain around his neck.

"Our attorney will look over your warrant," Castleman said. When the attorney was finished reading, he whispered to Graves, who listened and nodded.

"Sheriff," the attorney said, "our children are not abused, endangered, or neglected, as you will see. Mr. Castleman will give you a walking tour of the property, and then you may meet with Isaiah to ask all your questions. I will attend your interview with Isaiah to represent him."

"I'm sorry, sir, neither you nor Isaiah's parents will be allowed to attend our forensic interview. It is prohibited by law. We must interview Isaiah alone in his home."

"I want to remind Sheriff that this property is sacred, and you are interfering with precious religious liberty," Graves said in Russian-accented English. "I wish to register objection." With that, Graves stood, bowed, and left the room via the interior door. The door remained open momentarily, and Ulysses noticed a group of little girls in white dresses who crowded around their spiritual leader, offering bouquets. Castleman and the lawyer also stood when Graves left the room. "I will give you a tour of the property now," Castleman said.

Outside the Welcome Center, Ulysses and Angela were led along a walkway, past the freestanding kitchen and dining hall, where residents were streaming in for the first lunch seating. "We have three seatings for each meal," Castleman said. "One for men, one for women, and one for children." They could hear the people in the dining hall saying grace in unison. Behind the dining hall stood the house Ulysses remembered having belonged to the former Zen Roshi of Sleeping Tiger and, before that, to the Archbishop of Santa Fe, who built it. "Who lives in that house now?" Ulysses asked.

"I do, "Castleman replied, "Until my family's house in the Council Grove of the Wise is completed."

Castleman allowed them to peek into the nearby chapel, a former zendo. "We're proud to have returned it to a proper place of Christian worship," he said. Ulysses noticed that the interior had few ornaments, apart from a larger-than-life oil portrait of Daniel Graves behind the altar, a ten-foot-tall white cross on one side draped with an American flag, and large tablets of the Ten Commandments on the other. Castleman explained that they couldn't go inside because it was off-limits to nonbelievers.

On a hill above the dining hall, where a Benedictine monastery once stood, were two four-story apartment buildings, a school building, and an armory. Castleman showed them the new parking lot on the ground that had once been forest. "This lot is for people who live off-site," he said.

The apartments were cheap, utilitarian stucco structures that looked like student housing. "The units on the left are for single men, and the ones on the right are for married couples with children. Children are housed with their parents. Married couples without children and any divorced persons with children live off-site at present," Castleman said. "This is the Women's Pavillion for unmarried women and girls undergoing training." He gestured to two prefab buildings surrounded by chain-link fencing and stadium-style lights.

"Why are the women's quarters heavily fenced?" Angela asked.

Castleman looked at Ulysses as he answered. "For their safety," he said. "We respect women and take seriously their desire to remain pure."

"I'd like to see inside," Ulysses said.

"We cannot allow men inside as it would violate the modesty standards fundamental to our religion."

Ulysses decided not to pick this battle. *We can always return with paperwork specific to this building.*

"Here is our Elect learning center," Castleman said as they approached a squat metal building with a wooden bell tower topped by a sizeable old-fashioned bell. "We have two classrooms, one for boys and one for girls."

Inside the boys' classroom, a mixed-age group wearing black uniforms worked on math problems suitable for their skill level.

Two male teachers circulated in the room to answer questions. Castleman whispered to the lead teacher, who was helping a student, and then introduced him to Ulysses.

"This is Levi Patterson, Isaiah's father," Castleman said. Levi, who wore a full beard and was tall and thickly built, nodded toward Ulysses but did not speak or make eye contact. Castleman whispered to Patterson again. Patterson glared at Ulysses with undisguised hostility as they exited the classroom.

In the girls' classroom, a single teacher lectured on proper dress, grooming, and deportment to a roomful of girls in identical long, pastel-colored dresses.

"What is the significance of the headscarf color?" Angela asked. Castleman didn't respond. "I notice these girls are wearing white scarves, the teacher is wearing black, and other women have red scarves. Does that have meaning?" Again, Castleman ignored her, walking ahead on the path.

"You heard the question, Mr. Castleman. Please do us the courtesy to answer."

"Sheriff, white is for unmarried girls and women, red is for married women, and black is for widows or divorced women."

They arrived at a Quonset hut that Castleman said housed their armory. The hut was surrounded by fencing, barbed wire and more high-powered lighting. Two men with semi-automatic rifles stood by the door. "I need to look in there," Ulysses said. Castleman frowned, but Ulysses said, "I insist."

Castleman unlocked the gate and padlocked door. Angela fell behind the two men and took pictures of the exterior with her cellphone. Inside, the walls were lined with gun racks laden with guns and rifles of various types, gun safes, and large metal cabinets that held body armor, mace, tasers, night vision, and ammunition. Ulysses made a mental inventory to go alongside Angela's photos. One long metal cabinet bore a sign that said, "Explosives."

"What is in there?" Ulysses asked.

"Dynamite, C4, and blasting caps left over from construction."

"How do you keep this building secure?" Ulysses asked.

"The Servant and I have the only keys, and you saw the armed guards. They preside around the clock and report directly to our explosives expert, Levi Patterson, whom you just met..."

"Will I be able to meet with Mr. Patterson after we interview Isaiah?" Ulysses interrupted.

"Levi is needed in the classroom during that time. I will represent him."

The people who live here are under tight control, Ulysses thought.

After securing the armory, Castleman led them to a lookout situated on the property's highest point, where a cell tower stood. Castleman pointed out a "prayer garden," a football field, and a military-style obstacle course.

"Housing for the Council Grove of the Wise is being built over there," he said, indicating an area that remained wooded. "It has beautiful views. The Servant and his wives live there now." The land on the other side of the Grove sloped toward Picuris, but the fence was not visible from this vantage point because of a sharp drop-off above a cliff.

"The area around the Grove will remain natural: woods and meadows with walking trails for the Council of the Wise and their families. We plan to build a birthing center there in the spring." Ulysses considered asking to go down there, but a quick look at his watch told him they didn't have time.

"Unless you have other questions, we can walk over to the Patterson home now, and you can conduct your interviews."

They arrived at an apartment on the first floor and were introduced to Isaiah's mother, Merrily, who invited them into her cramped quarters. Merrily was pregnant and wore a floor-length pale blue dress with a white apron and a red head scarf. Inside, Christian praise music was softly playing. "Would you like to come into my kitchen?" Merrily asked Angela. "You can help me serve refreshments."

"You don't have to give us refreshments, Ma'am," Angela said.

Merrily nodded and went back into the kitchen.

"Shall I call Isaiah? Castleman asked. "His mother kept him home from school."

"How old is Isaiah?" Ulysses asked.

"Seventeen."

"Do you have a room where we won't be disturbed?"

"What about in here?" Castleman asked, indicating a small living room with a couch and two chairs that adjoined the kitchen.

"It's not private enough," Ulysses said. "What about his bedroom?"

Castleman looked pointedly at Angela, "It wouldn't be proper according to our religion."

"I tell you what," Ulysses said. "If you don't have a private room where I can interview your son, how about you and Mrs. Patterson leave the premises? Then we can meet in this room."

Once Castleman and Merrily Patterson left the house, Isaiah emerged from his bedroom. "Hello, Sheriff and Deputy," the young man said, shaking hands. "Mother mentioned you wanted to speak with me." Isaiah sat carefully, favoring his mid-torso and rib area.

"Hi, Isaiah," Angela said. "How're you doing?"

"Not too bad," he said.

"Did you get to sleep in this morning?" Angela asked.

"Yes, Ma'am."

"We're here to talk about what happened yesterday, but before we start, I'd like to get to know you better, okay?"

"That's fine."

"Tell me about your family," she asked. "Are you the oldest?"

"My parents adopted me when I was four. I have two little brothers, and my mother will have a baby girl, God willing, in about a month." Isaiah looked toward the kitchen.

"Are you hungry?" she asked.

Isaiah looked at her for the first time, registering surprise.

"Teenaged boys often are," Angela said. "And it's lunchtime."

Isaiah shook his head. "No, Ma'am. I'm supposed to wait to eat. I'm on a special fast."

"I have an energy bar if you'd like one." She took a protein bar from her pocket and handed it to Isaiah. He looked toward the front door, took the bar, opened the wrapper, and devoured it.

"You want a glass of milk or something?" Angela asked.

"Yes," Isaiah said. "If there is an open carton."

Angela went into the kitchen and poured Isaiah a glass of milk. "Okay, let's get started then," she said. "Yesterday, you came running toward the Welcome Center and seemed upset. What was going on?"

"Nothing, really," Isaiah said. "I was being insubordinate. I'm better now."

"Who were you insubordinate to?" Angela asked.

"Major Mark," he said. "He runs the training exercises. And Colonel Gideon, who is the Major's commanding officer."

"What kind of training exercises?"

"Calisthenics, marching, firearms training."

While Angela talked to Isaiah, Ulysses assessed the young man's appearance. Isaiah was small and thin, with brown skin, pimples, short black hair, and a facial tic. He was wearing pajama bottoms and a vintage Jesus Christ Superstar t-shirt. His bare wrists bore scars and recent cuts, and he had a bruise on his upper right arm.

"Why did you get into trouble?" Ulysses asked.

"I'm not good at training. Major Mark and his honor guard call me a sissy, and one of the guards pantsed me."

"What does that mean?" Angela asked.

"They pulled my pants down." Isaiah looked like he might cry.

"Really? That's not good."

"I hate them," Isaiah said. "The honor guard is a bunch of bullies."

"Then what happened?" Angela asked.

"I started to run away, but Major grabbed my arm and threw me down. Then, an honor guard kicked me." Isaiah lifted his tee shirt and showed a large red bruise on his torso.

"Ouch," Angela said. "That looks like it hurts."

"It does. Especially if I cough or sneeze."

"You might have a broken rib," Angela observed. "After the boy kicked you, what happened?" Angela asked.

"I ran down the hill yelling for help. But that was stupid. No one would help me."

"Why not?"

"Discipline is supposed to make me stronger."

Angela nodded. "You said you were on a fast, Isaiah; what does that mean?"

"It's the punishment for insubordination. I'm not allowed to eat for 24 hours. Please wash this glass and return it so they can't tell it was used. And could you take this wrapper? Please don't throw it in the trash. If I get caught, I'll have to fast for three days. Don't tell my parents I ate!"

"Isaiah, how many times have you been made to fast, and when did it start?"

"Lots of times. It started when I was ten."

Angela looked at Ulysses. She mouthed the words "child abuse."

Ulysses said, "Angela, please call our liaison at CYFD in Santa Fe to learn about the next steps." Angela took her cell phone and stepped out of the room.

To Isaiah, Ulysses said, "Son, I'm worried about your well-being. I want to take you to Taos to have your injuries evaluated. You can stay at our teen shelter, a supervised group home. I don't think you are safe here."

Isaiah said nothing. He looked frightened.

"You'll be with a group of boys about your age and supervised by adults. You'll get plenty to eat there."

"Will I be able to come back here?"

"That will be determined based on an investigation."

Isaiah swallowed hard, but he said nothing.

"My parents are going to be angry with me," he said. "I do everything wrong. Now, I'm going out to mingle with the nonbelievers. They won't ever let me come back."

The door opened, and Merrily Patterson came in. "Did you feed him?" Merrily asked Angela, who didn't reply. "How dare you interfere with our family?"

Ulysses stood up. "Mrs. Patterson, we are taking custody of Isaiah on suspicion of child abuse. A representative from Children, Youth and Families Department will contact you to arrange visitation. Why don't you help Isaiah pack the things he'll need for the next three days?"

"You can't do this, Sheriff. We are a church. We have the freedom to raise..."

"I'm exercising my authority as Sheriff to remove Isaiah from a dangerous environment and protect him from abuse and neglect. Now help him pack a bag, or I'll take him as he is."

Merrily escorted her son into his room, whispering to him. Castleman came into the house, talking on his cell phone. Ulysses and Angela heard him say, "Send back-up." Angela unsnapped her holster and checked her weapon. Castleman noticed this but said, "Sheriff, I have called my security to block your action."

"Sir, you should reconsider. You might manage to have Ms. Romero and me leave today, but we will return in greater numbers tomorrow, and the consequences could be severe. If I were in your position, I would call off your security and allow us to perform our lawful duties."

Isaiah came downstairs fully dressed, holding a small duffle bag. He said, "I'm ready to go, Sheriff." To Ulysses, his face registered relief. "Goodbye, Mother," Isaiah said as they approached the door. "Tell Father I said bye."

Mrs. Patterson stood by the kitchen door, arms crossed over her pregnant belly. She neither answered nor glanced at her son.

On the way into Taos, Isaiah fell asleep in the back of the cruiser. Angela called ahead and obtained the needed permissions and the address of the intake center. They picked up a burger, fries, and milkshake for the young man and delivered him to meet with the lead social worker. She would take over and make sure Isaiah was evaluated medically and psychiatrically before being taken into temporary foster care.

"That was rough," Ulysses said once they were alone in the car.

"What did you think of the Elect setup?" Angela asked.

"It's creepy," Ulysses said.

"That kid is traumatized," Angela said. "Do you think Major Mark is former deputy Mark Shea?"

"Possibly. Please find out all you can about him. We should be able to charge him with assault on a minor. I'm most worried about that armory, though. Dynamite is unstable, and I don't know if they are storing it properly. It can't be exposed to water but must be kept at a certain humidity level. It looked haphazard to me. When we return to Headquarters, I'll call the ATF."

After Ulysses spoke with Bill Samuelson, special agent at Alcohol, Tobacco, Firearms and Explosives, he met with his deputy Zach Wright. Zach had found murder victim Jesse Porter's next of kin, his sister Aisha, a schoolteacher who lived in East St. Louis with her husband and two daughters. When Zach called to inform Jesse's sister that her brother had been murdered, she was devastated.

Jesse had lived with his sister's family for the past year since he and his wife divorced. He had no children. Jesse, who was thirty-three, had worked as a nurse's aide in a youth detention center before joining the Malcolm X Brigade and going underground. Aisha said Jesse had been depressed and isolated since his divorce. She didn't know any of his contacts in New Mexico. Jesse's father was dead, and his mother was disabled from a head injury due to a fall at work.

Ulysses also briefed Zach on the visit to the Elect compound and the interview with Isaiah.

"Sir, isn't Mark Shea living out there with his son, Patrick? I read it on a Facebook page, 'Taos through the grapevine,'" Zach said. "You know how staunch Mark has gotten lately. I wonder what his ex-wife thinks?"

"Call Marcie," Ulysses said, "and ask her what she knows."

LizBeth arrived as Zach went out. "How was your visit with the Elect?" she asked Ulysses.

"They've got quite the stockpile of weapons over there at their 'sanctuary,' as they call it, including a good bit of dynamite. Castleman said they acquired it when they were building the place. I spoke with Bill Samuelson at ATF about it. He wants to talk with you."

"I had my assistant pull all their permits," LizBeth said. "They purchased dynamite just before the election. And they used it several times when they were building." LizBeth opened her laptop and brought up a satellite image of the area on the other side of the fence that trespassed onto Picuris land. It showed a road going downhill to a gate into an underground facility.

"Did anyone from Picuris report hearing blasting?"

"I asked Ray, and he said he had heard some but didn't register what it was. He said he heard it two or three times. He said he would ask if any other tribal members had noticed."

"Where did you get this satellite image?" Ulysses asked.

"President McDade gave the FBI access to military satellites over Texas, New Mexico, and Oklahoma. That's where this came from. Nancy, my boss, has asked for a special team to go inside. They could be hiding illegal stuff in there."

"No wonder they put up a fence. It was stupid to put it on Picuris land."

"It could also be a command-and-control center or safe housing for some of their population, particularly their VIPs. Nancy is facing fierce opposition to us going in there."

"What kind of opposition?" Ulysses asked.

"There is a lot of political turmoil in Washington over how to interpret the powers of the emergency declaration made after the violence at the inauguration. McDade hasn't invoked the Insurrection Act, and his coalition is divided over how much to prioritize security over liberty. The security crowd, including him, wants to do extreme things like suspend the Fourth Amendment and habeas corpus. The liberty crowd, mostly in Congress, doesn't. They want to preserve civil liberties at all costs unless we go to war. Ultimately, it is the president's call, but first, he'll probably test the limits of the emergency declaration."

"Does the FBI field office director decide whether to make an incursion?" Ulysses asked.

"Because of the fence, I believe so. The fact that they placed that fence on Picuris land gives the FBI jurisdiction. Nancy wants to be sure all the rules are followed, and she hasn't given a green light yet."

Ulysses leaned back in his chair and crossed his arms over his chest. "The property is in Taos County," he said. "I could argue that I have a right to go in there with force."

"I had considered asking you to do that. But I'm worried it would be more than your team could handle if the Elect resisted."

"They do have a good many armed men hanging around," Ulysses commented.

"Tomorrow, I'm convening the Rapid Response Team at the SCIF at the Roundhouse at 9 a.m. I'd like you to attend. I've already invited Ray and Matt. We will discuss new threats at LANL, and I will present this satellite data."

"Will the Governor be there? What about the National Guard commander?"

"The governor's representative and the Adjutant General of the Guard are supposed to be there. I'm unsure these people can be trusted, and I'd like to exclude them. But that won't work, as I'm sure you know."

After LizBeth left, Angela came into the office to report on her visit with Isaiah at his group home. She arrived bringing extra socks, underwear, and snacks and found him settled into a double room with an empty bed. He was sleeping when she arrived. Angela met with the mental health worker who lived at the group home and the supervising social worker. "It's not a bad place," Angela said, "but Isaiah is confused and fearful. We agreed he could rest and adjust for a few days before starting at Taos High School. His mother is allowed to visit over the weekend."

"Are you feeling okay about our intervention?" Ulysses asked.

"Yes," Angela answered. "But it's hard to see how confused the kid is."

"I can't imagine he'll be going home anytime soon," Ulysses said, "It sucks to be involved in separating a family. But I didn't see any other choice."

"There wasn't any other choice." Angela paused and shifted in her chair. "Agent Tallichet just told me her office has hired Eli Martinez to work with them as a cyber specialist in counterterrorism."

"Really? That's good news, isn't it?" Ulysses noticed that Angela wasn't smiling.

"I don't know, Sheriff. I haven't heard from Eli myself, so I'm not sure. But it's good news for him."

Zach knocked on the door and came in. "I just spoke with Marcie Shea. She said Mark lives at the Elect compound, where he goes by 'Major Mark.' Their son Patrick chose to live with her, but he's out there with his father on visitation days."

"Angela, you and Zach, get out to the compound and question Mark tomorrow."

"Yes, sir, we will."

"Isaiah also mentioned a dude named Colonel Gideon. Check him out, too."

"Sir, could he be Gideon Strum, the leader of the Santa Fe Knights?"

"Find out," Ulysses said.

That night, Ulysses arrived home in time for dinner with his family. Rosemary placed a casserole of green chile chicken enchiladas on the table and bowls of calabacitas, Spanish rice, and arugula salad. The children were excited to have their father home for dinner and to eat their favorite meal, which Frances called "the soft and gooey."

"Daddy, I helped Mommy make goat cheese today," Frances said, waiting for her portion to cool. "I chopped the chives and parsley!"

"That's great, Pookie," Ulysses said, using his nickname for his youngest. "I can't wait to try some. Hey, I've got good news. Eli is coming back to New Mexico."

"How does Angela feel about it?" Rosemary asked.

"She just found out," Ulysses said. "He's been offered a job working with LizBeth at the FBI."

"Well, that's closer than Washington," Amelia said. "It could be good, maybe?"

"Monty, how was your day?" Ulysses asked. Monty had his phone in his lap, which was against the rules.

Monty chewed for a minute, swallowed, and said, "Fine." He turned his phone face down.

"Did anything interesting happen?"

"Nope. Not a thing."

"Do you have homework?"

"A little."

Ulysses made a note to talk with his son after dinner. "Amelia, how was your day?"

Frances interrupted, "Mommy, this chile is hot, hot, hot!"

"It isn't hot at all!" Monty said.

"You can handle it, Frances. Eat your dinner, and don't interrupt."

"It was better the past couple of days without Patrick Shea preaching at us," Amelia answered.

"How many days is he suspended for?"

"He comes back tomorrow. I'm not looking forward to it."

"Tell Daddy what you did today, Amelia," Rosemary said.

"I tried out for JV basketball," Amelia said.

"That's great, Bean! You know I played basketball at Taos High. I was…"

"I know, Dad."

"Did you get a callback?" Ulysses asked.

"I did. I'm hopeful."

"How was your day, Mama?" Ulysses asked his wife.

"Very good," she said. "I pulled up the frost-kill, shredded some, and made cheese with my daughter. But I am exhausted."

"I've got the bedtime routine," Ulysses said. "If you want to turn in early."

After dinner, Monty cleared the table, and Amelia washed the dishes while Ulysses helped Frances get into her pajamas, wash her face, and brush her teeth. Then he tucked her in bed and read a chapter from *Pippi Longstocking* to her. While Rosemary dozed on the couch in the living room, Ulysses went upstairs. He knocked on Amelia's door. She was already in bed in her pajamas, texting on her phone. Ulysses kissed her goodnight.

Monty was still in his clothes, playing a video game on his bed. When his father came in, he turned the game off.

"Hey, Son," Ulysses said.

"Hi, Dad," Monty said.

"Did you get your homework done?"

"No. I have a report to write on the Confederacy."

"What part of the Confederacy?"

"Why they seceded from the Union."

"Do you want any help?"

Monty yawned. "No, I've got it."

"Do you want to get started? Like, make an outline?"

"No, Dad, I don't. I hate writing. It's like my least favorite thing in the world."

"I understand, Buddy; I used to hate it also. My mom used to help me write my reports."

"I've done all this research and taken notes, but I don't know how to start writing. It all swims around in my head. I don't think I'm very smart."

"I know you are plenty smart, Monty. You have a terrific memory, notice everything, and are good at fixing things like your mother. Maybe you are just struggling with academics."

"I hate school," Monty said. "I always have."

"I know you hate school. Your teachers want to have you tested for a learning disability. Mom thinks it's a good idea. What do you say?"

Monty lay flat on the bed, put a pillow over his head, and said nothing.

"I'll take that as a yes," Ulysses said.

"How did Grandma teach you to write?" he said from under the pillow.

"She would give the first paragraph to me, then have me write three more, and then we'd read what we wrote aloud, and then we'd edit that, and I'd write some more, and pretty soon, I could feel how it was done."

"Feel how it was done?"

"Yeah, you know, sense it inside of me."

"She would dictate to you?"

"Yeah, at first. Just the first paragraph. It worked. Eventually, I could do it on my own."

"Isn't that cheating?" Monty asked.

"It got me going. Like priming the pump."

"Will you do that for me?"

"Sure, I will. Tell you what: Why don't you shower, brush your teeth, and get in your pajamas and we can start tonight?" Monty got out of bed reluctantly and went into the bathroom. When he came back ready for bed, Ulysses helped Monty write the first paragraph.

About an hour later, Ulysses checked in with his son, who was still working on the following three paragraphs.

"How is the paper coming?"

"Terrible," Monty said. "It makes no sense." He showed Ulysses a page and a half on his computer.

"Good job writing this much, Son," Ulysses said. "It's much better than a blank page. Why don't you read it aloud to me."

Monty slammed the table with his hand when he finished reading and said, "See what I mean? It's crap."

Ulysses said, "Wait a minute. It just needs a little organizing. You said you were most interested in why the Confederacy seceded, right? So, what sentence most clearly states your understanding of why they left the Union? That is what you call the theme sentence."

When Monty found his theme sentence, Ulysses said, "So put that sentence at the end of the first paragraph."

"Then I'll have to rewrite the whole paper!" Monty said.

"Just do it," Ulysses said. "I'll hang in here with you while you do that."

After another hour of work, Monty had rewritten the paper to answer the critical question of why the states of the Confederacy seceded. All that was left was the conclusion. Monty immediately got tense and angry. "I don't know how to write a conclusion," he said.

"Look, Son, a conclusion is a summary plus at least one new thought. What new thought occurs to you when you look at what you've written."

Monty thought for a few minutes. "That the states that seceded in 1860 aren't that different from those that have seceded since McDade was elected? They don't want to follow laws they disagree with. So, if they can't change the laws, they want to secede."

"Do you think the Union will go to war this time to force them to remain in the Union?"

"No, I don't think it will. I think the whole thing is going to crumble. What do you think, Dad?"

"I don't know, but I'm pretty sure we'll be stuck with each other no matter what happens."

Later, when Monty was in bed with his lights off, Ulysses came downstairs and got in bed with his wife.

"How did your talk with Monty go?" Rosemary asked.

"I helped him with an essay due tomorrow for history class."

"He let you help him? He always says no to me."

"I think he needs more of his Daddy."

"You are right about that, Ulys."

"I wish I had more time to give him. This job is wearing me down."

Rosemary lay her head on her husband's chest. "I know you've been feeling blue lately. What's going on?"

Ulysses wrapped his arms around his wife and kissed the top of her head. "I feel like all I see is the dark side of human nature. I've been fantasizing about a career change," he said. "Are you hiring?"

Rosemary laughed. "What did you have in mind? Do you want to grow vegetables, raise milk goats, or make chutneys and cheese?"

Ulysses sighed. "As long as I don't have to deal with crime day in and day out, I'll do just about anything. The problem is, I don't think I can work for just any boss. But I could work for you!" He kissed her.

"I would hate to be your boss, you big alpha dog. But seriously, Ulys, what's causing you to feel this way?"

"The feeling has been coming on for some time, but this most recent homicide hit me harder than usual, that young man killed in town. And yesterday at Headquarters, I had a visit from Pete Dowd, which shook me up. I had a bad dream about it."

"Is Pete still sober?" Rosemary asked.

"I think so, but he has liver cancer."

"That's terrible. What stage?"

"I don't know but he looked sick. Thin and sallow. And smoking like a chimney."

"What brought him to Taos?"

"Something about the murder of a Catholic priest in Santa Fe."

"Rita Wainwright talked about that on her podcast today," Rosemary said. "Father Timothy Flynn?"

"That's him," Ulysses said.

"Rita said he'd been involved in anti-nuclear activity for years," Rosemary said. "A source told her the Santa Fe Knights threatened him."

"It's crazy right now with all these armed fanatics," Ulysses said, scooting down in bed and pulling up the covers. "But if I talk about it, I'll get worked up and probably won't sleep. I have an early meeting in Santa Fe."

Rosemary reached over and turned off the light. "Come here, Babe," she said, wrapping her arms around him. "Just this moment, right?" she said, reminding him of his mantra.

Ulysses began to repeat his mantra and fell asleep.

Angela drove home after dark, anxious and exhausted from work. Before she pulled into her driveway, she noticed a car with government tags parked in front of her house. As she approached her shadowy front porch, a man stood up from the swing, causing her a moment of panic. Then she realized it was Eli Martinez, her old boyfriend. She took a deep breath and said, "Hi, Eli, what are you doing here?"

"I'm sorry if I startled you. I just got to Albuquerque yesterday and wanted to see you as soon as possible."

Eli came down the steps and embraced her. Angela pulled away slightly, but when Eli kissed her, she struggled not to kiss him back. "I fished my wish," he said. I've got an appointment at the Albuquerque office doing counterterrorism. And they are sending me to Santa Fe to work with Agent Tallichet."

"That's good news, Eli," Angela said. "Have you seen your family yet?"

"Not yet. I came right here."

"Where are you staying?"

"I was hoping I could stay with you," he said.

Mr. T, Angela's elderly Siamese cat, came out of the bushes and meowed loudly.

"He's hungry," Angela said. "Come in while I feed him."

Eli followed her inside, leaving his small backpack on the porch. Angela put down her briefcase, took off her holster, loosened her belt, and stowed her gun in the safe. While she fed Mr. T, Eli stood, his arms crossed over his chest, watching her and saying nothing. Angela noticed he'd shaved off his goatee and cut his hair. *He's just as handsome, but I miss his braids.*

"Are you glad to see me?" he asked.

"Yes, but I'm not sure I'm ready to pick up where we left off," Angela said.

"That's reasonable. A lot has changed since we were last together."

Angela nodded.

"My feelings for you haven't changed," Eli said. "I still want us to be together."

"Have you eaten?" Angela asked, changing the subject. "I have some good green chile stew and fresh tortillas. There's beer and kombucha in the fridge."

"That would be wonderful. Then, if you like, I can get a room in town. We don't have to rush anything." Eli took a bottle of porter out of a six-pack and opened it.

"That would be good," Angela said. "I'm not ready."

"I want us to talk," Eli said. "Please tell me what you are feeling."

Angela heated the stew and warmed the tortillas. When she put it all on the table, she said, "I'm feeling a lot of things, Eli. I'm scared of how much it hurts to be apart from you. I'm wondering if any of this will work, given our jobs in these crazy times."

Eli quietly ate his stew and tortillas. "This stew is delicious," he said. "When did you learn to cook?"

Angela laughed and drank from her beer. "I got it from the Co-op," she said.

"We both work too much," Eli said when he'd finished eating. "It will be hard for us to have much time together. But can't we try? I've missed you so much."

Angela could feel resolve wavering. *Do I want to give this up?*

Eli gathered the dishes and took them to the sink. Angela wiped off the table. Eli came up behind her and kissed her on the neck. She felt chills and arousal, but she didn't turn around to face him. He whispered, "Thanks for dinner," kissed her neck again, then turned to walk out the door.

"I'll call you," Angela said as he departed. He waved without turning around.

Chapter 8

Ray had been dozing on the couch after dinner when Matt came in to review the War Council's plan to scale the fence at the Elect compound to see what was stored in the newly created bunker on Picuris land. Ray got up and turned off the television. He offered his son coffee and cookies, and the two sat in the quiet living room. Matt seemed nervous.

Matt had selected his two most fearless members of the War Council, his cousin Miguel and an older Iraq war veteran named Frank, to accompany him. Besides the War Council, Ray, as governor, was the only other person who was informed about the mission.

"What time are you heading up there?" Ray asked.

"A little after midnight. We'll wait for the moon to set. We're heading up the big arroyo to take the trail to Lizard Head," he said, referring to a sinuous ridge that ended in sandstone cliffs and appeared like a giant lizard from a distance. "Just on the other side is where their fence corners, but there aren't any lights or razor wire, so that's where we'll enter."

"How much gear are you taking?"

"ARs, ammo, and night vision. We'll wear Kevlar and ski masks, and I'll carry the infrared camera I bought last summer. Miguel is bringing a dosimeter from work. It fits in his pocket."

"You know that place is bound to be well guarded," Ray said.

"I know. We are carrying side arms and tasers. We plan to incapacitate any guards first, then see if we can get inside. Then we'll take measurements and pictures of what we find." Matt cleared his throat, sipped coffee, and picked up a cookie.

"Be careful not to speak Indian," Ray said. "We don't want them to know we broke into our own land." He chuckled. "They'll probably blame it on the anti-nuclear crowd. And for God's sake, don't use names!"

"Dad. I know."

"That's good. You are a good leader, Matt, but watch out. Frank is headstrong, and Miguel always pulls a fast one. He'll be up and over the fence before the two of you even get started. All that track and field."

"Plus, he's ten years younger than me and twenty years younger than Frank."

"But Frank has experience—two tours in Iraq. Son, you may be in command, but you've never done anything like this before. Be careful out there!"

"I will, Dad. Relax."

"What did you tell Sarah?"

"I told her we were doing maneuvers with our new night vision."

"She's got to know you are lying." Ray sighed. "She's not going to be happy with you."

"I'm not looking forward to her wrath," Matt said. "But this has to be done."

"Yeah, it's part of the job."

Matt left his father's house and walked home to put Micah to bed. The night was cold and still. Clouds had settled over the mountains, and the season's first snow was expected. Matt thought about his wife, Sarah, and their son, Micah, who had turned seven during the summer and was now in first grade. He was leading this mission for them, even though his risk-averse wife opposed any illegal activity. Once he and his father saw reconnaissance of the bunker and heard what might be stored in it, Matt knew he had to see what was happening with his own eyes. Neither he nor Ray believed they could wait for the FBI to take the necessary steps. Either way, the health and survival of the pueblo were at stake. Matt understood that he, Miguel, and Frank could be injured or killed.

The team met just after midnight and hiked up the arroyo to where the fence crossed onto Picuris land. About 100 yards from the fence, a large, recently completed house occupied the high ground. Another new house was under construction. For about 200 yards up the slope, the property was dark, quiet, and thick with spruce, fir, and Ponderosa pines.

The wind blew, and snow fell as the three men scaled the fence. On the other side, Matt paused to listen and look around for any threats. He didn't see any guards. Matt led the way in the dark, first downhill and then up again, through brush and boulders. It was slow going, even with night vision. They crept along to where the fence angled to come around the steep, rock face of a hill, the high point of the boundary. Behind the rock face was a bunker. The snow grew heavier, further restricting visibility.

As they neared the bunker, Matt spotted two men with guns crouched beneath a roof that overhung the metal door. The door was large, heavy-duty, garage-style, and closed.

Miguel and Frank were behind Matt. They were shielded from view by the slope. One guard appeared to be asleep. The light of a phone showed the other guard's face.

"Frank and I will go in, guns drawn. Miguel, if they fire on us, return fire. I'll do the talking. I'll try to get them to open the door. Frank, cuff them both. Taser them only if necessary. Miguel, you take dosimeter readings outside. If we get inside, continue to take readings, and I'll take pictures. Activity at the door may bring lights, sirens, and other guards. Frank, you go up the fence first and cut the razor wire, then cover us from up there. We'll need to get over the fence as quickly as we can. Okay, let's go."

Matt ran toward the guards with Frank and Miguel following close behind. The man with the cell phone screamed in fear and grabbed his gun but quickly put his hands in the air. The one who'd been asleep, scarcely more than a boy, dropped his weapon and sat still. Frank cuffed them together back-to-back. Matt saw a code pad mounted near the door.

"What's the code to open the door?" Matt asked the men in a whisper.

"We don't know," the boy said. "Don't hurt us!"

The other guard said nothing. Frank stepped over to him and showed his taser. "It's 1488," he said, responding to the threat. "But if you open it, all hell will break loose."

Standing outside the door, Miguel looked at his dosimeter in disbelief. "This place is red hot," he said. Frank pressed the code into the pad. Immediately, klieg lights came on. The heavy metal door did not open at first, but when Frank pressed it again, it shuddered and lifted, and a siren began to sound. Matt ran inside a concrete-floored room about twenty feet by thirty feet full of metal crates.

"This thing is pegged at "dangerous to human health," Miguel said. Matt took pictures with the infrared camera and several with his cellphone. Frank scaled the fence and had begun cutting the razor wire when they heard the first gunfire. Miguel went over the fence and down quickly. As Matt climbed, there was more gunfire. Frank covered the last of Matt's climb with his AR, but as Matt came over the top, he missed his footing and fell hard on the rocks below, dislocating his shoulder. When Matt stood up, Frank started to run downhill, one arm holding his side.

Miguel and Frank made their way downhill as ordered, with Miguel running and Frank moving more gingerly. Fueled by adrenaline, Matt ran after them, afraid a horde of angry soldiers would follow them. He was in excruciating pain and stumbled several times on the way down, but fueled by adrenaline, he moved fast. When the three came to the top of the arroyo that led down to the village road, they saw the rest of the war council gathered, staking out positions to fire on any pursuers. Behind them, they could still hear the siren and see the lights, but no pursuers.

On Blueberry Hill, Serena Hurley sat up in bed and listened. *What woke me up,* she wondered? She heard only her daughter's gentle breathing and a log settling in the wood stove. The fear that seemed to have become her constant companion made her heart pound. A pack of coyotes howled again nearby. Serena shivered. Ever since childhood, when coyotes had killed a beloved cat, she'd hated that sound. *It's only coyotes,* she thought. *They can't hurt us.* Serena got out of bed, pulled on her clothes, and lit a kerosene lamp. She opened the damper on the stove and added a few logs. She took her gun out of its bag, checked the safety, and set it on the table near her phone. It was only 4 am, but she knew she'd never get back to sleep.

Serena pulled a rocking chair close to the stove, tucked a blanket over her legs, and tried to calm herself. Her mind drifted back to her political awakening eight months earlier. Before then, Serena had never paid attention to politics or even voted. Busy at her job and with her daughter, she had barely noticed the rising tide of political violence. Then came President McDade's close victory over Nationalist candidate Duke Hadest, followed by weeks of civil unrest. Like many watching McDade's inauguration, Serena saw the horror unfold as the Supreme Court Chief Justice administered the oath of office to the President-elect. Snipers opened fire, killing the Chief Justice and President McDade's wife, Julianne. She was a mother of a daughter Kaylee's age. Dozens were injured, including the Democratic-Republican Speaker of the House, who died three days later.

Serena began to pay attention, and since then, she'd grown more fearful as the country divided into armed camps of partisans. Wyoming, her home for ten years, had voted overwhelmingly for Hadest and followed Texas and Oklahoma in secession from the Union. First, there was a news blackout. Then, the governor declared martial law, suspended the state constitution, and began drafting young men into his "Righteous Guard", as Nationalists called their force made up of National Guardsmen and new conscripts.

One day, as Serena sat in traffic in front of the Capital complex, she saw dozens of protesters loaded into buses at gunpoint. She learned the protestors were held in old barracks at the Air Force Base where she worked. Wearing her identity card, she got close enough to see the dilapidated wooden buildings, muddy yards, and fences topped with razor wire where detainees, including women with small children, milled around or huddled in small groups in light rain, obviously cold and miserable. She recognized one of the women from Kaylee's daycare. Serena had become radicalized that day.

Kaylee was still sleeping soundly. Serena filled the kettle and set it on the wood stove. She dug around in a cabinet and found a box of tea, powdered milk, cocoa, and sugar packets. When the water boiled, she made herself a cup of tea and cocoa for Kaylee. Then, she sat back in her rocking chair and thought about the events that led her to flee Wyoming for New Mexico.

It all began with finding a website called Nuclear Peace and Justice. The site was decidedly left-wing, and most of its ideas were unfamiliar to Serena. Still, she spent hours reading the news, analysis, and commentary posted and following the links provided, especially at night after her husband and daughter were asleep. She became familiar with the people who were frequent contributors, and eventually, she responded to one of them, a man who used the handle "Malcolm."

Malcolm wrote often about how the Nationalists had infiltrated Los Alamos National Lab and were planning to use nuclear materials to regain power. He called for a "People's Cadre" to prevent this calamity. Serena, whose stepfather, Nick Boyar, oversaw LANL's plutonium pit production facility, began to fantasize about joining the fight. What better way to get back at her abuser than to expose him as a terrorist? However, she told Malcolm nothing about her stepfather because she had even more meaningful information to share.

Around the same time, she discovered Nuclear Peace and Justice, Serena had become suspicious of her boss, Brigadier General John Baynes, an avowed Nationalist and Klan member. Warren Air Force Base housed the Minuteman III missiles. Just before the election, they had received the first shipment of the most up-to-date materials from LANL for a newly commissioned missile deployment program called the Crusader.

The previous summer, Baynes had Serena place daily calls to secure compounds in Texas and New Mexico. She was never allowed to listen to those calls, but from loose talk among the men, she learned that Baynes was talking with Duke Hadest, Daniel

Graves, also known as the Servant, and other men. Whatever they were talking about was top-secret and urgent.

One day in September, Serena was in the office when security and a technician arrived with an odd-looking metal case they loaded into the vault. Baynes handed Serena a file of information and asked her to prepare a document with all the specs for the case, including its contents, storage requirements, and other safety details. That was how she discovered that the case, or "toolbox," as Baynes called it, contained almost a pound of finely processed weapons-grade plutonium. According to Baynes' safety specs, weapons-grade plutonium was safe to handle or transport if it remained in its packaging. Serena, whose job required her to open Baynes's vault regularly, resolved to steal the case, bring it to New Mexico, and give it to Malcolm. By now, she knew that Malcolm's real name was Jesse Porter and that he lived in Taos.

Serena fantasized about being the heroine of a story in which Baynes was thwarted, her stepfather was exposed, and the kind, brave, and handsome Jesse became her lover. Even though she cherished her husband and didn't want to leave him, the fantasy exhilarated her and encouraged her to take more risks.

Serena felt sick when she thought of everything that had transpired since fleeing Wyoming. Jesse was dead, and she had allowed the activists to take the toolbox. Where had Monica and that man taken it, and what kind of harm might it cause? Jesse had told her it would only be used to negotiate peace, but was that true? Serena felt confused. She wished she had never gotten involved. *How could I have been so foolish?* She glanced over at her daughter, who had awakened and was now sitting up in bed.

"Mommy, can we go home?" Kaylee asked. "I miss Daddy!"

"Soon, sweetheart," Serena said. "I miss Daddy, too. Come, sit on my lap. I've made you some cocoa, and it's just the right temperature for you."

LizBeth Tallichet was sound asleep at the Sagebrush Inn in Taos when the room phone woke her. It was her boss, FBI special agent Nancy Levine, calling from Albuquerque.

"You didn't answer your cellphone, LizBeth," Levine said.

LizBeth picked up her phone from the bedside table; it was dead. She quickly plugged it in. "I'm sorry," she said. She looked at the hotel clock. It was 3 am.

"Don't let that happen again. I'm glad I knew where to find you."

"I'll be more careful. You must have some big news."

"Oh, boy, do I. The report on Santistevan's helicopter crash is being released through secure top-secret channels at 8 am Eastern Time. Santistevan was assassinated. Governor Hobbs and his chief of staff are in custody and about to be indicted as accessories. President McDade has federalized the National Guard and removed the Adjutant General, who is also implicated."

"Holy shit," LizBeth said. "We won't have the Rapid Response Team meeting I planned for this morning."

"No, indeed," Levine said. "We must streamline that group. I am deploying you to Santa Fe full-time. I've arranged for office space for you to establish a command center at the Roundhouse."

LizBeth took a deep breath and stood up. "Who is the Acting Governor?" she asked.

"Since there's no lieutenant governor, it's the Secretary of State, Barbara Garcia. She's from Las Cruces, about seventy, and not a Nationalist. She was sworn in at midnight."

"I've met her," LizBeth said. "She seems like a reasonable person."

"Who do you want on your team at the Roundhouse?"

LizBeth began to pace. She didn't know the answer to that question.

"Getting rid of Governor Hobbs and Adjutant General Gruber is a good start. Sheriff Bustos of Rio Arriba is not trustworthy because he is a militia member, although he denies it. And Sheriff Marjory Blanca seems unreliable."

"Who *do* you trust?" Levine asked.

"I need a lot of consultants who I can't take away from their important day jobs, like Santa Fe Sheriff Villalobos, Bill Samuelson from ATF, Attorney General Lex Sisneros, and my old colleagues Sheriff Ulysses Walker of Taos and Governor Ray Pando of Picuris."

"Get them to commit to regular meetings with you and to prioritize your direction."

"Okay. It's too bad we don't have people on the ground at LANL. Do you have anyone undercover up there that you haven't told me about?"

"Let me get back to you on that," Levine said.

"It will be a smaller team," LizBeth said, "but more trustworthy. I want to bring Eli Martinez along. And the four agents who have worked with me here in El Norte. I'll give you a list."

"I will send the people you request, plus your office staff from Albuquerque. We'll move them to Santa Fe, starting tomorrow."

"Where are you going to be?' LizBeth asked.

"There's skirmishing on the Texas border around Hobbs, and the President wants me to keep him abreast on that conflict. Today, he's going to invoke the Insurrection Act."

This situation just got a lot scarier, LizBeth thought

"Monty, did you finish your paper?" Ulysses asked when the boy came to breakfast dressed for school. Amelia had already eaten and gone upstairs. Rosemary was milking the goats with Frances in tow.

"Yeah, but can you review it before I print it?" Monty asked.

"Okay. Get it on your computer for me to look at."

When Ulysses read the boy's paper, he was surprised at the writing's quality. "Monty," he said, "this is a very good paper. I corrected a few misspellings and added a comma or two. Print it, turn it in, and rest easy."

"Are you sure?" Monty asked.

"I am sure," Ulysses said, feeling gratified that he'd managed to help his son.

Ulysses arrived at Headquarters, and Angela was at her desk. Ramona had made coffee and warmed some apple empanadas.

"Sheriff," Ramona said, "your meeting in Santa Fe was canceled. Agent Tallichet wants you to call her."

Ulysses went into his office and closed the door. LizBeth picked up on the first ring.

"Glad I caught you," LizBeth said. "That meeting is canceled, but can you come to my new office this afternoon for a different meeting? It's at the Roundhouse at 3."

"Yes," he said, considering checking in with Pete Dowd while he was in Santa Fe.

"Listen, Ulys. Is your line secure?"

"As far as I know."

"Governor Hobbs and his chief of staff have been arrested. And the Adjutant General of the National Guard, William Gruber, has been replaced."

"Wow. What is the crime?"

"The assassination of Governor Santistevan. Hobbs and his chief of staff have been charged and are in custody. Gruber has not been taken into custody yet."

"Who took over as Governor? We never had the special election for Lieutenant Governor."

"The Secretary of State. She was sworn in this morning."

"Barbara Garcia," Ulysses said. "She's a good egg."

"Ulys, I could use your help with something. We received anonymous intel about what's in that bunker on Picuris land."

"Anonymous intel?"

"Picuris went in with a team and broke into the bunker. They took very high dosimeter readings. Like dangerous to human health readings. And they have photographs."

"Ray and Matt weren't willing to wait, I guess."

"Just between us, I don't blame them," LizBeth said. "I need you to talk to Ray. He denied the raid to me, but I was hoping you could get him to own up to it so we can work together. Call on him and find out what they know."

After Ulysses hung up the phone, Angela knocked on his door. "Sir, can I tell you about our interview with Mark Shea?"

"Come on in," Ulysses said. "Did you arrest him?"

"No, we didn't have enough evidence to arrest. He came

with the Elect lawyer and denied everything. He accused Isaiah Patterson of inflicting wounds on himself. He said the boy had done it before, and the lawyer referenced a release he had for hospital records saying as much."

"Who signed the release?"

"Isaiah's parents, of course," Angela said. "The kid has been psychiatrically hospitalized three times. He's been diagnosed with several conditions, including autism." Angela gave a dubious look and shrugged her shoulders.

"That seems like a dodge," Ulysses said.

"What are your next steps?" Ulysses asked.

"Zach wants to interview the boys who may have witnessed the incident and their 'trainers,' but some are minors, so we'll have to be accompanied by a social worker. He also plans to talk with the doctors who examined Isaiah after this most recent episode."

"Keep me posted, Angela," Ulysses said.

Ulysses then called Ray Pando but got his voicemail. "I'm on my way to see you," Ulysses said to his voicemail. "I should be there in thirty minutes."

On the drive to Picuris, Ulysses pondered the increasing instability in New Mexico. Carlos Santistevan, a gifted orator, had been beloved by Hispanics and trusted by Anglos and the Native population. A landslide re-elected Santistevan after his administration had presided over four years of relative prosperity. His tragic death in a time of national turmoil was traumatic for many in the state.

Hobbs wasn't a popular governor and was viewed with suspicion by many. Only Nationalist sympathizers and militia members saw him as one of their own. How would they react to his arrest? Texas felt very close, a state that had seceded from the Union and provided a haven for Duke Hadest and his army. Would Texas militias swarm over the border? Ulysses shook his head as if to rid himself of dark thoughts. *I had better keep my wits about me and not succumb to paranoia.*

Ulysses thought about his meeting with Ray this morning. Ulysses had always known Ray to be a thoughtful, even cautious man. But this situation was bound to put the tribe on high alert. What would Ray, as governor, want to do about it? And what would Matt and the younger tribal members want? *I'm glad this isn't in my jurisdiction,* he thought as he pulled onto the reservation. *I can be a friend and not law enforcement.*

Ulysses parked the cruiser and got out. The plaza in front of San Lorenzo Church was empty but for a few elderly people chatting together under a big elm. He heard chanting from somewhere, maybe a kiva, one of which stood in the upper plaza behind and to the rear of the church. Ulysses walked toward Ray's home, an adobe that faced the church with a wide porch on the west-facing side. As he approached the front door, a woman came out, drying her hands on a dish towel. "Come in, Sheriff Walker; Ray got your message. He should be here in a little while. I'll get you some coffee." They shook hands.

Ulysses remembered Billie Arguello, the tribal secretary who had helped him in a previous investigation. He followed her inside to the comfortable living room, where he'd spent time visiting with Ray when Clarice was alive and a few times since Ray had been widowed.

"Have a seat, Sheriff," Billie said. "Cream and sugar?"

"Sure," Ulysses said. Cable news was on the television. An announcer was discussing the swearing-in of the new governor.

"Big news day," Billie said, handing Ulysses a mug of hot coffee.

"That's for sure," Ulysses said. "Where is Ray?"

"He's in the kiva," Billie said.

Ulysses didn't say anything. He sipped his coffee and picked up a peanut butter cookie from a plate she set on the coffee table. "Did you make these?"

"Yeah. Ray is a better cook than me, but I'm better at cookies." She laughed.

They sat in comfortable silence, listening to the television and sipping coffee. Billie sat in Clarice's old rocker, her eyes on the television. Ulysses wondered if Ray and Billie were having a relationship. He ate his cookie, and when the ad interrupted the news, he asked, "What do you think about Hobbs being arrested by the FBI?"

Billie shook her head. "I don't know what to think, Sheriff. Around here, we call it 'WMB,' which stands for 'white man's business.' But it is bound to bring more instability, and that's never good for us."

"I hope not," Ulysses said.

Ray came in the front door. "Hi, Ulys," he said. "What brings you here this morning?"

Before Ulysses could answer, Billie stood up. "I have to get back to work," she said. "There's a pot of fresh coffee if you want any, Ray."

Ray went into the kitchen and emerged with a mug. He then took a cookie and sat in his recliner. "I guess you spoke with LizBeth," he said.

"Yes," Ulysses said. "She told me there was a raid last night. She said you denied it."

"It's hard to 'raid' your own land," Ray said with a scornful laugh. "Someone tipped her off."

"Who do you think?"

"Not saying," Ray answered.

"Was anyone hurt?"

"Frank, Billie's cousin, got shot, but it was just a flesh wound. Matt dislocated his shoulder. They'll both recover."

"Look, man, I'm not here to get on your case about going in there. I'm just glad no one was killed. Those people are dangerous."

"You don't think I know that? They were shooting at our men on our land. We are in danger *right now*, Ulys."

"I know, we all are."

"Listen here. They have dynamite and radioactive material stored not two miles from us. What the hell?" Ulysses had never seen Ray so angry before.

"Ray, calm down. I'm on your side."

"Don't tell me to calm down, and don't say you are on my side unless you are ready to go to war with those fanatics."

"Okay, I hear you," Ulysses said. "I am just trying to understand what happened last night and what the tribe plans to do."

"I can answer the first question but not the second one. The truth is, I don't know what we will do. Everyone is either scared to death or crazy angry. I'm still trying to settle down enough to think."

"I understand. I feel the same way. Tell me about last night."

"Matt and the boys conducted a reconnaissance operation. We didn't hurt anyone."

"What did you find?"

"Inside the bunker, the dosimeter readings were in the 'danger to human health' range. We have pictures. Big containers full of God knows what. Together with the dynamite you told me about and all the other weapons they have, they can murder us all whenever they want. We have plenty of weapons here, but they have more and stuff we don't have." Ray ran his fingers through his grey hair and stuck strands loose from his braid behind his ears. He stood up and started to pace. "I've never been faced with this level of threat before. Honestly, I don't know what to do."

"Have you spoken with LizBeth?"

Ray frowned and shook his head. "I told her it wasn't us, but I guess she didn't believe me."

"No, I don't think she did. Ray, you've got to level with her. She and her team are our best hope. No one will fault you for entering an illegal facility on your land."

"Are you sure? I'm not. Some think we should take matters into our own hands, maybe get the other tribes in the region to rise with us and go in there. But that seems like a fantasy to me."

"It sounds like a way to get a lot of people killed." Ulysses set his coffee cup on the table and stood up. "LizBeth wants me to meet her at the Roundhouse this afternoon. Will you come with me?"

"What is the meeting about?"

"About what to do next, I'm pretty sure. She wants our input. It would be good for you to be there."

"I have to return to the kiva now," Ray said. "I'll think about it, and if I'm coming, I'll drive myself."

Nick Boyar welcomed his subordinate, Philip Devin, into his office. He offered him an Eames chair in front of a floor-to-ceiling window that overlooked the Pajarito Plateau, with the snow-capped Sangre de Cristo Mountains visible in the distance. Philip removed clips from his trousers and placed them in his fanny pack. He had broken a sweat on his bike ride to LANL from White Rock, and he wiped his forehead with a bandana.

"Enjoying your leave time, Phil?" Boyar asked.

"Yes, and why not? It's coming out of my account, isn't it?"

"That's the way it works, bro."

"So, what's up?" Devin asked.

"Not much," Boyar said, remaining standing. He rocked back and forth on the heels of his expensive shoes. "I need a favor from you." He smiled, showing white, even teeth. "It's a private matter. I hope I can rely on your discretion?"

Devin laughed. "Of course you can. Don't you always?"

"My stepdaughter and her six-year-old child are somewhere in the area. My wife is desperate to see them. I want you to locate them so I can bring them to her."

"How would I know where to find your stepdaughter?" Devin asked.

"We believe she's staying with that crowd I asked you to watch."

Devin laughed again and crossed his legs. "I see. She's part of Nuclear Peace and Justice?"

"Perhaps not formally," Boyar said, unbuttoning his suit jacket and sitting across from Philip in an identical chair. "But I believe she is, what do they call it, a fellow traveler? Can you find her?"

"I'll do my best," Philip answered. "What do you want me to do with her when I find her?"

Boyar thought for a moment. "Just tell me where she is. I'll pick her up and facilitate the reunion. Elena is being impossible about it."

Philip shifted in his chair. "Is there anything else?"

"There is something more important than Elena's daughter that I want you to locate."

"Okay, tell me about it."

"My stepdaughter used to work at Warren Air Force Base in Cheyenne. When she came here, something went missing. Duke Hadest has been pretty worked up about getting it back. He's sending his ops team to look for it. I'd like you to find it *and* her before they do. "

"What is it?" Devin asked.

"That's above your pay grade, my friend," Boyar said. "Suffice it to say that it is essential enough to the mission that Hadest himself is involved in getting it back."

"Well, what does it look like, then?"

"It's a box with a handle, the size of a carry-on suitcase. It weighs about forty pounds."

"Sounds interesting. Is it dangerous to handle?"

"No, it shouldn't be."

"Okay, but what's in it for me?"

Boyar smiled. "The kind of reward you like best. Cash. Six figures for both."

"I'd like six figures each," Devin said.

"I'll see what I can do."

"What do you think about Hobbs getting arrested?" Devin asked. "Are you in any trouble?"

Boyar gave him a sharp look. "Why would I be in trouble? I've had nothing to do with Hobbs since he took office, and now he's headed for the supermax in Florence, Colorado. Gruber and all his senior staff escaped to Texas, so we'll likely hear no more from either of them." There was a knock on the door, and a young man brought Boyar's lunch on a tray. "Okay, Devin, that is all. Begone. Let me know what you find." He looked at his watch. "I have a meeting in the SCIF in half an hour."

As Devin got up to leave, the waiter said, "Dr. Boyar, the Director wants to speak with you before the meeting. He said it was urgent."

Boyar looked annoyed but said nothing as he cut into his petit filet.

After lunch, Nick Boyar knocked on the nearby office door

of Dr. Jonathan Shapiro, the LANL Director. Shapiro was a year away from retirement and frequently out of the office, using up his ample personal leave time. This left Boyar in charge, which was how he preferred it. Shapiro had a reputation for being a micromanager. "Come in, Nick," Shapiro said. "I want to discuss something with you before our SCIF meeting."

"Of course," Boyar said. "How can I help?"

"The worker you had arrested, uh…" he looked at a top-secret briefing he held to check the name. "Charlotte Foster. She was employed here for four years and reported to Philip Devin?"

"That is correct," Nick said. *I hate this man,* he thought. *I wish he would go ahead and die before he finds a way to pin something on me.*

"When Foster was arrested, you said she was a Nationalist sympathizer, right? What was your intel on her politics?"

"Her husband was an officer in the Santa Fe Knights. They attended Flags of Our Fathers, and she was a Nationalist precinct captain four years ago."

"Yes, I see all that. But you didn't review her security clearance before placing her in the pit production facility?"

"No, at that time, she had no offenses and wasn't up for re-evaluation. Sometime after the election, she divorced her husband and left the church. So, we felt that her Nationalist ties were neutralized. And Devin was pleased with her work."

"Then she brought a whistleblower complaint in September. What was that about?"

"Old pit waste was missing from her unit. She filed a safety complaint. It was a routine procedure. We investigated the matter."

"Then you charged her with stealing the material she reported missing? She had a perfect work record. Did you have anything else on her?"

"One of her co-workers mentioned that he had seen her snooping around in a restricted area of the facility, where the missing materials were stored, before filing the complaint. His interview is included in the materials you are holding."

"I read the interview," Shapiro said. "She had clearance to be in that part of the facility. There wasn't anything in that interview that justified arresting her. Did you know she'd been affiliated with Nuclear Peace and Justice for about six months?"

Boyar's face remained impassive. "I heard that same rumor, Jon, but Devin checked it out, and it's false," he said. "She's never been affiliated with the anti-nuclear movement. She has some enemies here at LANL, though. People don't like her and don't trust her. They think that where there's smoke, there could be fire."

"That's not a reason to target her. Or anyone," Shapiro said. "Look, we must be vigilant right now. The potential for infiltration by the Nationalists has never been higher. But we must follow the rule of law."

"I understand, Jon. I have never done otherwise!"

"Nick, in our meeting today, you will be asked whether you targeted Charlotte Foster because she was a whistleblower, which is against the law."

"Truly? Relax, Jon, I did not break the law. My team had her arrested because of legitimate concerns, and when we didn't have enough to indict her, she was released," Boyar said with a shrug.

Shapiro looked distressed. His red-rimmed eyes were watery, and his skin had an unhealthy pallor. "Don't be cavalier, Nick. You know what is at stake here. We are closing in on what happened on 285 South when the waste truck was intercepted, and the material was stolen. I wanted to give you a heads-up. I hope you understand."

"What are you trying to say, Jon?"

"Nick, you are a person of interest in this investigation."

Undersheriff Angela Romero and Deputy Zach Wright drove through the gate at the Elect compound and parked in front of the Welcome Center. Lisa White, the social worker assigned to assist with the interviews, was standing by her car, talking on her cell phone. She ended the call and came over to shake their hands.

"Thanks for the case summary," she said, indicating the folder she was holding. "Is there anything else I should know about?" White, with a weathered face and bright blue eyes, wore corduroy slacks and a sweater featuring a smiling jack-o-lantern.

"Did you see the records from Isaiah's hospitalization?" Angela asked.

"The boy has a severe trauma history," she answered. "He's made a very serious complaint. I'm glad you are going to be interviewing some witnesses. Who will we see today?"

"Mark Shea, a.k.a. Major Mark, and two boys who witnessed the incident, Jacob Graves and David Valdes. Shea worked closely with Angela and me for many years. We've asked to speak with Mark's commanding officer, Gideon Strum, but I'm not sure he's available. Strum wasn't there during the incident in question."

"Is that Gideon Strum of the Santa Fe Knights?" White asked.

"Yes," Angela said. "He's the commander, I think. And an ex-con. Okay, if you two are ready, let's do this," Angela said.

As they entered the center, Zach presented their paperwork and introduced Lisa White. At the same time, Angela ensured the room's camera was not operational so that no one could monitor the interviews.

First to be questioned was Mark Shea, a former deputy and subordinate of Angela. Mark entered and sat down without acknowledging his former colleagues. He wore a military-style cap and a black uniform adorned with a red emblem of a cross and flag. He did not make eye contact with Angela or Zach.

"Were you present during the training exercise when Isaiah alleges you and a member of your honor guard injured him?" Zach asked.

"Yes," he said.

"Did you grab Isaiah Patterson and push him to the ground?"

"No, I did not. We never discipline children in anger."

"What kind of discipline is appropriate for minor children here?"

"Our religion specifies that we use the rod on hands, the backs of knees or buttocks."

"Have you ever disciplined Isaiah Patterson?"

"Yes."

"More than once?"

"Yes. He is a troubled youth."

"Isaiah has reported that after you knocked him to the ground, another boy kicked him in the ribs. A medical examination showed cracked ribs and bruising. Did you witness this?"

Shea rolled his eyes. "No. But I do know that Isaiah has faked injuries in the past."

"These injuries were not faked," Angela said. "I have the medical report here." She slid the paper copy across the table. Shea neither looked at her nor the paper.

"Mr. Shea," Lisa White asked, "have you ever seen Isaiah bullied by the other boys?"

"What does she mean by bullied?" Shea asked.

"Just answer the question, Mark," Zach said. "You know what bullying is."

"No. But the boys don't like him. He is not a good team member."

"That'll do, Mr. Shea," Angela said. "We will have more questions for you later."

Shea stood up, looked briefly at the camera, and left the room.

"He looks like a zombie," Zach said.

"I'm so glad I never have to work with him again," Angela said, shaking her head. "But let's move on. Zach, go get David Valdes."

David was about fourteen and had lived at the compound with his parents for six months. He was short and compact, with the beginnings of a mustache.

Angela introduced herself. "You aren't in any trouble, David," she said. "We want to ask you some questions. Please answer as truthfully as possible." David nodded and swallowed hard.

"How do you know Isaiah Patterson?"

"He is a fellow cadet."

"What do you think of him? You can be honest."

David looked around the room and at the camera. "Is that on?" he asked.

"No," Angela said. "It has a red light at the bottom if it's on."

David's adam's apple bobbed as he swallowed again. He cleared his throat. "I feel sorry for him."

"Why is that?" Angela asked.

"Nobody likes him. Boys come up behind him and pull down his pants. Then he cries. Crying is a punishing offense."

"What happens if you cry?"

"Maybe the rod. Maybe a fast."

"Have you witnessed the rod administered?"

David looked at the camera again. "Are you sure that is off?"

"Yes, I'm sure."

"I've seen it a lot. I hate it." David's lips were twitching

"Has it happened to you?"

"Yes. But it happens to Isaiah the most." His voice was almost a whisper.

"Why, do you think?"'

"Lots of reasons. They say he's crazy. He doesn't believe in God. Anyway, I feel sorry for him. He practically lived in the dungeon last summer." Tears were welling in David's brown eyes.

"What is the dungeon?" Lisa asked.

"It's a children's detention center," David said. "I've never been there, but I've heard about it."

"Did you see the Major knock Isaiah to the ground? Did you see anyone kick him?"

"I don't want to answer any more questions," David said. "Can I go now?"

Angela looked at the social worker, who nodded permission. "Can you just answer those questions? Did Major Mark knock Isaiah to the ground?"

David nodded his head.

"Then did one of the boys kick him?"

Again, David nodded yes. "Please don't tell them I told you!"

"We won't, David. This is just between us," Angela said.

"Do you feel safe at home?" Lisa White asked.

"Yes, Mom and Dad know all about this. My parents are sick of this place. We want to leave."

"If you need help, David, day or night, you can reach me at this number." White gave her card to the boy before he left the room.

"These children are in danger," White said after David left the room. "We need to remove David as soon as possible. I will report this situation to the governor. But she's certainly got a full plate right now."

"It's mass chaos everywhere," Zach said, shaking his head. "How will we ever get back on track?"

"We just have to do the next right thing," Angela said, patting him on the shoulder. "Over and over. Go get Jacob."

Jacob Graves came in behind Zach, looked at the camera, and smiled. "You got it turned off?" he said. "How'd you do that?" Jacob was eighteen, tall and athletic, with buzz-cut blonde hair. He was wearing a cadet uniform like the one worn by Mark Shea. It had a patch on his upper arm that said, "Honor Guard."

"Have a seat, Jacob," Zach said. We have a few questions for you."

The boy gazed confidently at the deputy and ignored the two women. "Sure thing," he said.

"How long have you lived here?"

"Since it opened," he said. "My mother is the Servant's first wife."

"Do you live with your mother and father, then?"

"Yes, but when I turn eighteen, I'll get an apartment in the single men's housing."

"How well do you get along with your father?"

"Very well. I am his oldest son."

"Do you know Isaiah Patterson?"

"Yes. He is one of our cadets. His father is second in command to Mr. Castleman. Who is, of course, subordinate to the Servant."

"What do you think of Isaiah?"

"He is troubled, I'd say. He struggles."

"Have you ever seen him bullied?"

Jacob stroked his chin and then said, "No. The boys are kind to him for the most part. They try to live our creed. 'Lift up the lesser ones.'"

"Do you consider Isaiah 'lesser?'" White asked. Jacob didn't answer.

"Answer the question, Jacob," Zach said.

"In some ways, yes. He is of unknown origin, being adopted. Some think he is mixed race. He is not manly. He is disobedient. And he lies." Jacob looked at his watch.

"Were you present when it is alleged that Major Mark struck Isaiah during a training exercise?"

"Yes, I was there. But I did not see the Major hit anyone."

"What did you see?" Zach asked.

"I saw David Valdes push Isaiah down and kick him while the Major and I tried to break up the fight. Eventually, Isaiah got up and ran toward the gate, accusing the Major instead of David, who he'd thought was his friend. But, as I said, Isaiah has a history of lying and resisting authority."

"What were David and Isaiah fighting about?" Zach asked.

"Isaiah had recently tried to get David to have sex with him. They deny this, but they were both disciplined for their sins before the fight."

"How were they disciplined?"

"The rod to the buttocks, witnessed by the cadets. It was a good lesson in what will happen with same-sex attraction."

Lisa White shook her head as she took copious notes.

"Can anyone verify what you are saying about the fight?" Zach asked.

"Anyone who was there," Jacob said confidently. "If they tell the truth, that is."

Before Angela and Zach left, they tried to get permission to speak with David Valdes' parents, but their request was denied. Instead, they left David's parents a note in a sealed envelope expressing their concerns and providing instructions on how to contact law enforcement. On their way back to Headquarters, Angela and Zach remained silent until Zach finally said, "I feel sick after that interview."

"Me too," Angela said. "And I'm worried about David Valdes."

"We should shut the place down somehow," Zach said.

"Easier said than done," Angela answered. "I'll talk with Sheriff about arresting Mark Shea."

Ulysses left Picuris and drove to Santa Fe to meet with LizBeth Tallichet. On the drive, he took a call from his former police partner, homicide detective Pete Dowd.

"Hey, Ulys, do you have time to meet today?"

"I'm on my way to Santa Fe right now. I can come to you. I have a meeting in about ninety minutes. Is that enough time?"

"It should be," Pete said. "Meet me at Tio's. It will be empty at this time of day."

When he arrived in Santa Fe, Ulysses parked the cruiser on a side street a few blocks from the Santa Fe Plaza, leaving his gun in the vehicle lockbox. Tio's, a landmark bar on the corner of Alameda and Don Carlos was dark and empty. Ulysses pushed open the batwing doors. The place smelled of stale beer. Pete sat in a shadowy booth near the kitchen door, drinking a glass of lemonade.

"Thanks for coming," he said as Ulysses sat across from him in the booth. A young bartender dried glassware, her air pods in place, singing along to music only she could hear.

"Sure thing. What's going on?"

"I've just been relieved of my badge and gun," Pete said, swatting at a fly. "I'm on unpaid administrative leave and am a person of interest in the murder of Timothy Flynn."

"I'm sorry to hear that," Ulysses said. "What do they have on you?"

Pete's face was ashen, and his hand was trembling. Ulysses wondered if there was vodka in his lemonade. Tio's was one of Pete's favorite haunts when he was drinking. Now, with this latest development, had he relapsed?

"Tell me what you know, Pete," Ulysses said.

"Last night, I finally accessed the locker room and used a UV light to examine my locker. There were prints in the interior, at the bottom, and new drill holes. I lifted some belonging to a new detective assigned to the locker behind mine. So, I figured this guy had entered my locker from his and taken my taser. The new detective is Booth Baca, Chief Baca's homeboy, a member of the Santa Fe Knights, and a deacon at Flags of our Fathers. Then, this morning, they 'found' my taser in the rose garden at Our Lady of Sorrows, Father Flynn's parish."

"And your prints are all over it, right?"

"That's right, seeing as how it belonged to me. But they don't have a motive. At least not yet. I think that's why they didn't arrest me."

"Do you have an alibi for the night Flynn was killed?"

"I went to a six o'clock AA meeting, then I went home, ate dinner, and went to bed."

"Did you cook or get takeout?"

"Take out. I went to the Baha Tacos drive-through on Cerrillos about 7:15."

"What was Flynn's time of death?" Ulysses asked.

"Sometime between eight and eleven pm."

"Is there any motive they might try to pin on you?"

"I can't think of one. People know I was no fan of the anti-nuclear bunch, as you know, but I didn't hate them enough to kill one, especially not Father Flynn."

"Did you ever have an argument with him that anyone witnessed?"

Pete finished his lemonade and softly burped. He took a deep breath and said, "Cathy and I had a couple's session with him once in his office at the rectory. His housekeeper, Josefina, was cleaning upstairs. She may have overheard me and Flynn having words when he got after me for my drinking. I think I said, 'Fuck you!' or something like that. I didn't threaten him. But she gave me the stink eye when we left his office, so I knew she heard something. That woman idolized Flynn."

"They might say you believed Flynn had turned Cathy against you. You should get a lawyer, Pete, today. Do you know someone good?"

"I do, but she's expensive. I don't know how I'll pay for it."

"Just call her. Promise me you will. These folks are ruthless, and they are targeting you. It's only a matter of time before you are arrested."

"Okay, I will. I know you're right, Ulys. I don't want to be the fall guy for them." Pete reached into his pocket and came out with a chess piece, which he put on the table. "I found this in my locker," he said. "What do you think it is?"

"A murderer's calling card," Ulysses said. "I found a similar item at a recent murder in Taos. I'm worried for you, Pete. Flynn's killer is warning you."

"What should I do, Ulys?"

Ulysses said, "Contact the lawyer and your sponsor, too, Pete. Then batten down the hatches. You are headed for some heavy weather."

"This is just a slip, not a relapse."

"Call a lawyer and call your sponsor. Promise me."

"I will."

"Good, stay in touch."

A few minutes later, Ulysses parked in the legislative parking lot and walked into Lizbeth Tallichet's new offices in the Roundhouse near the SCIF. A receptionist greeted him and directed him to a conference room. LizBeth, Ray, Lex Sisneros, Sheriff Villalobos of Santa Fe, and State Police Chief Javier Santiago were seated around a table. LizBeth introduced Governor Gutierrez of Santa Clara Pueblo, Governor Montoya of San Ildefonso Pueblo, and agent Bill Samuelson of the ATF.

"Let's get started," LizBeth said. "We haven't got a moment to lose. As you can see from the confidentiality agreement, nothing we say can be shared without my express permission. I'd like for everyone to sign the agreement, and then I'll take questions."

"Have any further arrests been made at LANL related to the missing materials?" asked Bill Samuelson, after signing the confidentiality agreement.

"No, there have been no further arrests," LizBeth answered. "And the previous suspect had to be released."

"No one else has been charged with removing radioactive materials?" Governor Montoya asked. Montoya, who was elderly and on oxygen, was paying close attention, taking notes and occasionally talking quietly with his counterpart from Santa Clara, Governor Gutierrez.

"Not yet," LizBeth answered.

"Why was the suspect released?" asked Governor Gutierrez, a thin middle-aged Indian man wearing a suit and bolo tie. "We were told that Los Alamos Sheriff Blanca had a confession from the woman."

"Unfortunately, sir, the story about a confession was later rescinded. It appears that Dr. Foster was wholly innocent in the theft of nuclear waste. In fact, she is resuming her work at the pit production facility in the next day or so, if she hasn't already." LizBeth noticed that the Santa Clara Pueblo governor looked irritated at this news. "Sir," she asked, "do you have a question or concern about this information?"

"I am concerned about what is going on in the Los Alamos County Sheriff's Offices," Governor Gutierrez said. "There seems to be a competence problem."

"We have an eye on that situation, Governor, and we will do our best to cover any deficiencies up there."

Ray Pando raised his hand. "What information do you have on the Texas/New Mexico border militia activity?" he asked.

"Governor Garcia is in contact with the Texas governor. As of my last briefing, the Texas militia has agreed to stand down."

"Is it true that Adjutant General Gruber of the New Mexico National Guard has escaped to Texas?" Ray asked.

"He and several of his top-ranking officers fled to Texas last night to escape prosecution as accessories to murder."

"Who will take over at the Guard?" Ulysses asked.

"The President has nationalized the Guard and replaced the entire leadership. We can expect them to arrive tonight and be on board tomorrow. The Guard will receive support from the Army Rangers to manage the more complex aspects of operations here in our region."

"What kind of operations?" Ray asked.

"I'm about to tell you," LizBeth said. She hoped that Ray's testy attitude didn't introduce more distress into the conversation. The other two pueblo governors looked anxious enough already. "Okay, everybody, listen up. I've brought you together to alert you that we have evidence of a domestic terrorist operation centered in

Los Alamos, Santa Fe, Taos, and Rio Arriba Counties. We believe that individuals are storing illegal and dangerous materials they intend to use for an attack. We have stepped up our surveillance at LANL and in the vicinity of Picuris Pueblo. We want you to increase vigilance in your jurisdictions."

"What kind of materials are they storing?" Governor Gutierrez asked. "What should we be worried about?"

"The FBI is looking for nuclear waste. We will inform you if we are concerned for public safety in your jurisdiction. But we need you to be vigilant about anything suspicious on your pueblo or in your law enforcement area. Step up your surveillance and report anything out of the ordinary directly to my office."

"Are you still worried about a possible RDD?" Sheriff Villalobos asked.

"What is an RDD?" Governor Montoya asked.

"A dirty bomb," Ray answered. The governors began talking to each other in low voices, and Ulysses noticed the fear on their faces.

"Yes, we remain concerned," LizBeth answered, "but we must stay calm. The good news is that we have a strong team. New Mexico Governor Garcia is in daily communication with the White House. We will soon have a new, competent, loyal command at the New Mexico National Guard. There is nothing..."

"How do we protect ourselves from a dirty bomb?" Ray asked.

LizBeth paused, wary of the tension obvious in Ray's tone.. "In case of a detonation, the protocol would be to evacuate. Director Levine has directed shelters to be readied. A team is preparing public videos that will be shown on local channels and specific websites to help people prepare and cope. But we don't want to start a panic before something happens."

"What signs would indicate an attack was imminent?" Ray asked.

"Governor Pando, I assure you we are monitoring this situation closely and have intelligence, including radiological intelligence from regular drone surveillance. We will keep you informed. Okay, folks. That is all for now. We will be in touch again, very soon. In the meantime, remain vigilant. Sheriff Walker and Governor Pando, please, I'd like a word."

Ulysses and Ray followed Lizbeth into her office. Eli Martinez, whose small office was nearby, joined them. He shook hands with Ulysses and with Ray.

"Ray, I'm glad you could come today. I'm sorry you thought I wasn't taking the threat to Picuris seriously enough. I can assure you that you have my attention."

"Tell me Picuris will be fully informed about and involved in whatever operation you are planning," Ray said.

"You have my word," LizBeth said. "Eli, what information can you give us about the law enforcement officers you have been investigating? Ulysses and Ray, this is highly confidential intel."

"Marjory Blanca, Acting Sheriff of Los Alamos County, is to be considered suspect due to the Nationalist connections of her husband and her membership at Flags of our Fathers, the Elect-aligned church in Santa Fe. The two Governors, from Santa Clara Pueblo and San Ildefonso Pueblo, are respected members of their tribes who have served in tribal government in various capacities. Governor Montoya is being treated for colon cancer, which is a concern but not a red flag. Governor Gutierrez has gambling debts, but they are not significant. We have eliminated Sheriff Bustos of Rio Arriba County due to his militia activity and Nationalist ties. I investigated how to remove him and Blanca from office and discovered no way to do that. We can only remove sheriffs if martial law is declared nationally." Eli looked at Ulysses. "Turns out you sheriffs are powerful dudes, Sheriff Walker."

"I told you we were," Ulysses said, smiling at his former employee.

"What can you tell us about Nick Boyar, Eli?" LizBeth asked.

"More information is needed on Boyar," Eli said. "One thing we know is that he has ties with the Elect and seems personally beholden to Max Castleman. There are also concerns that he might have intentionally targeted the woman he arrested at the pit production facility. She was a whistleblower with safety concerns and had a perfect work record. She had nothing to do with the missing material. Dr. Shapiro, the LANL Director, got her released."

"Great information, Eli, thanks. A plan is underway to raid the bunker at Picuris where radioactive material is stored."

"When is the raid?" Ray asked.

"Very soon. You will be notified."

"Should we be prepared to evacuate our people?"

"I can't answer that yet," LizBeth said.

Ray stood up, shaking his head, and left the meeting. "Contact me when you know what you are doing," he said.

Chapter 9

Ulysses missed a call from Rosemary while he was in the meeting. He called her back as he left downtown Santa Fe on his way to Taos.

"Ulys," Rosemary said, "are you near home?"

"Why, what is up?"

"Did you know there will be a demonstration on the Taos Plaza?"

"What kind of demonstration?"

"A group called 'Nuclear Peace and Justice' is demonstrating against Elect activities taking place at Taos High."

"Where did you hear about this?"

"It was on Rita Wainwright's radio show. It's all about Taos High School. The Elect have banned books, instituted a dress code for female students, and they've been harassing a trans girl who plays JV Volleyball."

"Rosemary, where is Amelia? Is she at this demonstration?"

"That's why I called. Amelia left me a voicemail that she had a project after school and not to expect her home until seven-thirty. Now she's not answering her phone. I'm sure she's going to the plaza. The protest is at five, and it's almost five now. I can't leave Monty and Frances to go get her, and I can't take them either."

"I'll call Angela, Rosemary. Don't worry. I'm on my way there now."

Angela picked up on the first ring. "Yes, Sheriff," she said. "What is up?"

"Do you know about this demonstration on the plaza?"

"I just now heard about it from the Taos City Manager. A city clerk who was unaware of the jurisdiction change gave them a permit! Zach and I are mobilizing the team."

"The city should send police back up since they allowed this to happen. It could get ugly. And Angela, Amelia is probably there. Please look out for her, will you? I'm on my way."

As Ulysses drove north on NM 285 in the October afternoon, sunlight spilled onto the Sangre de Cristo mountains, lighting up a swath of golden trees. The season's beauty seemed like an unreal blur, lost to everything happening: an imminent raid at Picuris to recover materials for an RDD, his former partner at the Santa Fe Police framed for murder, his daughter in a demonstration against the Elect on the Plaza. Ulysses took a deep breath and began breathing with his mantra, but it didn't touch his distress. He turned on his flashers when he reached the Rio Arriba County line and sped north in the passing lane.

His mind drifted to a familiar escape fantasy. He imagined locking his house, taking their savings, loading his family into Rosemary's market van, and driving to Canada. In the fantasy, Canada would welcome them with open arms. They'd find a cabin in the mountains where they could live for next to nothing, and for a few years, or at least until things settled down in the States, they would live in peace. Rosemary would home-school the children, and he would get a job in construction to make ends meet. Whatever the case, he'd never return to law enforcement. Ulysses knew it was only a fantasy. Canada was already turning Americans away at the border. And it wouldn't be fair to disrupt Amelia and Monty's lives. But perhaps he could get out of law enforcement? For a moment, he saw Jesse Porter's still-warm body lying dead on the rug and the feeling of revulsion he felt at the time. *Do I want to run away and let his killer go free?* He asked himself. The silence he felt inside surprised him. *It's like I don't care anymore*, he thought. *Maybe I never did? Maybe it was all bravado and testosterone.*

Ulysses entered the Rio Grande canyon just outside of Velarde. He noticed a large mixed flock of ducks and geese on the river, recently returned from their breeding grounds in the far north to winter in New Mexico. A man in waders stood in the teal-colored river, fishing. Overhead above the narrow canyon, two ravens flew in tandem along the rimrock. *I belong here,* Ulysses thought. *I need to get a grip.* He returned to his mantra.

Ulysses arrived at Headquarters, where his secretary, Ramona, was alone in the front room. In the back, a 911 staffer spoke with a caller. Phones had been ringing all afternoon as merchants on the plaza called to complain about the demonstration. They said the city police had yet to arrive, and they were worried.

"Sheriff," Ramona said, "at least two hundred protestors, teenagers and adults, are already there, and more are arriving by the minute. Counter-protestors are also arriving. What are you going to do?"

"Stay calm, Ramona. I'm going there right now," Ulysses said, putting on his bulletproof vest. "Call the mayor again and demand backup in the strongest possible terms. Tell callers to remain calm. We have this in hand."

Ulysses took his semi-automatic rifle and put it on the gun rack in his cruiser. He flipped on the flashers and siren. When he arrived at the plaza, he parked in the police pullout on the south side and got his bullhorn. He saw Angela with three deputies on the bandstand and Zach with seven more deployed around the mostly enclosed plaza.

Over a hundred people carrying signs and chanting marched on the sidewalks, and some stood chanting near the bandstand. "No banned books!" they yelled, "No burkas!" Activists in red tee-shirts and bandanas chanted, "No More Nukes" and "Fuck Religion!" Ulysses scanned the plaza for Amelia and finally saw her with a group of her friends near La Fonda. She held a sign that said, "Trans Rights are Human Rights!" *We could easily be overwhelmed,* he thought as he began walking toward the bandstand. *This is a setup for a disaster.*

Ulysses climbed onto the bandstand and clicked on his bullhorn. "This is your sheriff speaking. You must disperse now for your safety. This demonstration is unlawful!"

The crowd roared, "No!"

Two Taos city police cars arrived near the east corner, and four officers got out. They stood there, looking around, but stayed by their cruisers, lights flashing.

"Exit the plaza now," Ulysses said firmly. "The permit for this demonstration is improper. Your assembly is illegal. Please disperse or you will be arrested."

An armored vehicle sped in from the west and abruptly stopped at the corner of the plaza. Seven heavily armed men in black clothing and masks jumped out of the truck and moved aggressively toward the demonstrators. Another armored vehicle, this one a Rio Arriba County deputy's car, pulled in from the south and disgorged four more militia members. The counter-protestors moved toward the students, swinging baseball bats. Two students were knocked to the ground. Angela approached the city police and ordered them to protect the students, but they hesitated. Protestors surged toward their fallen friends, but a counter-protestor threw a flashbang grenade at them, and chaos followed. Several students fell, grabbing their ears and screaming, and some were trampled in the stampede. The city police lobbed tear gas toward the counter-protestors, who were undeterred because they were wearing gas masks. The counter-protestors used bear spray on the city police, who fled back to their cruisers.

"Get on the radio and tell Zach to bring all the deputies to meet us at the entrance to La Fonda," Ulysses said to Angela. He waded into the crowd with his billy club, followed by Angela and several city police. Counter-protestors fled from them. He looked around for his daughter but didn't see her anywhere. When he arrived at La Fonda, he saw that many distressed students were sheltering there or trying to rinse their eyes after exposure to tear gas.

"Why did you gas us, pigs?" one girl yelled. Another girl yelled, "Shut up, Tyler, you idiot! They didn't gas us! The militias did!"

"Have any of you seen Amelia Walker?" Ulysses asked the girls, some of whom he thought he recognized.

"She and Phoebe Stein left before we got tear gassed. That loud grenade scared them," one answered. Ulysses felt a wave of relief. *Please let this be true.*

When the deputies and remaining officers had gathered, Ulysses ordered them to sweep the area for counter-protesters and arrest them, but most of the counter-protesters had already left the scene. Paramedics arrived to assist the injured. The plaza was littered with debris from the protest, including water bottles, shoes, clothing, and fallen signs. Taos deputies arrested some counter-protesters who came in the Rio Arriba County car and took them to the city lockup for processing. Zach and his deputies placed two young men from the militias in handcuffs as they attempted to flee. One was Jacob Graves, whom they had met earlier that day at the Elect compound, and the other was Patrick Shea, the son of their former colleague, Mark Shea.

Ulysses surveyed the situation, angered by the city officials who had allowed this to happen and the police who had done nothing to stop it. He knew he would be blamed, but he thought, *so be it.*

While Joseph and the other Taos deputies swept the plaza for remaining threats, Angela and Zach took the two young men to Headquarters to be charged and interrogated. Ulysses drove home. He called Rosemary, who told him Amelia had arrived home shaken but unharmed and was in her room. "I told her, 'Wait until your father gets home,'" Rosemary said with a rueful laugh. "For once, you get to be the bad cop."

"How are you feeling?" Ulysses asked his wife.

"Relieved. But still angry and scared."

"That sounds about right," Ulysses said. "How are Frances and Monty?"

"Frances is oblivious to the news, thank goodness. Monty is in a grumpy mood. I could use some help with him. I have eggplant parmesan ready for dinner. Our last eggplants."

"I'll be home shortly," Ulysses said.

Ulysses arrived home in time to kiss Frances goodnight. He ate dinner with Rosemary and then went upstairs and knocked on Monty's door while Amelia cleaned up without being asked.

"What's up, Monty?" Ulysses asked.

"Nothing," the boy said without opening the door. Ulysses entered the room, where Monty played a video game on his computer.

"Mom said you had some questions about the demonstration?"

"Not really." He continued playing the game and didn't look at his father.

"Close your computer, Son, and look at me. Are you worried or angry?"

Monty looked sullenly at his father and shrugged. "Angry, I guess."

"What is making you angry?"

"I don't know," Monty said. He started to open his laptop, then closed it again. "I'm sick of everything."

"Me, too," Ulysses said. "I've been feeling a little low myself lately."

"What about?" Monty asked.

"I'm fed up with all the chaos. The assassinations, the bullying, lawless behavior, demonstrations and militias, the secessions, all of it. It's exhausting to deal with."

"Me, too, Dad," Monty said. "Even at school, there are bad fights now. It doesn't feel right."

"I know, Son. It feels terrible. But I believe it will get better. As Angela says, we have to do the next right thing. Over and over. That's our job."

"That's probably BS, Dad."

Ulysses hugged his son and kissed his cheek. "It might not be."

Then he walked across the hall and knocked on his daughter's door.

Amelia answered in a sleepy voice, "What?"

Ulysses opened her door a crack. Her light was out, and she was in bed. "We'll talk in the morning, Bean," he said.

"Okay, Daddy. I'm sorry about today. Thanks for trying to keep me safe."

LizBeth Tallichet arrived home to find Dawa and Pema asleep on the couch in front of the television. The kitchen was a mess, and the remains of Dawa's meal were on the table. LizBeth helped herself to a bowl of spicy mutton stew, a traditional Tibetan dish at which Dawa excelled. LizBeth poured a beer, considered whether to awaken her wife, and decided against it. Instead, she ate the stew and listened to the local news at eleven, which featured a story about a demonstration against the Elect in Taos that had turned violent due to the presence of armed counter-protesters. Halfway through the broadcast, LizBeth turned it off. Dawa was snoring lightly, and little Pema was deeply asleep against her mother's breast. LizBeth turned off the family room lights, covered her wife and child, and began cleaning the kitchen.

LizBeth was afraid. Nothing she had ever experienced had prepared her for the responsibilities now resting on her shoulders. After this evening's meeting with her boss, Special Agent Nancy Levine, LizBeth realized she was expected to lead the raid at Picuris as the agent in charge, primarily assisted by ATF Director Bill Samuelson and fifty Army Rangers dispatched from Fort Carson, Colorado. Levine understood the urgency of the operation, but she was too deeply involved in monitoring the standoff on the southeast border between Texas and New Mexico to focus on another threat hundreds of miles away. The President had tasked Levine with ensuring the remaining Nationalists were removed from the New Mexico National Guard ranks. She was also expected to oversee the newly appointed adjutant general. The Guard had to be prepared in case of an incursion from Texas.

Levine told LizBeth that she trusted her to handle the nuclear threat in El Norte by herself. After LizBeth requested assistance from LANL, Levine revealed the identity of an undercover informant who had been working for the FBI for about a year. LizBeth was shocked to learn that Matt Pando's wife, Sarah, the mother of a young child and a public relations specialist, was secretly spying on Nationalists within LANL for the FBI. Levine informed her that Sarah Pando was the anonymous "tipster" who had alerted the FBI about the War Chief's raid on the compound bunker. Why hadn't Levine mentioned this earlier? Did Matt and Ray know about Sarah's work?

LizBeth was already worried that her relationship with the tribe was at risk because of the slowness of the FBI's response to the threats posed by the compound above Picuris. How would their relationship be affected if the governor discovered his daughter-in-law was an informant? Ray and Matt might see the FBI using Sarah as an informant as intrusive into tribal integrity and putting Sarah in harm's way. LizBeth had only met Sarah Pando once and remembered her as quiet and reserved, the kind of woman who faded into the background. How helpful could Sarah Pando be with efforts to root out the threats at LANL? LizBeth would find out, and she didn't feel as confident about her role as she was accustomed to feeling.

LizBeth finished cleaning the kitchen and began getting ready for bed. Her mind turned to Ray Pando and his question about evacuating his people from their ancestral home at Picuris Pueblo. She couldn't tell him to evacuate until the last minute for reasons bound to be evident to him. An evacuation would reveal to the Elect that a raid was coming, giving them time to prepare in ways that could be deadly for everyone involved. Ray's anger and distrust bothered LizBeth, who had come to see Ray and his son Matt as friends and allies. Still, she realized it was perfectly reasonable for Ray to distrust the entire power structure when it came to protecting Indian people. *Who can blame him, given history? In his shoes, I'd feel the same way.*

Ray and Billie sat together on the couch before a wood stove in her snug living room after eating a late supper of fresh elk cutlets and the last green beans from her garden. Ray had spent the evening meeting with the Tribal Council about the nuclear materials on Picuris land and how to proceed. The War Council, aware of the tribe's lack of specialized equipment and training to handle radioactive material, advocated that they join with the FBI effort led by Agent Tallichet even though it was proceeding slowly. The Tribal Council accepted their proposal but agreed they would begin evacuation in three days. Though sorely tempted, Ray had not given up the top-secret information that an imminent raid was planned.

"This is like the bad old days," Billie said in a hushed voice. "We have to leave our homes to be safe, like after the Pueblo Revolt."

Ray pondered for a moment. "Well, it's somewhat like that. We might have to flee. But the last time we had to escape, we had at least confronted the Spanish Government. These fools seized our land because it facilitated weapon storage. We didn't attack them; we merely conducted surveillance. But here we are anyway."

Billie appeared amused. "Feeling a bit grumpy?" she asked.

Ray said nothing. He carried their plates into the kitchen and began washing them. A log settled in the wood stove. "It's late, Billie. Do you want me to go?"

"No, Ray, why don't you stay the night again?"

"I need to be up early, so I'll go home."

"Don't go away mad," Billie said, patting the couch beside her.

He sat back down and put his arm around her. "I'm not mad," he said, "just frustrated."

Billie rested her head against his chest and said, "I keep thinking about the Pueblo Revolt. Our ancestors had twelve good years without the Spanish, but when they returned, our people fled. Our pueblo lay abandoned for almost ten years. Many never returned, and we became a much smaller, poorer community after that."

"That's true," Ray said. "And if whatever is in that bunker up there goes off, we may never be able to return."

Having decided to resume her relationship with Eli, Angela lay in bed beside him, with Mr. T curled at their feet. "I can't believe we get to sleep in the same bed again," she said. "I had given up on this."

"Didn't I tell you this would happen?" Eli said. "You need to have more faith in me."

"Of course you would say that!" Angela said. "But what were the chances of getting the job you wanted in Santa Fe?"

"I guess it takes a civil war," Eli said.

"Is this a civil war? It feels more like pure chaos. It makes the real Civil War look organized."

"The states that have seceded are mostly from the old Confederacy: Texas, Oklahoma, Louisiana, and Mississippi."

"Don't forget Wyoming and Idaho," Angela asked. "And they aren't contiguous. They are surrounded by 'enemy territory.'"

"And now that they've lost access to federal dollars, all will be hurting. There will be hell to pay as soon as the first hurricane hits Louisiana!"

"How did we get here?" Eli asked.

"Hell, if I know," Angela said. "But the better question is, where do we go from here?"

"Hell, if I know," Eli repeated. "If worse comes to worse, you and I can hide in the mountains behind Taos."

"That's a fantasy, Eli. And not my fantasy." She laughed. "Imagine me living rough. My mother would roll over in her grave."

"If she's in her grave," Eli said.

"Okay, this is getting out of hand," Angela said, turning off the light. "Aren't you forgetting something I promised you?"

Eli crawled under the covers and began kissing Angela's warm belly.

Serena had spent a long, anxious day indoors at the house on Blueberry Hill, waiting to hear from whoever was supposed to pick them up and take them to the next safe house. Kaylee was bored and fretful. Serena had few resources to entertain her, bringing only three books they'd already read several times and no toys or games. They told stories and sang songs, drew pictures with paper and pencils Serena found, took naps, and listened to several CDs Kaylee selected from a dusty rack by the bed.

They'd been warned against going outside where they might be seen and had even been encouraged to stay away from the windows. They'd also eaten most of the food in the refrigerator, including all the remaining fruit, vegetables, milk, and eggs. The only things left were potatoes, instant oatmeal, bread, butter, and sliced turkey. Kaylee refused to eat anything but bread and butter, which would soon be gone.

At dusk, Serena noticed her anxiety rising almost to panic, as it did every evening now. When Kaylee began begging to talk with her father, Serena impulsively called Russell, who picked up immediately.

"Serena is that you?" the old man asked.

Serena said nothing, but Kaylee yelled, "Daddy!" and took the phone.

"Can you come to get us?" the little girl cried. "I hate it here."

"I'd love to come get you. But I need to know where you are."

"We are in this terrible, smelly house and can't go outside, and there's nothing to eat!"

Serena took the phone, "Hi, Russ," she said.

"Hi, Serena. I'm so glad you called! Where are you?"

"Somewhere outside of Taos," Serena said. "I don't know where exactly."

"Are you and Kaylee alone?"

"Yes. Russ, someone killed my contact, the one I came to meet."

"I know that, Serena. I'm in Taos, too. I've been to see the County Sheriff. He's trying to find you." Sirens were approaching the small house, including a fire truck with a blaring horn.

"I don't know where I am. I came here in the dark. I think I am in the west of town, which is rural. All I have is this old flip phone they gave me. There isn't a camera or GPS or anything."

"Are these people holding you prisoner?" Hurley asked.

"No. They are trying to keep me safe. But I'm scared, Russ."

"I'm sure you are, Darlin'. But don't worry. We will find you and Kaylee and bring you home safe."

"I can't ever go back to Wyoming. I took something from the Air Force Base. Something hazardous."

"What is it, Serena? What did you take?"

"Weapons-grade plutonium to trigger the new nukes at Warren," Serena swallowed. Saying this aloud made her sick to her stomach. "I took it from General Baynes's vault." Kaylee watched her mother with puzzled eyes. There were more sirens, but Serena couldn't see anything from the windows, which faced away from the road.

"Where is it now?" Russell asked.

"I gave it to the Nuclear Peace and Justice activists."

"Oh, my God, Serena. Whatever did you do that for?"

Serena began to cry and said nothing. There was a long silence.

"Don't worry, Serena," Hurley said finally. "I will find you, even if we have to go door to door. Then we'll go somewhere safe together. I'm going to call the sheriff now. Try to get some rest. Let me say goodnight to Kaylee."

After saying goodnight to her father, the little girl cried herself to sleep, and Serena fell asleep soon after, relieved by having spoken with her husband.

In the middle of the night, someone kicked in the outside door. Two men in tactical gear and masks entered with bright flashlights, guns drawn.

"Get up," one man said, pulling Serena by the arm. "Get your shoes on. And give me that," he said, snatching her cell phone. He handcuffed her. The other man ransacked the tiny house, throwing Serena's gear and clothes into a bag.

Kaylee screamed, "Mama!" The other man grabbed her. "Shut up, kid," he said. He taped her mouth closed while she kicked and squirmed. Kaylee tried to grab her teddy bear, but it was under the covers wedged between the bed and the wall, and she couldn't reach it.

"Where is the item you stole from Warren Air Force Base?" the first man asked.

"It isn't here," Serena said. "Someone took it."

"Who took it?"

Kaylee began to whimper.

"A man. I don't know his name." Serena thought of Jesse. *Are they going to kill us too?*

"What did he look like?"

"I never saw him. It was dark."

The men went outside, and Serena could hear them tearing apart the shed where the toolbox had been stored. After about fifteen minutes, they came back, and Serena and her daughter were blindfolded, pushed out the door, and put into a waiting van.

Monica Lovato and Philip Devin drove to the Tsankawi ruins at Bandelier National Monument with the toolbox they'd stuffed into an oversized backpack. Since national parks and monuments were closed due to the political emergency, Devin had figured this remote location near LANL would be an excellent place to stash their prize.

At midnight, Monica let Philip out near the entrance. He lifted the backpack to his shoulders and ran out of sight along the path past Anasazi dwellings and the ancient Puebloan ruin of Tsankawi Village. Monica sped away, planning to return to pick him up when he signaled her.

In the pitch dark after moonset, Philip used a headlamp to jog straight for a series of ladders that led him to a well-preserved dwelling where he loved to play as a child and imagined living an idealized life as an indigenous boy. Philip paused to catch his breath before climbing the final ladder. The night was cold, but bright stars felt close in the bowl of the sky.

Philip considered the material in the pack on his back and felt a thrill as he climbed. *I have always wanted to make history, and now it is within my reach!* He deposited the toolbox behind a blackened boulder in the ancient dwelling. He wiped it free from fingerprints and traces of DNA and said, "I'll be back for you later, my friend." Then he texted Monica and ran back to the road.

"All safe?" Monica asked.

Philip nodded. "Good to go."

"Now we need to get Serena. I hope we aren't too late."

"Me too. I need a win to please Boyar."

"It's more than just pleasing him, Phil! We must ensure her and her child's safety. She has contributed so much to the movement."

"Of course," he said, patting her thigh.

They sped off. Forty minutes later, they arrived at the snail house on Blueberry Hill, but Serena was already gone.

Chapter 10

Ulysses was up before dawn helping Rosemary pack the van for the final farmer's market of the season. Frances was up early, too, excited about going to the market and dressed in coveralls that matched her mother's. They loaded cabbages, acorn and butternut squashes, seven dozen eggs, four cases of chutneys and jams, twenty-two pumpkins, and enough goat cheese to meet the high demand for Rosemary's dairy products. Rosemary also had a dozen fresh ristras and wreaths made by her neighbor, Pilar, whose artistry and low prices attracted a lot of customers. Rosemary's farmer's market business had been booming all summer, but she was ready to finish the season's heavy farm and market work.

Frances hugged her father before climbing into the truck to wait for her mother, who was locking the pack house. "Daddy," she said, looking up at him, "I dreamed Bad Rabbit took a girl in a pink hoody."

"Really? Was it a scary dream, Pookie?"

She nodded. "It woke me up, but I went back to sleep and dreamed about my Halloween costume."

"What do you want to be for Halloween?"

"I want to be a scary soldier. Like Bad Rabbit."

"Is Bad Rabbit a soldier? I thought you never saw him?"

"I saw him last night. He wore a black cape and a mask. I want Mom to make me a costume like his."

"Good luck with that, Pook," Ulysses said. "Mom is busy these days. Maybe you can start on it yourself."

"Okay, but I *will* need some help, Daddy." She gave him one of her stern looks.

When Rosemary and Frances drove off at sunrise, Ulysses entered the house and poured himself some coffee. A pot of oatmeal with apples and cinnamon simmered on the stove. Amelia and Monty were both sleeping in, it being Saturday. Ulysses served himself a bowl and ate while considering Frances' dream. Was Frances the girl in the pink hoody? Was Bad Rabbit a person now? *I wish I knew how to talk to her about her dreams without scaring her.*

Ulysses' cell phone rang. It was Russell Hurley.

"Sorry to call so early, Sheriff, but I need your help. I heard from my wife, and she's in trouble."

"Did she call you?"

"Yeah, last night. She and Kaylee are in something she calls a 'safe house.'"

"Where?"

"She couldn't tell me exactly, but west of Taos in the country somewhere."

"That covers a big area, Mr. Hurley. Have you tried calling her back?"

"She's not picking up. Serena told me something else."

"What's that?"

"You know she was secretary to the Warren Air Force Base general. The one who handles the new nukes?"

"You said something about that."

"Well, she took something from them when she left her job. Some nuclear trigger material."

"What?"

"A case with weapons-grade plutonium, Sheriff. It's not very big, but it is dangerous in the wrong hands. She called it a 'toolbox.' She's pretty sure they will be looking for it."

"Where is this stuff now?" Ulysses asked.

"She gave it to a Nuclear Peace and Justice activist friend. For safekeeping, I guess. She doesn't mean any harm. She's a good girl, Sheriff. She lacks common sense. But we must find her and get her out of there."

"Come by headquarters in about two hours, and I'll meet with you. In the meantime, don't tell anyone else what you just told me. I have to get going now."

"Okay, Sheriff."

Ulysses ate his oatmeal and scanned the news on his computer. *Taos News* had a scathing article about last night's mêlée at the protest, but at least the reporter had his facts straight. The headline read, "Permit Mix-up between City and County Results in Violent Protest on Plaza." He also reported that militia from Rio Arriba County, south and west of Taos County, were involved in the counter-demonstration and primarily responsible for the violence. Ulysses finished eating as Amelia came down to breakfast.

She helped herself to oatmeal and ate quietly at the kitchen table. When Amelia finished, she took her bowl to the sink and started up the stairs.

"Just a minute, Amelia," Ulysses said, "we need to talk."

Amelia sat back down but didn't look at her father.

"What gave you the idea that it was okay to go to that demonstration without our permission?"

"Daddy, I didn't know there would be violent people there. I wanted to support friends the Elect have targeted. I have a right to speak up, don't I?"

"Of course you do. But you don't have the right to defy your mother. You are only fifteen, Amelia. You could have been hurt by those people who came out to oppose you. Things aren't like they used to be."

Amelia started to say something but seemed to think better of it. "I won't do it again," she said. "Daddy, are those people going to take over Taos?"

"No, Bean, I assure you, they will not. Not as long as I'm sheriff. Amelia, you are grounded until your mother and I decide you've learned from this."

"I have learned a lot already," Amelia said. "I can't be free in my hometown or at my school from people who want to force me into their religion."

When Ulysses arrived at headquarters, Joseph came in to say there had been a suspected arson the night before on Blueberry Hill, west of Taos. "Someone deliberately burned an old shed behind an abandoned yurt. No one was injured. Hondo/Seco brought two ladder trucks and put it out at about 9 pm. We don't have any leads yet."

"Did you see anything suspicious?"

"ATV tracks, beer cans, and an anarchy symbol spray-painted on the door of the yurt."

"Okay, thanks, Joseph."

Ulysses asked Angela to gather the senior deputies for their weekly conference in his office. He rolled out the whiteboard and began the briefing.

"Everything we discuss this morning is on a strictly need-to-know basis," he said as he started the meeting. "Let's start with Monday's murder victim, Jesse Porter. What do we know?"

Angela walked to the whiteboard. "Jesse Porter, aged 33, was killed Monday night at the apartment where he was staying. The post-mortem listed the cause of death as strangulation, but Porter had been tased before being strangled. The bloodwork showed cannabis and antidepressants. Porter came to New Mexico from Texas last summer and worked as a field officer for the Malcolm X Brigade, the more militant arm of Nuclear Peace and Justice. He is survived by his mother, sister, and ex-wife. Porter had no prior convictions. His apartment was leased by Monica Lovato, a field commander for Malcolm X. We have not yet been able to contact Lovato. She is 38 and biracial, was born in San Jose, California, and raised in Livermore. She is divorced with no children. She graduated from Cal Tech, receiving a degree in electrical engineering. She was employed for four years at Lawrence Livermore Laboratory in California until she was fired for insubordination last spring. She has no arrest record. According to neighbors, Lovato owns a house in Santa Fe but has not been seen there for at least a month. She may be involved with a man named Philip Devin, a lead engineer at the plutonium pit facility."

"What ways have you tried to contact her?" Ulysses asked.

"I've done all the usual searches, Sheriff, but with no luck. This morning, I asked Eli Martinez to look into it."

"Okay, let me know as soon as you find out anything. She knows we are looking for her. I don't like that she hasn't contacted us."

"Deputy Zach, do you have anything to report about the Patterson child abuse case?"

"Yes, Sheriff. We interviewed Mark Shea, a.k.a Major Mark, at the compound along with two witnesses. Shea acknowledged that he was involved in the physical discipline of his 'trainees,' but he said it was a standard practice and minimized it. He denied striking Isaiah Patterson on that day. Of the two witnesses, one was a juvenile, and one, Jacob Graves, is eighteen. Graves denied witnessing physical violence. He is the religious leader Daniel Graves' oldest son and was arrested at the protest last night. Graves was charged with unlawful assembly and released. Graves was with Patrick Shea, Major Mark's son. Patrick was also arrested and later released to his mother. Shea is seventeen.

"The second witness was David Valdes, fourteen, who said he had witnessed Mark Shea strike Isaiah Patterson and that another boy had kicked Patterson when he was lying on the ground. Valdes said his parents wanted to leave the compound. Before Angela and I left the compound, we tried to contact Valdes' parents but were unable to do so. We left them a note that we were concerned for their son's safety."

"Are we prepared to make an arrest?"

Zach looked at Angela, who nodded. "We will proceed with an arrest today."

"It would be good to meet with the Valdes parents beforehand and ensure they have a safety plan."

"Yes, sir."

"Okay, I have some things to report," Ulysses said. The woman whose car was left on the shoulder of 522 has surfaced. Serena Hurley, 32, and her daughter Kaylee, 6, are somewhere near Taos, staying in housing arranged by activists. She recently called her husband, Russell Hurley, and told him she was in a safe house west of Taos, though she didn't know her exact location. She also said she had property belonging to the Warren Air Force Base in Wyoming, which she turned over to the Nuclear Peace and Justice activists. Since that conversation, Russell has not been able to reach Serena. We need to find her. Others with bad intentions may also be searching for her.

"We believe the property Serena turned over to Nuclear Peace and Justice is very dangerous, and we are eager to find her and the material.

The deputies started calling out their questions.

"One at a time, folks. Zach, you go first."

"How are we going to find this material, Sheriff?" Zach Wright asked.

"I hope to get help from Monica Lovato when we find her," Ulysses said. "Russell Hurley should be here soon to meet with us regarding his wife's whereabouts. She may have been moved. She isn't answering her phone."

"Sir, what is the material? Can you tell us?"

"No, only to say it could be used in a dirty bomb."

"Sheriff, is Taos in danger?" Dakota Wilson, 911 dispatch supervisor, asked.

"Not presently, no. The only way you can get radiation poisoning from the material itself is to eat it. To make a dirty bomb, you need something like dynamite to disperse it. A dirty bomb spreads low-level radioactive material, which creates fear and chaos and keeps an area off-limits until it can be cleaned up. Still, it is unlikely to kill anyone unless the dispersing blast itself kills that person." The deputies were talking in low voices among themselves.

Ulysses reminded them not to tell anyone about what they had learned. "If you tell anyone, including family members, and I find out that you did, not only will you lose your job, but I will also see that you are prosecuted. Please understand that information like this, if leaked, could cause a panic."

"Okay, let's talk about the action steps. Angela, contact Agent Tallichet and tell her about the material that Lovato or her associates may have. Then you and Zach arrest Mark Shea. Joseph, you focus on finding Serena Hurley and her child. Angela, when does the new deputy, Rosie, start?"

"Monday, Sheriff."

We could use her right now, Ulysses thought.

The deputies began to file out of Ulysses' office. Michael from dispatch approached Ulysses with a worried look. "Sheriff," he asked, "Do you know anything about the murder of Father Timothy Flynn in Santa Fe? My cousin works as an admin for the Santa Fe Police. She told me that a Santa Fe Police detective, Peter Dowd, was arrested for the murder."

The law enforcement grapevine is brutal. "I knew it was coming," Ulysses said. "I saw Pete yesterday in Santa Fe. He is my old partner, and it was his case."

Michael frowned and said, "I'm sorry to hear that, Sheriff."

And he's being framed, Ulysses thought but didn't say. "Thanks, Michael," Ulysses said. "I think he's innocent."

Shortly after the meeting broke up, Russell Hurley came to the door of Ulysses' office.

"Good morning, Sheriff," Hurley said. His clothing looked disheveled, and he hadn't shaved in several days. "I still haven't heard from Serena, but I might have found some useful intel."

"Have a seat, Mr. Hurley," Ulysses said. "Tell me what you found."

"When I spoke with Serena last night, I heard sirens and a fire truck in the background. This morning, I called the fire department and found out where the fire was. It was in a rural area west of Taos called Blueberry Hill. I drove out there this morning and looked around. This might be where she is, at least in the general area. Can we go door to door and see if we can find her?"

"You didn't go near any of these buildings, did you?"

"No, sir."

"Speak with Deputy Joseph Maes. He was out on Blueberry Hill this morning checking out a suspicion of arson with that fire. Tell him what you found. He is planning to go back out, and you can follow him. Stay in your car. Let him do the door-to-door. These people are dangerous."

Serena Hurley was numb with fear. She had no idea where she was or who had kidnapped her. Her daughter had been taken from her when they arrived at their destination, blindfolded in the van with their kidnappers. She spent the night in a cold underground chamber. There was a bare mattress on the floor, a bucket for a toilet, and a single overhead lightbulb. The men didn't reply to her questions or pleas and bolted the door from the outside.

Now awake after a fitful night, Serena surveyed the shadowy room where she was imprisoned. One wall was bare rock, and the other three were cinderblocks. The ceiling was made of fresh-cut pine logs. Stacked against one wall were four additional mattresses, a stack of buckets, a case of bottled water, and some folding chairs. *They plan to use this dungeon for more than one prisoner. Am I the first one?*

Serena was glad she had the presence of mind before being abducted to put on her heavy down jacket and wool hat. The room was icy, and there was no sign of a heater, blankets, or even sheets for the mattress. *Are they going to interrogate me here?* She wondered.

The fear she was feeling took her back to her days as a teenage runaway. At first, she and Josh, the boy she ran away with who she barely knew, lived with his father in Cheyenne, Wyoming. It was during a gas boom, and Josh and his father both worked in the gas fields. During the day, Serena studied for her G.E.D., which she quickly passed, and then attended business school online while cooking and cleaning for Josh and his father. On weekends, she bussed tables at Cracker Barrel and turned her wages over to Josh's father. She met Russell Hurley at the restaurant. Hurley, who had retired from a career as an insurance adjuster, ate breakfast twice weekly with a group of well-heeled older men who left good tips. Russell took her to dinner one night and told her about his wife of forty years, Lee Ann, who was dying of ALS. He was caring for her at home with help from an undocumented Mexican woman. Russell and Serena became friends.

After about a year, Josh's father started trying to initiate sex with

Serena, and when she rebuffed him firmly, he said, "I support you, little puta. If you are so ungrateful, you should leave my house." The next day, Josh bought Serena a ticket and put her on the bus to Chicago. She never had a chance to say goodbye to Russell.

Serena got a job as a waitress at a Waffle House near the bus station and rented a room at the cheap motel across the highway that her boss had told her about. She struggled to get enough tips to pay for her room and feared becoming homeless. When her boss approached her with a job opportunity that would make her more money than waitressing, Serena decided to learn more. The boss introduced her to "Mr. Kutznets," a bald, elegantly dressed middle-aged man with a foreign accent, who told her he wanted her to "audition" for him as an escort.

"Just give it a try, and we'll see how you do and if you like it," the kind-seeming man said. "No pressure." In the meantime, he paid her rent for a week and gave her a wad of cash. "All you have to do is look pretty and sweet," he said, smiling and chucking her under her chin. "This is easy for you."

Serena was dimly aware of what an escort was, and since the abuse she'd suffered from her stepfather from the time she was twelve had included intercourse, she knew something about sex. At first, being an escort was not a lot different than being abused by her stepfather. Later, when Kutznets moved her into "The Stable," as they called it, she discovered it was much worse. She became a prisoner.

During the year she lived at The Stable, Serena became familiar with Kutznets's extended family network of Russian gangsters who sold drugs, engaged in human trafficking, and some of whom, she'd heard, were hired assassins. Some gangsters were devoutly religious, attending a Russian Orthodox Church with a charismatic priest. Once, a young man brought her to church with them. Later, he was severely reprimanded and blamed Serena for his mistake. That painful year now seemed like a blurry nightmare.

Eventually, Russell found her and helped her to escape, but not before she had suffered trauma that gave her nightmares.

When Serena emerged from her trance, she was shivering from the cold and fainting from hunger. She had no idea what time it was. She heard voices outside her door, and then the bolt shot back. The door opened, and a man entered.

"I hope you slept well," he said, smiling. He was wearing a black uniform with a cross and flag insignia. "I'm sorry about how rudely those men behaved toward you. They thought you were a fugitive rather than a guest. Won't you come next door and have breakfast?"

This was different from what Serena expected. She asked, "Where is my daughter?"

"The little girl is in good hands. Please don't worry! You'll be able to visit her very soon. But come, breakfast is waiting."

Serena followed the man out the door and across a narrow hall into a room with tables and chairs, cameras, and rings on the floor to restrain shackled prisoners. Serena was familiar with such rings.

A plate of eggs, bacon, toast, and a cup of coffee was on the table.

"Sit and eat before food gets cold," the man said. "I have questions for you."

Serena was hungry. She did as she was told.

"Have we met before?" the man asked.

"I'm not sure, sir," Serena answered.

He studied her briefly, then said, "You have been brought here at the behest of worldly powers. This is the home of Daniel Graves, the Servant. He is God's Messenger on Earth. You are lucky to be here, Serena."

"Okay," Serena said. *He knows my name.*

"If you cooperate, you can stay here. We will protect and provide for you, and you will dwell in the Women's Pavilion and have plenty to eat."

"I just want to find my daughter and go home," Serena said.

He smiled and said, "You cannot leave unaccompanied." Serena noticed that his eyes were misaligned. *Which eye do I look at?* She remembered these eyes from somewhere. *Does he recognize me somehow?*

Serena said nothing for a few minutes. During her year being trafficked, Serena was constantly vigilant about her survival. She learned to judge a man quickly. This man was familiar somehow. His accent and demeanor reminded her of the Kutznets gang. Perhaps she had seen him in Chicago? She defaulted to the behavior she'd learned there. Always look submissive and don't make eye contact. "What do you need from me?" she asked.

"Good girl," the man said. "Light of wisdom has shone upon you. Tell me where you have hidden material you brought from Wyoming."

Serena realized it wouldn't be as easy as she'd hoped. She swallowed. "I am not sure what you are talking about," she said softly.

The man leaned across the table and grabbed her wrist. "Never lie to me," he said, twisting it.

"Sir, I'm not lying," Serena said, tears in her eyes. "Are you talking about the toolbox?"

"Yes, child," he said, stroking her wrist with his middle finger. "Tell me where you hid the toolbox."

Serena thought for a moment while faking sobbing. "I can take you to it," she said. "But first, I need to see my daughter."

When Angela and Zach arrived at the Elect Compound with an arrest warrant for Mark Shea, they were told he was "out of state." A young woman in the Welcome Center told them Mark wasn't expected to return anytime soon. She also said that David Valdes and his family had been absent for morning prayers and that a team of "brothers" was seeking them on the property.

"Did they take their car?" Zach asked.

"At their rank, personal vehicles are not allowed on the property," she answered.

When they returned to the car, Angela's phone rang. It was Eli. "I have a bead on Monica Lovato," he said. "She is hiding in a house in Dixon. That's a little village on the road to Peñasco."

"I know where it is," Angela said. "Do you have an address?"

"Private Road 1110," Eli said. "I'm sending you a pin."

"Thanks, Eli," Angela said, putting on her seatbelt. "We are going over there now."

"Glad to help," Eli said. "Let me know if you need anything else."

"See if you can locate Mark Shea," Angela said. "At the compound, they said he was out of state."

Angela called Ray and told him to look for the Valdes family. "They are on foot and might have pursuers," she said. "If they come your way, please help them. They could be fleeing for their lives." Ray agreed to her request, and they hung up.

Joseph Maes drove to Blueberry Hill, with Russell Hurley following in his car. They started from the arson site and worked their way south. Maes knocked on doors, showing those who answered a photograph of Serena and her daughter. Many houses had no one home, and one or two appeared abandoned. None of the five people Joseph spoke to had seen Serena or Kaylee. Eventually, he knocked on the door of a small stucco house with a greenhouse on its south side. Russell parked on the road while a fierce-looking border collie watched him suspiciously from outside the car. A small woman in overalls, her gray hair neatly tied in a bun, came to the door. "Step inside," she said. "I don't want to let the cold in."

"Have you seen this woman or child?" Joseph asked her, coming into the humid warmth of her greenhouse.

The woman, who gave her name as Suzanna Griego, looked at the picture a long time and finally said, "I don't know for sure."

"Have you seen anything suspicious in the neighborhood, such as people you don't know coming and going from a house?"

"Well," she said, "that's a broad question. Why do you want to know?"

"Ma'am, this woman and her child are missing, and we think they might be being held against their will somewhere in this neighborhood." He showed her a picture.

"I haven't seen anyone like them but see that driveway on the other side of the road?" She pointed east, toward the mountains.

Joseph nodded.

"There is a house down that road, and people always come and go from it. Last night, I got up to let my dog out about midnight, and I saw a van pull out of the drive and take off going south."

"Is that unusual?" Joseph asked.

"Maybe. There's nobody there for days at a time, and then a van with two men in front and their lights off pulls out in the middle of the night. Is that suspicious? You tell me."

Out front, the dog beside Russell's car was growling and showing her teeth.

"Okay, thank you, Mrs. Griego. Can you call off your dog?"

"Here, Jenny," she said. Jenny licked her chops and trotted toward her mistress, wagging her white-tipped tail.

Joseph and Russell drove down the long, rutted drive toward an abandoned, ramshackle foam shack. The outbuilding behind it stood open, with items like an old mattress, a wheelbarrow, and the contents of several cardboard boxes strewn across the ground. After knocking, Joseph drew his weapon and tried the door. It swung open. Finding no one inside, he invited Russell to come in, and together they searched the one-room house, which had meager furnishings. Russell pulled back the covers of the bed that stood against one wall and ran his hands along the sides of the mattress. When he discovered Kaylee's teddy bear stuck between the bed and the wall, he held up the toy. "They were here."

Angela and Zach drove down from Peñasco as the snow began to fall and entered the unincorporated village of Dixon, a picturesque town on the Rio Embudo, established in the 1700s by close-knit Hispanic families. The long-time residents were joined by hippies, artists, homesteaders, and retirees who began arriving in the 1960s. The town is famous for its annual art studio tour held each November. *I wish things would settle down enough for Eli and me to attend the tour,* Angela thought, feeling nostalgic for more peaceful times.

Angela did not know the town well because it was off her beaten path and in Rio Arriba rather than Taos County. They passed Private Road 1110, not much more than a dirt track, and had to turn around. The road led past an abandoned trailer and another with a truck outside, under which a chained dog sought shelter from the light snow. They drove past an agricultural field, over a flowing acequia, and into a bosque of large golden-leafed cottonwoods where a small adobe with a metal roof stood in a clearing surrounded by riparian woods. An elaborate treehouse perched in one of the enormous cottonwoods in the back. Angela saw a familiar black Tesla parked in front.

"Zach, you get out here. Make a large arc and come around the back of the house while I go to the front. I don't want her skipping out on us."

Zach got out and took off jogging on a small trail toward the river. Angela slowly got out of the cruiser.

A walkway lined with sunflowers led to a wooden door with round windows on either side. Angela thought she saw a woman look out of the far window. In the back, Zach apprehended someone running out the back door. Angela could hear Zach introduce himself to a man. The front door opened, and a pretty young woman with cornrowed hair wearing blue jeans and a flannel shirt came out. "Hello," she said politely. "You must be the Sheriff."

"Undersheriff," Angela said. "Are you Monica Lovato?"

"Yes, won't you come in? I know you want to ask me some questions."

Angela entered the house, which consisted of a living room, kitchen, and small bathroom. A ladder from the living room led to a sleeping loft. The house was tidy and full of savory smells from the soup on the stove. "Would you like a cup of coffee? I can make some," Monica asked as Zach entered the back door.

"Who were you talking with?" Angela asked.

"It was Philip Devin. He was headed to the outhouse," Zach said.

"Is anyone else here?" Angela asked Monica.

"No," Monica said. "Just the two of us."

"I wouldn't mind some coffee," Zach said.

While Monica made the coffee, Devin came into the house and cleared space by closing two laptops, stacking papers on the table, and putting them out of sight. Angela noticed that the documents were schematic drawings.

"How can I help?" Monica asked, setting down a tray with a large French press, a pitcher of cream, and four cups.

"You rented the apartment where Jesse Porter was killed," Angela began. "How did you come to know him?"

"I work as a Nuclear Peace and Justice field commander," Monica said. "The Malcolm X Brigade. Jesse joined up some months ago and needed a place to stay, so I let him have an apartment I used for work in Taos. I live in Santa Fe."

"And this place?" Zach asked.

"I'm cat-sitting for a friend who's in Mexico and taking a little retreat. My work has been stressful lately."

"What do you do as a field commander?" Zach asked.

"It's like community organizing," Monica said. "I recruit people to help with our anti-nuclear weapons campaign. I've been involved in anti-nuclear work as a volunteer for many years."

"You recruited Jesse?"

"Yes, and I trained him and gave him a place to live. I'm devastated by his death. Do you have any leads on who killed him?" She pushed down the plunger on the coffee press and said, "Help yourself." Zach and Philip both poured cups for themselves.

Angela said, "The neighbor, a man working a gallery nearby, heard a lot of commotion and said he saw a man in a mask running down the stairs from the apartment. That's all we have. What about you? Do you have any ideas who might have killed Jesse?"

Monica shook her head. "There are many people who hate us," she said. "I used to get death threats on my phone all the time until I got rid of it. But I don't know who would want to kill Jesse. He was a sweet, gentle man. Somebody killed our comrade Father Tim in Santa Fe, too."

"Yes, I know," Angela said. "Do you know anything about that?"

Monica shook her head. "No. Unless it was someone from the Santa Fe Knights., Tim and I had been movement friends for years. Everybody loved him."

"Tell me who you think of as enemies."

"Groups like the Knights and La Militia in Española who have infiltrated the police. The Nationalist Party has undercover agents here who target groups like Nuclear Peace and Justice. Also, the militarized churches, especially the Elect."

"Do you have any names of people who have threatened you?"

"Sheriff Bustos in Rio Arriba, Gideon Strum of the Knights, Police Chief Maurice Baca in Santa Fe, somebody called 'The Rook.'"

Angela wrote down the names.

"You've been involved with anti-nuclear work for quite a while, yet you used to work at Lawrence Livermore Lab in California, correct?" Angela continued.

"Yes. I mostly worked on the nuclear winter project there. We did analysis and computer simulations of what would happen in the event of an exchange of nuclear weapons between the United States and another nuclear-armed power."

"Why were you fired?"

"I published an article that alluded to some of the unclassified parts of my work. The administration called what I did insubordination and fired me. But I sued for wrongful termination and won a settlement."

Angela looked at Philip sitting in a leather club chair with a marmalade cat on his lap. He looked calm and comfortable.

"Are you still working at LANL?" she asked him.

"Yes, but the pit facility is closed, so I am on six weeks of annual leave."

"Are you involved in anti-nuclear work?"

"Hardly," Devin said. "I produce nukes." He chuckled.

Monica got up and went into the kitchen. "Would anyone like a lemon bar or some water?"

"Yes, please," Zach said.

"I'll have a glass of water," Angela said. "Do either of you know Serena Hurley?"

"No," Monica said. "Who is she?"

"She and her seven-year-old daughter came here from Wyoming about ten days ago. Now they are missing. We believe she was staying with Jesse Porter when he was killed."

Monica looked at Philip, and they shook their heads. "I hope you find her," Monica said.

"Do you know anything about stolen nuclear material circulating in Taos?"

"What kind of nuclear material?" Philip asked.

"Tell me what you know," Angela said.

"There was material stolen from the pit facility where I work," Philip said. "They had a suspect but didn't have enough to incriminate her. Is that what you are talking about?"

"No. But what material went missing there?"

"It's classified, so I can't say. But I can give you the name of someone who can."

"Let's focus on the nuclear material that came from Wyoming."

"I don't know anything about that," Philip said. "Have you alerted the FBI?"

The cat jumped down from Devin's lap and went out the cat door.

"Yes, we have," Angela said. Where can I find the suspect, Charlotte Foster?"

"I don't know where she is," Devin said. "I can give you her phone number."

"Explain something to me," Angela asked. "What is an anti-nuclear activist doing with someone who makes triggers for nuclear bombs?"

The two laughed and exchanged glances. "We're bridge partners," Philip said. We play in online tournaments. I'm a bronze life master, and Monica is a regional master."

Too cozy for words, Angela thought.

After Devin gave Angela Charlotte Foster's contact information, Angela stood up. "Do you like your Tesla?" she asked casually as she opened the front door.

"Yeah," Monica said. "I just bought it last summer."

Angela noticed a look of dismay cross Philip's angular face. *This is a romantic relationship,* she thought. *And for some reason, he doesn't want me to know it.*

When Angela and Zach drove off, a petite woman with short grey hair and bottle-thick glasses climbed carefully down from the treehouse and went inside. "What do they know?" she asked.

"Not much," Philip said. "They are looking for the toolbox, though, and Serena Hurley."

"I hope the special ops team from Texas didn't find Serena," Monica said. "I hope she and Kaylee are okay."

"They won't hesitate to play rough if they think she knows where the toolbox is," Philip said. "But she doesn't know a thing." He smiled.

"There isn't anything to smile about," Monica said.

"Sorry," Philip said. "You're right." His smile faded into a smirk. "Hey, Charlotte, when do you start back to work at LANL?"

"Tomorrow, I'll go in for an extensive debrief; if all is in order, I can start right away. They need Chemical Analytics up and running, and I'm the only one who can do that for them."

"You are a rock star, Mom," Monica said, hugging the older woman. "Indispensable to pit production and on the right side of the fight."

Charlotte smiled. "Just doing what we do! Listen, though, I think Boyar may be aware that we know he arranged the theft of the high-level waste."

"What makes you say that?" Philip asked, frowning.

"Just a hunch," Charlotte said. "You know I'm a Cassandra. I foresee the future, but no one believes me."

"Stay out of Boyar's way, okay?" Philip said. "I need you on the inside."

"I'll do my best," Charlotte said.

Philip went out to smoke a cigarette while Charlotte finished the minestrone simmering on the stove. Her daughter came up behind her and put her arms around her neck.

"Mom, I'm not too keen on you doing the op with Philip," she whispered.

Charlotte turned around and looked at her daughter through her thick glasses. "What are you worried about?"

"I've been seeing more of who he is and figured out I don't trust him."

"You aren't infatuated with him anymore?"

"Not anymore. You heard how he talked about that woman and her child. He doesn't care. He's obsessed with his plans and doesn't care what or who gets in his way. He's cold-hearted."

Charlotte was quiet for a few moments. "Commandos are like that," she said. "But we need them, Monica, if we are going to be successful." She stirred the soup and replaced the lid. "There's parmesan in the fridge. Would you get it for me?"

Monica handed her mother the cheese and a grater and said, "I know. But I'm feeling uneasy about him. I don't even like him."

"Stay strong, Monica. And trust me."

Do I trust her? Monica thought about her mother, who had re-entered her life five years ago. She marveled at how similar their career paths and politics were. For the first time, Monica, who had a lonely childhood in her adoptive family, felt like she belonged. Her mother had told her about the painful decision to give her up. Monica thought she had forgiven her, but had she?

Charlotte told Monica she'd met her father, a Nigerian, when they were both graduate students at Caltech. When he was unfaithful, Charlotte left him only to discover she was pregnant. When she was five months along and barely showing, she accepted a demanding job as a junior chemist at Lawrence Livermore. Determined to raise her child, she hired recent immigrants, who moved in with her and cared for the house and Monica.

Before Monica turned one, Charlotte was offered a better position at Oak Ridge, Tennessee. Unable to imagine how she could continue to juggle motherhood and work, Charlotte arranged for her daughter to stay with her caregivers in California. Later, she paid the Mexican couple, the Lovatos, to adopt her daughter. Monica never felt she belonged with her adopted family and experienced her childhood as unhappy. Meeting her biological mother had been a surprising turn of events for Monica, but the fact that her mother had given her away remained a painful reality.

Chapter 11

Cathy Dowd, Pete's ex-wife, greeted Ulysses at the door of a modest bungalow in Santa Fe, where she and Pete had lived together before they had separated more than fifteen years earlier. Ulysses had visited the home when he worked as a homicide detective for the Santa Fe Police. Cathy now lived there alone; their two children were grown. "I can't tell you how much I appreciate what you've done for Pete," she said softly, holding the storm door open for him to enter. "I was afraid he would die in detention." Cathy, thin, with hennaed hair, large tortoise-shell glasses, and a worried expression, had recently retired as a pediatric nurse practitioner.

"Thank the Attorney General," Ulysses said. "Lex arranged for Pete's release. I just had to ask. He understands that the case against Pete is weak." He took off his hat and put it on the coat rack. "How is Pete doing?"

"Not good, Ulys. Hospice was just here to make an assessment. They're coming back tomorrow with a team to set up full services. They said it could be a matter of days. One of our sons is getting him a home care hospital bed." She led him down a hall to the back bedroom, where Pete was resting in his ex-wife's queen-sized bed, attached to an I.V. and with an oxygen cannula under his nose. He opened his eyes and lifted one hand in greeting. He was jaundiced, and his belly was swollen with fluid.

Ulysses sat in a chair by the bed and patted his former partner's arm.

"It's good to see you here, Pete."

158

"Thanks to you, bro," Pete said. "I didn't want to die handcuffed in a hospital room."

"Anything I can get for you?"

"No, but I need to tell you something," he said urgently. "Pete paused to catch his breath. He swallowed hard. "Father Flynn was killed because he was in deep with some anti-nuclear activists who Chief Baca has been monitoring. Whoever killed Flynn probably also killed that guy in your jurisdiction." Pete licked his dry lips. Cathy offered him a drink of water, but he shook his head. "Let me finish," he said.

"Go ahead, Pete. Are you talking about Jesse Porter?"

Pete nodded. "Yeah. The killer was looking for something, first with Flynn and then with Porter. And these guys don't mess around. I thought Baca was the killer, but he's a small fry. The big fish live out at that religious camp in Taos County."

"The Elect compound?"

Pete nodded. "That's the one. Those people are directly connected with Duke Hadest and the so-called Texas Republic."

"Let me get this clear. Someone told you that whoever killed Timothy Flynn also killed Jesse Porter, and this person wasn't anyone in the Santa Fe police but someone from the Elect compound?"

Pete nodded. "That's what my informant told me. And that thing in my locker, the 'calling card?' That's associated with someone called 'the Rook.'"

Ulysses pondered what he had just learned. The chess piece, commonly referred to as a castle and occasionally as a rook, served as a perfect symbol for Castleman. "Pete, I need to speak with your informant. I will do my utmost to keep him safe. The killer is still at large and will strike again. This person could assist us in apprehending him. Who is he?"

Cathy came in and sat at the foot of the bed. "Tell Ulysses, Pete," she said. "Give him the information he needs to catch the guy. It will make you feel better."

Pete sighed deeply. "It's Elena Boyar," he said. "Nick Boyar's wife. She came to see me because she's frantic to find her daughter,

Serena. She told me Castleman has a hold over her and her husband. It's some kind of blackmail, but she planned to defy him."

"When did you talk with her?" Ulysses asked.

"The day I last saw you," Pete said. "When I got back to work, she was in my office. After she left, Baca arrested me for Flynn's murder."

The doorbell rang, and Cathy got up to see who it was.

"Thanks for the information, Pete. But what about you? Who knows you are here?"

"No one, as far as I know. Both my sons will be staying here, and they will keep me safe," he said.

Cathy entered the room, followed by an elderly priest in a cassock. "Pete, Father Dolan has come to hear your confession," she said.

LizBeth requested a meeting with Ulysses, Matt, and Ray to discuss the operational progress of the assault on the Elect compound. Bill Samuelson, Eli Martinez, Angela Romero, and Sheriff Gary Villalobos also attended. They met in the conference room of the tribal government office at Picuris Pueblo. LizBeth introduced Army Ranger Colonel Jack Riggs to the group. Except for Colonel Jack Riggs, this operation was more like war than most had experienced. Riggs, wearing civilian clothes to avoid alarming tribal members, looked relaxed. He noticed Ulysses looking at him and gave him a friendly return gaze. *In other circumstances, I might be riding mountain bikes with him,* Ulysses thought.

After finding chairs for everyone, LizBeth convened the meeting.

"I want to remind everyone that this operation will take place, in part, on a sovereign Indian nation. The operation will include tribal members under the command of Matt Pando, War Chief of Picuris Pueblo, and Army Rangers under the command of Colonel Jack Riggs. Once we retrieve the nuclear materials, Agent Bill Samuelson will work with Army Corps of Engineers specialists to remove the radioactive material safely. Agent Eli Martinez and I will maintain command and control here in this building, which has been secured, assisted by Governor Ray Pando and my logistics team.

"Sheriff Villalobos of Santa Fe will bring approximately twenty deputies. Sheriff Walker will bring four and I will have around ten agents to add. We also have fifty Army Rangers here from Fort Carson, Colorado. We know that these domestic terrorists are well-armed and are unlikely to surrender without a fight."

LizBeth opened a slide show of reconnaissance images. "Colonel Riggs and his team have provided us with these photographs taken by drones in the last forty-eight hours," LizBeth said, using a laser pointer. "This map shows the shape of the 50-acre property and its adjacent road, NM 75. The compound is bounded on three sides by undeveloped public lands managed by the Bureau of Land Management, but its longest boundary is with Picuris Pueblo. The property slopes significantly to the south and is rocky and steep in places. The eastern and northern portions are forested, as is the southeast area down to the boundary with Picuris. It is fenced on the Picuris boundary and along NM 75. Otherwise, it is unfenced."

Lizbeth changed the slides to a photograph. "Here is a picture of the front gate and Welcome Center. To the right of the Center is the kitchen and dining hall, and behind them is the residence of Max Castleman, also known as Maksim Spak. Their church is in front of the dining hall. On the hills above the residence are three apartment buildings occupied by families. Near the southeastern border with the BLM is the home of Daniel Graves, a.k.a 'The Servant', and Daniil Golubev. This building is their command-and-control center. Graves is in daily contact with the Nationalists in the new 'Republic of Texas' led by 'Johnny' Duke Hadest, for whom he acts as a spiritual advisor. My boss, Special Agent Nancy Levine, informed me this morning that an invasion by Nationalist troops in the next week cannot be ruled out, so this operation is of the utmost importance.

"Before we discuss the operation," LizBeth said, "I'll turn this over to Agent Eli Martinez for background. Eli?"

Eli took the slide changer from LizBeth. "You are probably wondering about the leadership of the Elect compound, and I will share our intel on them." He changed a slide to a picture of a bald man in his sixties wearing a suit and carrying a briefcase. "This is Ivan Kutznets, a.k.a John Kutznets, who emigrated from Russia in 1996 and founded a criminal gang in Chicago. The Kutznets gang engaged in protection rackets, human trafficking, and selling cocaine and heroin. They were known to have assassins for hire, supervised by this man, Maksim Spak, alias Max Castleman. Five years ago in Chicago, Ivan Kutznets disappeared, and Castleman took over as gang leader. The Chicago FBI, who had been watching the gang, believed Castleman killed Kutznets. An arrest was never made.

"Capitalizing on political unrest and corruption in the federal government, Castleman transferred his operations' focus to megachurches, which began to proliferate as profit centers, especially the loosely coordinated Evangelical Church of the Elect. Castleman hired Daniil Golubev, alias Daniel Graves, a defrocked Russian Orthodox priest, as his frontman." Eli showed a picture of Graves, imposing in his clerical garb, including an elaborate headdress and ornate cross necklace. "Graves is a powerful preacher. His message correlates well with the evolving Church of the Elect message, which could be boiled down to obedience to religious and political authority, white and male supremacy, and the importance of tithing.

"With money amassed from his various operations and support from wealthy donors to Nationalist causes, Castleman dismantled the Chicago operation and moved to New Mexico, where he established his unique brand of the Elect and purchased the property as a secure hiding place for the cult leaders." Eli showed a smiling photograph of Spak/Castleman, taken recently.

"The last piece of the Russian connection concerns Nikolai Boyar, who we know as Nick. Boyar is the nephew of Ivan Kutznets." Eli showed pictures of Boyar as a baby with his parents, with Kutznets, and as a graduate of Duke University in front of the Duke Chapel, and at Stanford as a graduate student. "Nick's mother, Sofia, Ivan Kutznets's sister, married Peter Boyar, an American of Russian extraction who was never involved with the Kutznets gang.

Sofia slowly distanced herself from her family of origin. She died in Chicago when Nick was twelve. Nick's father then moved with his son to Washington, DC, where he worked as a statistician for the Department of Energy. After he received a master's degree in engineering management from Stanford, Nick was hired at LANL. He moved up the ladder to his current position as the head of the pit production facility. That is, until Spak, whom we know as Castleman, came on the scene. Castleman, a cousin, began blackmailing him, we believe, forcing him to join the Nationalist Party and leave the Catholic Church for the Church of the Elect. Castleman has obtained substantial influence at LANL through Boyar."

"Thank you, Eli, for that information," LizBeth said. "Now, let's return to the operation site details. In this picture, you can see what we call 'the bunker' and the large fence to its south. The dotted line," she pointed with her laser pointer, "is the Picuris boundary. You can see how far the fence they built trespasses onto Picuris land. The fence is between twelve and fourteen feet high throughout its entire length. In places, it is topped with razor wire. There are banks of stadium lights here and here that are linked to the bunker door.

"The bunker is roughly 25 feet square. Its steel-reinforced door is blast-proof. High-level nuclear waste material stolen from the Los Alamos National Laboratory's pit production facility is stored inside. The radioactive material was bound for the Waste Isolation Pilot Project (WIPP) facility near Carlsbad, New Mexico. We have determined it was stolen in a false-flag operation attributed to undetermined anti-nuclear activists and anarchist groups. We now believe the theft was actually carried out by Nationalist sympathizers at LANL who brought the material directly to the compound." LizBeth changed slides.

Bill Samuelson spoke up. "The pit production process produces some of the most dangerous nuclear waste, though usually only in small amounts. Our intel is that LANL had not transferred its waste to WIPP since June. The pit facility was shut down in early October, but there could be a lot of waste product stolen and now in the bunker."

"This facility is called 'the armory.'" LizBeth continued, changing slides. "Sheriff Walker of Taos County was able to see inside. Sheriff Walker, can you tell us what you saw?"

"Undersheriff Romero and I visited last week. In addition to extensive weaponry and ammunition, we saw a metal locker twelve feet long and four feet high labeled 'explosives.' When we asked, we were told it contained dynamite used during construction."

"Dynamite is the preferred dispersal tool for a dirty bomb," Bill Samuelson interjected. "A locker that size could hold enough dynamite to disperse a great deal of radiation over a wide area."

LizBeth continued. "This building immediately next door to the armory is called the 'women's quarters.' It houses single women and girls in the process of 're-education.' Security on the armory and the quarters is tight with fencing, razor wire, posted sentries, and stadium lights. The quarters have a detention facility in the basement, used to incarcerate women accused of violations of their strict gender laws, including any disobedience to male authority. The facility has only one door to the outside, bars on the windows, and surveillance cameras. I think its position next to the armory poses problems for us. The women in the quarters could be used as hostages. Similarly, beneath the bunker, there is a jail facility for men and boys as well as an isolation room for captives. Ray has some information from Elect members who escaped the compound. Ray?"

"The Valdes family, who escaped abuse at the Elect Compound yesterday, are safe here now," Ray said. "Marisela Valdes, David's mother, worked as a housekeeper at the home of Daniel Graves. Her husband, Leo Valdes, was a security team member at the bunker. Marisela has given us the layout of the command center. Leo told us how to disable the blast door. He also said that no children are in the basement facility at present, although he did not know if any adult captives were held there. He reported that a new child is being housed at the women's quarters.

"Leo said that a rumor on the compound is that they plan to disperse the dirty bomb on the Santa Fe Plaza. The dirty bomb attack would be a prelude to taking over the capital and shutting down the state government. And to underline Agent Tallichet's earlier words, they will not surrender without a fight." Ray cleared his throat, took a drink of water, and continued. "We plan to evacuate Picuris the day before our operation begins. We will go in groups of three to five at a time, starting with women and children. We will try not to alert anyone, which should be possible because of our remote location."

LizBeth resumed. "Now, we will turn our attention to our incursion into the compound. The evacuation of Picuris will begin tomorrow at dawn. Sheriff Ulysses Walker and his team will use court orders to remove children, who could be used as hostages, from the property. We will remove the children for 24 hours to take them to safety. The rationale for removing the children is to do wellness checks based on abuse information given to us by the Valdes family. We will also search for any persons held at the compound against their will and try to remove them. Once the children and other noncombatants are removed, FBI agents will arrest Max Castleman and charge him with murder. Matt Pando and his team will begin bulldozing the fence. Then, Colonel Riggs and his team will mount their attack on the bunker, beginning with a drone assault. Their goal is to drive off the Elect combatants, secure the material, and with help from the Engineers, remove it safely. Let me pause there and see if anyone has any questions."

At that moment, Ray's office phone rang, and he answered it. "Billie?" he said as he walked out of the room. He motioned urgently to Ulysses, and he and Angela followed him outside.

Serena followed her interrogator out of the underground quarters where she had been held for two days. As they emerged into the sunlight and passed by armed guards, she saw her surroundings for the first time in daylight. In front of her stood a tall, slatted fence topped with razor wire. Behind her, near the top of a wooded hillside, stood an expansive three-story building. A sentry was stationed in a gatehouse outside the wall that surrounded the house. To her left, further uphill, Serena spotted several square concrete buildings resembling barracks.

Nearby, an old church with a steeple stood. A driver drove them up the hill, past a school and a playing field where boys were being drilled. They stopped in front of a building surrounded by fencing.

"Now you can look in on Kaylee," the man said. "Briefly. Then, you will fulfill your end of the bargain."

"What do you mean 'look in on Kaylee.' You said I could visit my daughter!"

"Since you cannot yet stay with her, it would only upset her to see you. Once you have proven yourself, we will permit an actual visit. Not until."

The guards at the gate surrounding the jail-like building saluted Serena's interrogator and held the gate open for him. Serena heard the gate clang shut as the main door opened. They were admitted into a bare anteroom lit by fluorescent lights. A middle-aged woman in a black headscarf awaited them. Inside the building, it was hot and stuffy.

"Good morning, Mr. Castleman," the woman said. She had a ring of keys on her belt.

"Good morning, Widow Jane. This is Serena. She is here to see her child, Kaylee. Please take her to the viewing room so she can see her through a two-way mirror. Serena is not to communicate with anyone, only to observe. I'll come for her in fifteen minutes."

"Yes, Mr. Castleman. The Servant is instructing the children now. Do you want to go in with him?"

"I would not want to interrupt his teaching. But tell me, has David Valdes and his family been found?"

"Not to my knowledge, sir."

"How many women are in detention?"

"Three," she said. "A discipline session is scheduled in half an hour." The woman looked at Serena. "Will she be witnessing the discipline?"

"Not today. Carry on."

The woman grasped Serena's arm, turned her around, and tied a scarf over her hair. Serena's survival instincts were heightened, and she started searching for ways to escape with her daughter.

The woman unlocked a gate and guided Serena down a hallway, where doors opened into sparse dormitory rooms with bunk beds.

"Who lives here?" Serena asked.

"Single women, widows, and unaccompanied girls."

"Where is everyone?"

"At work," Widow Jane said.

At the end of the hall was a laundry facility where women washed, dried, folded, and ironed clothing under the supervision of another matron. Around the corner was a set of double doors and a staircase leading down to a basement.

Widow Jane unlocked a door leading to a viewing room and turned on the lights. The small space featured a two-way mirror that overlooked a larger room where a group of girls sat in a circle around a bearded man dressed in black robes and a headdress resembling those worn by priests Serena had seen in Chicago. She noticed Kaylee sitting to the priest's left, as he stroked her black hair. Her little face, usually so animated, bore a blank expression. Serena felt a wave of nausea. She desperately wanted to knock on the window to let her daughter know she was there. However, Widow Jane stood in front of it, watching her.

The priest held Kaylee's chin and looked sternly at her while speaking. The other girls stared at their laps. Serena noticed tears on her daughter's face.

"Can you turn on the sound so I can hear what he's saying?" Serena asked.

"The Servant's spiritual instruction is not for your ears," Widow Jane said.

"He's making my daughter cry," Serena said, incredulity turning to anger.

"She is his daughter more than yours," the woman said.

"I can't watch this," Serena said.

"Suit yourself." The matron opened the door and pushed Serena out into the hall. At that moment, she saw two matrons open the doors to the basement and lead two handcuffed women toward the viewing room that Serena had just exited. A third matron led a woman with a shaved head down the hall toward the door to the room where Kaylee was. The woman's hands and bare feet were shackled. Serena's fear rose to panic. She felt like she couldn't breathe.

"I need to get outside," she said in a strangled voice. "Can I wait outside?"

Widow Jane took Serena's arm. She led her past the woman about to be punished, down another hall toward the antechamber where they entered. On that corridor, doors opened into children's dormitories. Serena noticed there were bars on the windows and no doors to the outside anywhere. Serena was sweating heavily and couldn't get her breath. *This is a prison with armed guards and only one door, just like The Stable.* She remembered escaping from the brothel with Russell and the men he'd hired to help her escape a year as a sex slave.

Finally, they arrived at the front door. The woman unlocked it, and fresh air rushed in and cooled Serena's face and neck. She breathed deeply and walked outside. The entrance to the women's quarters closed behind her, and its lock clicked. As Serena stood in the gravel yard surrounded by barbed wire and watched by sentries, her mind began to clear, exposing a dilemma. She knew she couldn't return to that building again but she could not escape and leave Kaylee here. Serena began to pray for help.

The man called Castleman arrived at the gate to retrieve her.

"Let's go," he said. "I want you to take me to where you hid the item you stole." He opened the back door of a black SUV, and she got in, sitting next to a man she recognized as one of Kuznets's enforcers. He was hard to forget: a pale redhead with a double-headed eagle tattooed on his neck. The car sped away downhill toward a large, ugly gate and then onto a secondary road that wound through the mountains. "You had better be telling the truth, Serena," Castleman said. "We don't tolerate women who lie to us."

Serena felt another panic attack coming on. Like a rabbit set upon by a pack of dogs, no matter where she dodged or hid, her predators would find her and tear her to pieces. As they passed the signs to Picuris Pueblo, she saw a gas station ahead.

"I have to use the toilet," Serena said. "Can we stop here?"

Castleman didn't answer but pulled into the parking lot. The tattooed man unlocked her door and let her out. He followed her into the convenience store, which was empty except for a tall and broad middle-aged Indian woman who stood behind the counter. Serena saw the women's bathroom in the back corner across from the walk-in cooler. She entered the bathroom, and the man stood outside the door. Serena splashed cold water on her face and tried to think what to do. She had told Castleman the toolbox was hidden in a shed next door to the house on Blueberry Hill where she'd been kidnapped. *Why didn't I think this through?* She had been so desperate to see Kaylee. There was nothing in that shed, but the windswept mesa behind the house would be a perfect place for them to kill her and leave her body. The tattooed man pounded on the door. "Hurry up," he said. Serena stood back from the door.

The bathroom door opened, and the store employee came inside. She looked Serena over. Serena whispered, "Please help me. The men outside kidnapped me. I'm being trafficked, and they have my daughter, too. They are armed and will kill me if I try to escape. Please call the police!"

The Indian woman had heard about the Valdes family's escape and asked, "Are you from the Elect compound up the road?"

"Yes, I am trying to escape. Please, help me." Serena began to tremble.

The woman locked the bathroom door's deadbolt, pulled a cell phone out of her pocket, and placed a call. "Ray," she said, "I'm covering for Esther at the travel center, and there's a young woman here who says she's being kidnapped. What should I do?" She listened for a minute, then hung up. "Help is coming," she said.

The man outside the door started pounding on it. "Honey," he shouted, "are you okay? Come out right now, or I'll have to come in." Serena and the Indian woman moved away from the door to the back of the three-stall bathroom.

"Is he armed?" the woman asked in a whisper. Serena nodded.

After a few minutes, the man began shooting at the door. At the same time, Serena heard multiple sirens coming nearer. The man shot at the door until he could kick it down. He grabbed Serena and pulled her out into the store just as a tribal police car and a sheriff's cruiser arrived. The Range Rover she came in was nowhere to be seen.

The man dragged Serena toward the front door as she kicked and screamed. They knocked into shelves. Cans and bottles tumbled to the floor. The man smacked Serena in the head several times. She bit him and pulled at his shirt. The law enforcement officers approached the building.

The tattooed man put his gun to Serena's head and moved her toward the door. He also noticed that Castleman's car was gone, and Serena could feel his grip on her tighten and smell the rank sweat of his fear. She was trying to struggle free when someone stepped up behind her captor, and Serena heard a shotgun's pump action. "Let her go, or I shoot," the Indian woman said.

Serena pulled away and ran behind the shelves. The tattooed man rounded on the Indian woman. He saw her shotgun but leveled his gun on her, saying he would kill her. But before he could shoot, she blasted him at close range, knocking him to the floor and killing him. Ray, Matt, and Ulysses burst through the door with Angela behind them. Angela put her arm around Serena, who stood numb and in shock.

Angela took Serena to headquarters and sat her in an interview room where they wouldn't be disturbed. She then gave Serena a blanket and hot coffee and called her husband. Within a few minutes, Russell appeared and embraced his shaken wife.

"Russ, they have Kaylee," Serena said. "What are we going to do?"

"Sheriff Walker has told me I can count on his help," her husband said. "I'm going to take him at his word." Hurley looked as if he hadn't slept and had tears in his eyes. "Are you okay, honey? Did they hurt you?"

"I'm not harmed," she said. "I'm out of my mind with worry about Kaylee. Russ, that place, the compound, is scary. It's like something out of a nightmare."

"I know, Serena. But don't think about that now. Are you hungry?"

"No. I only want to get our daughter." She began to cry again.

"Serena," Hurley said, "your mother has been franticly trying to find you. Do you want to speak with her?"

"Are you serious? She's frantic because of all I know about her and Nick. She doesn't care about me or Kaylee. No, I don't want to talk with her."

Angela came in with a glass of water. "Here, Serena, drink this. When you are ready, I will ask you some questions."

Russell Hurley stood up. "I don't think she's ready for that," he said. "I'll take her back to the motel so she can rest."

Angela shook her head. "Mr. Hurley, some very dangerous people are looking for Serena. I can't let you go back to a place where both of you could be kidnapped or worse. Plus, we need information from Serena. It will help us rescue Kaylee."

Serena drank her water and sat up straight. She wiped her eyes. "I'm willing to answer questions if it will help get my daughter out of that place."

Angela considered where to begin. She needed to find the toolbox, but Serena would be wary of telling her anything that might expose her to charges for stealing from Warren Air Force Base. *I need to run this by Sheriff.*

"Serena, who kidnapped you, and how did that happen?"

"I don't know. Men kicked down the door of the safe house and dragged me and Kaylee into a van. I never saw those men again."

"Where were you held?"

"In a dungeon under a bunker. I was there until a man came to interrogate me. I recognized him as one of the Kutznets gang. I think he recognized me, too."

"Why were you kidnapped?" Angela asked. She heard Ulysses entering headquarters with Zach and Joseph.

Serena hesitated. She didn't want to tell this deputy information that could land her in federal prison. But maybe the deputy already knew. And perhaps she wouldn't be sent to jail for what she did?

"I think I know, but I need to speak with an attorney before I tell you," Serena said.

"Time is of the essence, Serena. Finding an attorney will take vital time we can't afford to spare."

Ulysses came into the room. "I can get her legal representation," he said. "I can also assure you, Mrs. Hurley, that we will consider the information you give us about the whereabouts of the material you brought to New Mexico from Wyoming when we decide what charges to bring against you."

Serena looked confused. "You know about the toolbox?" she asked.

"We do. And so do the Elect and the Nationalists, including their special ops teams. We could be approaching a dangerous juncture where the radioactive material in the toolbox threatens public safety. We need to know the toolbox's current location. As the Undersheriff stated, your willingness to provide us with information will be considered. However, giving that information later – after an incident occurs – won't be as valuable to your case." Ulysses turned to Angela, "Have Zach call Juanita Burns at Legal Aid and see if she can come over right away," he said. Angela and Ulysses exited the interview room. Serena and Russell began to whisper to each other.

Angela asked Ulysses for a meeting in his office.

"Sir," she said, "I spoke with Lisa White, the social worker who came along when we interviewed David Valdes at the compound. She mentioned that she could prepare the paperwork for us as soon as we provided her with the names of the children we wish to remove and the reasons."

"We won't have names. We need a blanket authorization to remove every child on that property. But to do that, we'll need a good rationale that won't alert the compound we are about to attack."

"I remember when we took Isaiah, the key element was his forced fasting," Angela said. "Can we say that we have intel that they are still using fasting as a punishment?"

Ulysses thought for a moment. "Do we have that intel?"

"Not really," Angela replied. "But maybe we could say we did?"

Ulysses gave her a disapproving look. "Whatever it is, it needs to be true. See what you can come up with."

"I'll speak with Lisa about the precedent for that kind of check."

Billie Arguello lay on the couch at Ray's, feeling shaken. "I can't stop seeing that man's face when I blew him to kingdom come," she said. "I've never even killed a deer. Do you think I did the right thing?"

Ray brought her a mug of tea and a quesadilla. "Without a doubt," Ray said. "That man could have killed the girl he was holding, and you and the rest of us for that matter. But I know how hard it is to take a life, even the life of a criminal. It's a brutal experience." Ray sat down beside his friend and took her hand. "You were very, very brave, Billie," he said.

Billie shook her head in disbelief. "I didn't even consider," she said. "I saw him dragging that poor girl to what might have been her death and picked up the store shotgun without so much as a thought. That's not like me," she said. "I'm usually a maker of deliberate choices."

"Like when you chose to become involved with me?" Ray said, chuckling.

"Well, yes. I did think that through, but maybe a bit quickly," she patted his hand. "But this was different."

"Billie, it was a matter of life and death. You saw what was up. You took bold action. That's what you have to do in these situations. I've been in that spot many times."

"Have you ever killed anyone?" she asked.

"You know I have. I killed two men in one day during a raid on a drug house in Albuquerque. It was them or me."

Billie nodded and sighed. "Are you worried about this operation?"

"I'd be lying if I said I wasn't. But I'll be in the command center with LizBeth and the drone operators. It's Matt I'm worried about."

LizBeth sat down to a late dinner with Dawa, who had nursed

their baby to sleep several hours earlier. LizBeth was tired and anxious about the operation. Dawa was also worried and irritable and picked at her food. The couple ate in silence until LizBeth said, "I have to be up in Santa Fe tomorrow at 7:00 a.m."

"Lucky you," Dawa said. "Why?"

"Eli and I are going to make an arrest before I go to Picuris."

"I take it something big is going on up at Picuris?"

"Yeah, but I can't talk about it. What are you up to tomorrow?"

"Pema has a well-baby check at 11, and I have a consultation call at 3 during her most reliable naptime. Kind of a big day in my world."

"I wish I could come with you to Pema's checkup."

"I wish you could be here to take Pema during my call." Dawa reached across the table and patted LizBeth's hand. "But I know you can't, and it's okay. Tell me, is it true that Texas militias might invade New Mexico?"

"It's a possibility," LizBeth said. "The National Guard has been deployed to the eastern border."

"Will we have martial law?" Dawa asked.

"That is also possible. Even with the Insurrection Act in place, nothing is as straightforward as you might think. Are you feeling worried, D?"

"Yes. If the Nationalists take over New Mexico, I want to leave. I can't live under that kind of system. I want to go somewhere that accepts us."

"Honey, let's not think about this now or neither one of us will sleep a wink."

"I'm also worried about you. Are you going to be deployed in some kind of assault?"

"If that were happening, I would definitely tell you. But, as of now, I am behind the scenes."

"Liz, tell me, what is the biggest risk we face? In general terms."

"There are multiple threats we face. Invasion by Texas militias, terrorist acts by New Mexico militias, and turmoil at LANL are the scariest ones in my book."

"Yikes, what kind of turmoil at LANL?" Dawa asked.

"I can't say," LizBeth said. "But there is a power struggle there, and everything is sideways. I've not seen my boss so uptight about anything before."

"Who are you kidding?" Dawa asked. "Nancy Levine is uptight on a good day. Should I be worried about mushroom clouds?"

LizBeth took her wife's hand. "No. I don't think we are facing that kind of risk. Again, if we were, I'd tell you."

"Thank God," Dawa said. "But what if the militias manage to detonate a dirty bomb?"

"Why are you worried about this?"

"Liz, just answer me. There are a lot of rumors on social media."

"I'll do my best to answer your question, Dawa. With dirty bombs, the detonation itself is the most dangerous part. Dirty bombs use a significant amount of dynamite to disperse the material. The explosion alone could kill anyone nearby. Radioactive dust can lead to both short-term and long-term health issues, requiring a complex cleanup, depending on the level of radioactivity in the dust. We're discussing terrorist activities, so the impact on the public is also psychological, which poses a significant risk in times like these. There is a possibility of someone setting off a dirty bomb in New Mexico, but I truly believe you and Pema are safe here in Placitas. If I had information to the contrary, I'd let you know. Does that help?"

"Thank you, Agent Tallichet," Dawa said jokingly. "If you have to be up at 5, you'd better get to bed. I'll clean up the kitchen."

LizBeth heard Pema starting to wake up in the next room.

"No, I'll do it," LizBeth said. "Somebody's awake and sounds hungry."

When Angela came into her house, she was greeted by savory smells.

Eli was in the kitchen, sitting in a rocker with Mr. T in his lap. The cat had been fed, and Eli had the makings of huevos rancheros laid out by the stove, with his grandmother's red chile bubbling in a ceramic pot. "Ready to eat?" he asked.

"If I *can* eat," Angela said. "I have the jitters, big time."

"Understandable," Eli said as he put together their meal. "What in particular are you worried about?"

"Ulysses, Zach, and I are supposed to get the children out in the morning. We moved the time up to before lunch. That doesn't sound particularly dangerous, but it is bound to be emotional and messy, and we'll have to be careful not to spill the beans that an attack is coming. I'm also worried about leaving women there in danger."

"Don't you think those women are there voluntarily?" Eli asked, taking the eggs and tortillas from the skillet and placing them on top of black beans, sour cream, and salsa. "Do you want a beer?"

"I'll just have water," she said. Eli ladled red chile onto her plate and handed it to her. "Most of the women are there of their own free will. But Serena Hurley informed us that at least three women were being held in some dungeon in the so-called women's quarters. However, we don't have a rationale to free them that won't expose the operation. I worry about them and what will happen next." Angela took a bite of her dinner. "This is delicious, Eli," she said. "Especially the chile. Just what I needed!"

Eli sat down and began to eat. "How did you like my background on the Kutznets gang?"

"Fishing for compliments?" Angela asked. "It was outstanding. I think I'm beginning to understand who we are dealing with. I was most surprised that Castleman is the head honcho, not the Servant, Daniel Graves. Or are they in a power struggle?"

"Yes, I think so. Graves appears to be a true believer and something of a nut. But being an ordained Russian Orthodox priest gives Graves caché, even if he is defrocked. And I don't think Graves is as ruthless as Castleman. Castleman is an experienced assassin with a long history, going back to the early 2000s. He's taken out the competition before and he probably has a few loyal men working for him."

"Like that man Billie Arguello blew away, Lev Kalinin," Angela said, taking another bite of her dinner. "What do you think about Nick Boyar?"

"He is under the control of Max Castleman. Boyar has done well for himself in the real world, but he must have some dark secrets. Or someone in his family does."

"We know Boyar sexually abused Serena Hurley from the age of twelve," Angela said. "Could Boyar have killed Rafael Cadiz?"

"Boyar doesn't seem like a killer to me. Elena Cadiz, maybe. She has a history with the Kutznets gang, which makes me think she could murder. Boyar seems besotted with her. He also wants to keep their family crimes secret, so he doesn't lose his high-profile job. And he is next in line when Director Shapiro retires. Max Castleman knows all the skeletons in Nick's closet, his abuse of Serena, and whatever happened with Rafael Cadiz. That knowledge gives Max power over Nick Boyar and, thus, power over LANL. And that is very bad."

"What else can the Elect do beyond what they've already done?"

"LANL has more stamped triggers and explosives in the pit facility than any place in North America, and through Max Castleman, the Elect have access to it all."

Monica Lovato, Charlotte Foster, and Philip Devin sat in the living room of Philip's condo, located in an exclusive complex in Los Alamos. Floor-to-ceiling windows offered expansive mountain views to the east, where the full moon had risen, illuminating the surrounding canyons. The room was tastefully furnished with a leather sectional couch, designer lamps, and a modern glass coffee table. A gas fire burned in a massive stone façade beneath a rustic mantelpiece. On the teak dining table lay the remnants of a hurried meal of Chinese take-out.

"Did you rent or buy this place?" Charlotte asked.

"I rented it fully furnished. The new tenants have taken possession of my house in White Rock, and I've disposed of most of my stuff there. I am almost free as a bird," he said.

"Are you still planning to go to Mexico when we're done?" Monica asked.

"That's classified," Philip said, laughing. "Seriously, Monica, you don't want to go where I'm going. It's better that way."

But we planned that I would go with you, Monica thought. She felt angry and ashamed that she'd trusted this man, once believing she loved him.

"Let's get down to our discussion, shall we?" Charlotte said.

"Yes, let's," Philip said. "With the power vacuum at LANL, no one is paying much attention to us. Plus, the pit facility is closed and won't reopen after the holidays, so most of the staff is still on leave. You and I, Charlotte, are well-positioned with authority and clearance to carry out our plan. But we should do it very soon."

"I agree. Security around the Analytics group is quite thin right now."

Philip continued, "Over the years, I've stockpiled enough dynamite to disperse the toolbox contents nicely. We have what we need to carry this off."

Charlotte nodded. "You have more than enough. Well done, Phil."

Monica gazed at her mother in the flickering gas light. Though her face had softened with age, it bore an avid look she'd observed on other activists, particularly women who had dedicated their lives to the movement, often operating undercover. Her mother was unlikely to concern herself with collateral damage when faced with a mission deemed so critical. Monica suppressed the fear and regret that threatened to undermine the little resolve she still had to follow through with their mission.

"Here is what to understand about the so-called leadership," Philip said. "Strictly speaking, Nick Boyar is still powerful, though his history as a convert to Nationalist politics made him unpopular in the upper management. Since the inauguration, he has grown quieter about his politics. Boyar is not a believer in the Elect nonsense or any religion. Nick's wife, Elena Cadiz Boyar, is religious, but she has fallen from favor with the Elect. They see her as a loose cannon. The LANL Director, Dr. Jonathan Shapiro, who is at retirement age, is preoccupied with cancer treatment that isn't going well. He's often away from the office and is widely expected to resign. He used to be shrewd and competent. But since he became ill, he has been erratic. Still, I would consider him a wild card. Shapiro and Boyar don't get along. What are your thoughts, Charlotte?"

Charlotte smiled. "Shapiro is one of my allies. I've been grooming him since I arrived. He's the one who exonerated and reinstated me after Boyar tried to frame me for the theft of the high-level waste material. He leaves me alone as long as I appear to be making progress on his priority projects. In my opinion, Boyar is a snake and an opportunist."

"Boyar stole the waste, correct?" Monica asked.

"Yes, and arranged for its storage," Charlotte said. "With the Elect."

"That isn't certain, is it?" Monica asked. "I thought they'd taken it to Albuquerque."

Philip's phone dinged. He looked at it and said, "I've got to take this call. I'll go in the bedroom."

The two women cleaned up from dinner, and Charlotte put on the kettle for tea. "I hope we have time to review the game plan tonight," she said. "I have some critical questions for Philip. He's so hard to pin down!"

"When Philip gets a call that he 'has to take,'" Monica said, "things usually go off the rails."

"Who do you think called him?" Charlotte asked.

"Nick Boyar, no doubt. Boyar thinks Philip is investigating Nuclear Peace and Justice for him."

"I wonder how much information Philip is giving Boyar?" Charlotte asked.

"Just enough," Monica said, "and most of it isn't true. Philip is wily. And nothing is more important to him than this mission."

Certainly not me, Monica thought, feeling cold anger.

"That is why we work with him. We agree this must be done—don't we?"

Do I? I'm not sure that I do anymore. But I can't look ambivalent to Charlotte. Monica said, "Anything that destroys LANL for the foreseeable future is worth the sacrifice, right?"

"Yes, the ultimate sacrifice, if necessary," Charlotte said.

Ulysses lay in bed, unable to sleep. Rosemary slept soundly beside him in the chilly room. He looked out the window, trying to gauge the time by the position of the big dipper that shone particularly brightly now that the moon had set. It must be about three o'clock. He couldn't afford to get out of bed for another two hours.

Ulysses tried to push away thoughts as one worry after another pursued his attention. Foremost were concerns about the operation scheduled for the next twenty-four hours. What would they do if the leadership refused to let the children go? Would he and Angela be allowed inside the women's quarters? Would they be able to carry out their plans? If they couldn't remove the children, what would happen to them during the operation?

Ulysses rolled over and snuggled against Rosemary's warm back. Beginning in the morning, the people at Picuris Pueblo would be leaving their homes to escape the risks of a potential dirty bomb detonation on their boundary. He started to count his breaths to stave off worries, but the image of families evacuating kept coming to mind. Should his family evacuate? He'd already consulted with LizBeth and Eli and been told it wasn't necessary. If a bomb were detonated, there would be time before danger arrived in his neighborhood, if it ever did, depending on the prevailing winds. And, given the distance and surrounding mountains, radiation would not likely be in sufficient quantities to cause immediate health risks. But there were other threats beyond the material at Picuris. LizBeth's intel said that Nationalists had infiltrated the LANL pit facility and were closely connected with the people at the Elect compound. What threats did they pose with so much dangerous material at hand? LANL was a more direct downwind threat to Taos than the compound. And what about the toolbox? Who had it, and what might they be planning? Late yesterday, Serena Hurley, advised by her attorney, revealed that she no longer knew where the toolbox was. It had been taken by a man associated with Nuclear Peace and Justice whom she did not know.

I need to clear my mind, Ulysses realized and got out of bed. In the hall, he opened the damper of the woodstove and its door. The firebox was still full of wood, and it burst into flame. He climbed the stairs and listened outside his children's doors. Monty and Amelia were asleep, and no lights came from under their doors. Ulysses closed the stove, wrapped a blanket around his shoulders, and sat cross-legged on the couch. He began his mantra. "Just this" on the in-breath, and "moment" on the outbreath. He could feel himself settling. *I'm not in control of anything except my actions. I will do my best; the outcome will be what it is.* He repeated his mantra and gradually began to feel sleepy. Then he heard Frances' door open. She approached him and put her hand on his knee.

"Daddy, what are you doing?" she whispered.

"I'm meditating."

"Can I meditate with you?" She climbed on the couch. "I'll try not to bother you." She sat up and crossed her legs, imitating Ulysses.

"What woke you up, Pookie? Did you have a dream?"

Frances yawned. "I dreamed you were playing Pied Piper."

"I was? What was that like?"

"A whole line of children was following you while rats like the ones in the storybook were watching."

"Was it a scary dream or a nice dream?" Ulysses stroked his daughter's red curls.

"It wasn't scary. But it wasn't nice either. The rats had icky, yellow eyes."

"Well, you know what I always say?"

"It's only a dream," Frances said, yawning again.

"Frances, can you put yourself back to bed like a big girl? It's the middle of the night, and you need more sleep."

"Don't you need more sleep, Daddy?"

"Yes, but I need to have some alone time first."

"Okay," the child said. "I can go back to bed on my own. Goodnight, Daddy." She went into her room and closed her door quietly. He returned to his mantra and began again to settle his mind.

Chapter 12

Ray and Billie had spent the night together in Billie's cool back bedroom, where heat from the woodstove barely delivered warmth. They snuggled under flannel sheets and a down comforter, but both were awake before sunup. Ray heard Billie's coffee machine, set for 6 am, begin its cycle. He squeezed Billie's hand and put his feet on the cold brick floor. "I'd better get out to the plaza," he said. "Matt and the boys will be wanting me if anything comes up. How are you feeling?" he asked Billie.

"I'm okay," she said. "I slept fine. No dreams that I can remember." She shrugged her bare shoulders.

"Nothing from yesterday?" Ray asked. He knew from experience that shooting a man could be traumatizing.

"No, nothing. I'm surprised I don't feel more." She sat up and began brushing and then braiding her long black hair.

"Everybody's different," Ray said. "You might feel something when things settle down."

"I know," Billie said. "Don't worry about me. Do you want breakfast?"

She stood up, and Ray admired her tall, sturdy body, which looked younger than her deeply lined face. She put on a warm robe.

"Just coffee for now," Ray said. "I'll get it."

He dressed and poured them each a mug of hot coffee, stirring a little sugar into Billie's cup.

"Evacuation day," he said, as if Billie needed reminding. "Where are you going again?"

"The shelter there in Santa Fe with Ramona and her mother," Billie said. "My bag is packed, and we've planned to leave this afternoon. Do you need me in the office until then?"

"I could use you until around 4 if you can stay."

While Billie dressed, Ray went outside. Already, a few family groups were loading possessions into trucks and cars. The women, some draped in the colorful blankets they wore on feast days, whispered among themselves while the children ran around excitedly. When they saw Ray, the women waved, but no one smiled. Next door, an elderly tribal member sat in his truck, the motor running, while his wife locked their front door. *I hope Benito brings enough insulin with him,* Ray thought. Matt and the War Council were already going door to door throughout the village, ensuring everyone had somewhere to go and a plan for getting there. The solemn scene made Ray feel sad. His people were being forced to leave their homes, and no one knew when they'd be able to return.

Ray saw Ulysses' Expedition and another Taos deputy vehicle stopping in front of his house across the plaza. He walked toward his old friend, grateful he'd come to check on him. Ulysses and Angela got out of the front seat. A female deputy, whom Ray didn't know, sat in the back, texting on her phone. Zach and Joseph were in the second vehicle.

"Hey, man," Ulysses said, reaching to shake Ray's extended hand. "How is it going?" He was in a starched uniform and wearing a fawn-colored wool hat with a straight brim and a low crown. His sheriff's badge was gleaming.

"It's going," Ray said and sipped coffee. We'll have everyone gone by 3 pm. At least, I hope we will. Why are you up here so early?"

"We're on our way to the compound," Ulysses said. "We want to get the children out early."

"Good idea," Ray said. "Just the five of you?"

"Yeah, I had to leave most of my deputies at home to keep Taos County safe. LizBeth is sending some agents from the Albuquerque office," Ulysses said, "and the Santa Fe sheriff is providing backup. We'll have about twenty-five law officers at the gate. Only the deputies from Taos and I will go inside, though. We want the operation to look low-key."

"That's good. Where will you take the children?" Ray asked.

"To the youth intake center in Santa Fe," Ulysses said. "Social workers from CYFD will take charge of them when we arrive. We have a new hire, a deputy with experience in domestic violence, so she should be helpful."

"What is your rationale for taking the children off-site?"

"Complaints about neglect and abuse corroborated by the Valdes family. Angela and our new deputy, Rosie, got the paperwork for a twenty-four-hour hold. They have no legal grounds to resist us."

"What about illegal grounds? Like all those weapons they have?"

Ulysses patted Ray on the shoulder. "Take it easy, Ray. We're going to win this fight."

"I hope so, Ulys. Stay safe."

It was just after sunrise when LizBeth and Eli met at the office in Santa Fe and drove to the palatial residence of Elena and Nick Boyar, followed by two agents in another car to provide backup. When they arrived, they saw servants coming down the stairs with trunks, boxes, and suitcases, which they were loading into a Range Rover.

"Going somewhere?" LizBeth asked a man wearing a sidearm, who appeared to be in charge.

"Mrs. Boyar gave orders for these items to be placed in her car," he said respectfully in Spanish-accented English.

"Is she at home?" LizBeth asked. The man looked up at the open front door. Elena Boyar stood in the shadow, clutching a cashmere robe over her nightgown.

"Who are you?" she called down to them.

"FBI, ma'am," LizBeth said. She and Eli flashed their credentials. "We have some questions we need to ask you."

"This isn't a good time," Elena said. Can you come back in about two hours? I'll be available then."

"No, ma'am," LizBeth said. "This is an urgent matter."

Elena went back inside, leaving the door open. LizBeth and Eli climbed the stairs and followed her in. They traversed the two-story conservatory and entered the sitting room, where Elena sank onto one of the two soft leather couches. Her face was blotchy from crying. A uniformed maid appeared, but Elena waved her away. LizBeth and Eli introduced themselves.

"Have a seat, please. What is this about?" Elena asked. She took a cigarette out of a gold case and lit it.

"Tell us about Rafael Cadiz's death," LizBeth said.

"Are you serious? He died twenty-five years ago! How could anything related to his death be urgent?" She blew out a cloud of smoke.

"Mrs. Boyar," Eli said. "How did he die?"

"It was a suicide," she said. "As you no doubt already know. He overdosed on barbiturates."

Eli and LizBeth exchanged a look.

Elena called in her maid and spoke to her in rapid Spanish. Angela only understood the word "abogado," which means attorney. Elena picked up her phone and began to text.

"Cadiz had lacerations in his throat," Eli continued. "Your fingerprints and his DNA were found on surgical tongs in your kitchen."

Elena swallowed, and tears appeared in her eyes. "This was disputed in the inquest," she said. "His death was ruled a suicide. Rafael left a suicide note on his computer. He was distressed about a deportation case he was losing. Please, this is not a good time."

"At the time of your first husband's death, what kind of work was he doing?"

"He was helping Venezuelan refugees get green cards."

"Did you know Sergio Flores?" Eli asked. "Rafael Cadiz was handling his case. He was about to be deported because he was being framed for drug smuggling. Did you know him?"

"I neither knew Mr. Flores nor anything about drug smuggling."

"Is it true that you worked closely with the Kutznets gang out of Chicago, overseeing cocaine smuggling out of Venezuela and Columbia?"

"I did some consulting work for Mr. Kutznets. He had business interests in my former home country."

"Did your husband know about your smuggling business?"

"There was no smuggling business."

"Did you ever know Paloma Walker?" Eli asked.

"Who is she?"

"Paloma is an immigration lawyer in Albuquerque who worked closely with your husband. She took over the Flores case when Rafael died. But it was too late to save Mr. Flores. He was deported less than a week after your first husband died, and then he disappeared. We've combed through the case details and discovered some facts about your past, Mrs. Boyar. Facts that were suppressed in the inquest into your first husband's death."

"I want you to leave now. Please understand that I am struggling with a family problem. I will answer no more questions until my attorney arrives."

LizBeth stood up. "You are under arrest for conspiracy to smuggle illegal drugs and conspiracy to murder Rafael Cadiz. Anything you say can be used against..."

"I didn't kill Rafael!" Mrs. Boyar began to weep.

"Well, who did?" LizBeth asked.

Mrs. Boyar wouldn't answer. She just cried and shook her head.

"You'll have a chance to speak with an attorney," LizBeth said. "You should get dressed. You are going to the FBI headquarters in Albuquerque. There are agents outside who will transport you."

Elena looked terrified. "No, you can't make me go there. My husband will prevent this! He is very powerful. He will fire both of you!"

"You had better go get dressed while you can, Mrs. Boyar."

LizBeth and Eli drove back to the Roundhouse, New Mexico's capital building.

"She seemed genuinely grief-stricken even before we arrested her. I wonder where she was going. And where was her husband?" Eli said.

"I thought she might be grieving also. Maybe about her daughter? For sure, she was surprised at the evidence we had against her. I'm glad we caught her before she fled," LizBeth said.

"The information about lacerations in the victim's throat and her DNA on tongs was in the file," Eli said. "Paloma thinks someone from the Kutznets gang paid off the district attorney," Eli replied. "In those days, the gang was well-connected, and D. A. Buddy Rizzle was on the take. He's spending time in federal prison for similar crimes."

Ulysses drove through Peñasco, where the cottonwood leaves had turned from gold to bronze. At the Double Rainbow, which was closed, Sheriff Villalobos had staged several school buses to transport the children. The town was quiet. Skeletons and black cats had appeared in front yards, and a few porches displayed jack-o-lanterns. Jicarita Peak wore fresh snow from the night before. The aspens on its slopes stood bare, white and grey against the snow. As they approached the compound, Ulysses pulled over, and the other cruiser pulled in behind him. Ulysses and Angela put on Kevlar vests. Zach and Joseph followed suit.

"Put on your vest, Deputy," Angela said to Rosie.

"I love this time of year," Rosie said. No one answered her. Undaunted, Rosie continued, "Do your children know what they want to be for Halloween?"

Ulysses looked pointedly at her. "Listen up, Deputy. Today could get dangerous. We are removing these people's children. Stay focused. Ready your weapons.

Team, Undersheriff Romero and I will present our paperwork at the gate when we arrive. Zack, Joseph, and Rosie, exit the cruiser and stand together. No chit-chat. If the Undersheriff or I say, "Get back up," Zach, radio Sheriff Villalobos and the FBI to come on the double. If anyone resists, we will move with force to implement our plan but limit the use of deadly force except on my command. It may get hot; if it does, follow the chain of command: Angela, Zach, then Joseph. If all goes well, supervise loading the children and their mothers onto the buses. Make sure the information is recorded for each mother and child as specified on those clipboards you have. Let's do this."

As they approached the compound, Ulysses was gratified to see two squad cars from Santa Fe parked on either side, plus a black Chevy Suburban emblazoned with FBI in white. As he had instructed, no one had yet emerged from the vehicles, but Ulysses felt confident they were all good to go if needed. When he arrived at the iron gate, it swung open, and Max Castleman, accompanied by two armed guards, walked out. Ulysses put down his window.

"Good morning, Sheriff," Castleman said. He looked briefly at law enforcement vehicles parked on the road and leaned over the open car window to speak to Ulysses. "What brings you here today?"

Angela handed Ulysses a clipboard with the court order. "Due to allegations of widespread abuse, we have authorization to remove children under eighteen from your premises to conduct wellness checks," Ulysses said. Castleman took the clipboard and flipped through the official papers for several minutes. Then he stood up and gave a little mirthless laugh. "This is ridiculous, Sheriff Walker, and you know it. There is no abuse or neglect here. You have no reason to separate children from parents. This is about your prejudice against our religious faith."

Ulysses got out of the cruiser and closed the door. Angela followed. "Mr. Castleman," Ulysses said, "the children we are removing will be taken to a safe location and assessed for their mental and physical health. If we are concerned for a child's safety, temporary housing will be provided, and a process for their return will be established. Otherwise, the child will be immediately returned to their parents, and guidelines will be established to avoid concerns in the future."

Castleman scoffed. He looked at Ulysses with his good eye and shook his head. Then he stepped away from Ulysses and called someone on his cell phone. After a few more minutes, he said, "Sheriff, you have come to our peaceful sanctuary with weapons and threats. We are a nonviolent group. We have no choice but to comply with your wishes, but we do so under protest." He looked at his watch. "We expect every child you remove to be returned to us, safe and sound, in twenty-four hours, or you will greatly regret it." Castleman walked away, speaking into his phone.

Angela radioed Sheriff Villalobos and asked him to bring the school buses forward. The deputies got out of the car. But before they could go much farther, a bearded man in black robes and a veiled headdress came out of the Welcome Center. Ulysses recognized the Servant, the Elect's spiritual leader. The cleric approached Ulysses and asked to speak with him privately.

"Sheriff Walker," he said in a husky voice, "why are you persecuting us? Don't you understand we are only trying to practice our faith?"

"Sir, we are not persecuting you but rather protecting vulnerable children, which is our duty under the laws of New Mexico."

"How dare you try to assert authority over us! You have no such authority! My authority comes from God!"

"My authority originates from the laws of New Mexico, Mr. Graves," Ulysses stated. "Things will go better for everyone if you permit us to do our jobs peacefully."

Graves raised his right hand and shouted, "I curse you and your children," he said. "Almighty God, I call down your wrath upon this man because of what he does!" He spat on the ground at Ulysses' feet.

Ulysses stepped back, shocked. Then he took a deep breath.

"Sir," Ulysses said, "communicating threats is a crime. In the interest of completing our task here, I will not arrest you, but if you further impede our efforts, I will."

The priest turned and strode back to the Welcome Center, his black cassock flapping about his legs.

Angela said, "What a ridiculous man! I can't believe he just threatened your children."

"He's like something out of the Middle Ages," Ulysses said. Then he laughed. "It would be funny if it wasn't so full of hatred."

Another man, about forty and wearing the fatigues and boots, came out of the Welcome Center.

"Mr. Castleman has been called away," the man said. "He has asked me to direct you." The man had a bullet-shaped head and tattoos on half his face and neck. "Follow me," he said. Ulysses recognized Gideon Strum, commander of the Santa Fe Knights.

"I am not going anywhere, Mr. Strum," Ulysses said. "Bring the children to me, and we will load them on buses." Ulysses looked over his shoulder at the Santa Fe deputies who had emerged from their vehicles and were approaching the gate.

"That's Colonel Strum to you," he said. "Have it your way."

Meanwhile, children began emerging from the school building on the hill. Mothers with infants and preschoolers came out of their apartments and walked toward the gate to board the buses. At the same time, half a dozen men with rifles, led by Levi Patterson, came out of the armory. Angela signaled to Zach, who radioed the FBI to back them up. "We have a situation here," Zach said. Come right away," she said.

"Tell your men to put down their weapons," Ulysses said to Strum. "Let us load the children safely. Strum stood still, arms crossed over his chest. "Believe me, Colonel Strum, this is not a fight you want to have. Women and children will be harmed." Not breaking contact with Strum's angry eyes, Ulysses heard the doors to the Suburbans slamming as FBI agents in battle gear got out of each one. They ran toward the gate, weapons drawn.

"What's all this?" Strum asked, his expression changing. "You don't need to intimidate us further. We are complying with your demands."

"Tell your men to disarm," Ulysses said. "Right now!"

The sound of crying children and women echoed up and down the hill.

"My brothers," Strum said through a bullhorn, "put down your arms. We will get our revenge later."

Ulysses snatched the bullhorn from Strum. "Men. Unless you want to be arrested, every weapon must be on the ground in five seconds."

"Do we really need to be doing this?" Rosie Bischoff whispered to Angela, looking distressed. "It seems unnecessary!"

"Focus, Deputy, and keep quiet," Angela said in a low growl. Meanwhile, recognizing that they were outnumbered, the men from the compound placed their weapons on the ground. The Santa Fe deputies loaded mothers with small children onto the school bus, followed by the older children. Zach assisted them in maintaining order while Joseph and Rosie searched the dormitories to make sure all the children were out.

When Ulysses and Angela walked to the women's quarters, they found the doors standing open. A group of girls under fifteen were in the fenced yard. Ulysses looked them over but didn't see anyone young enough to be Kaylee Hurley. They were all young teenagers. In a separate fenced area, four adolescent boys brought up from the rooms under the bunker stood blinking and rubbing their eyes as if they'd been in the dark a long time.

Ulysses and Angela searched all the rooms of the prison-like building, including the lockup in the basement, where the cell doors stood ajar. They saw no trace of Kaylee Hurley. When they emerged from the quarters, all the children in the yard had been loaded. Deputies were aboard each bus, registering the children and their mothers.

"Mr. Strum," Ulysses said. "I understand that Daniel Graves has three wives and seven children. Will you accompany me to get them evacuated?"

"No, Sheriff. I don't want to assist you with your cruelty."

Ulysses ignored the belligerent man and radioed Zach to come and assist them.

As they walked away, Angela told Ulysses, "Sheriff Villalobos said Gideon Strum has several vehicles full of militia members headed this way. He said he'd radio you if they arrived.

They approached a three-story house, several FBI agents accompanying them and paused at the perimeter of the building. Ulysses saw Daniel Graves standing on the front porch, surrounded by his wives and children. Ulysses noticed that the bottom story, which was partially underground, was bustling with activity.

Fluorescent lights illuminated a large room full of computers, and men gathered in small groups to examine charts. A guard stood at the door checking credentials as men and women entered, carrying boxes. *This must be their headquarters,* he thought.

Ulysses turned his attention to Daniel Graves, who stood glaring down at him, holding what looked like a bishop's staff. Two of Graves' wives stood next to him. The younger one had a girl of about six by the hand. These wives looked like sisters, blonde, stocky women with stern faces. They wore similar long dresses and kerchiefs covering their hair. The youngest wife, a thin woman with pale eyes who wore sweats and a headscarf over her shaved head, sat on a porch swing holding a sleeping infant while a crying toddler held up her arms to be picked up. Among the older children, Ulysses recognized Jacob, the boy arrested at the plaza protest. There was also a grown daughter whose face was splotchy with rosacea. She looked much like her mother, the oldest wife, with the same set jaw and blonde hair. Two boys, about nine and possibly twins, sat on the steps, whispering to one another. At last, Ulysses spotted Kaylee, shivering in a dirty cotton dress and sneakers, standing alone just inside the open door.

"Kaylee Hurley, please come with us so we can reunite you with your family," Ulysses said. Kaylee looked fearfully around her and then ran down the steps. Angela smiled at the child and held out her hand.

"Which of you children are over eighteen?" Ulysses asked.

Jacob Graves said, "I am, and so is my sister." He indicated the girl with rosacea. "She's nineteen."

"Everyone else, come with me. Mothers should accompany children six and under."

"My wife, Katya, the one with the baby, is unwell," Graves said. "She and her children will stay here." He stamped his staff on the porch floorboards for emphasis. "You cannot take her."

"No, Mr. Graves. Your wife and her small children will come with us. I will make sure she gets medical attention if she needs it."

"Guards!" Graves yelled, and two armed men came out of the house, pointing their rifles at Ulysses.

The FBI agents came forward, weapons drawn and shields in place.

"If you don't put down your weapons, they *will* shoot you," Ulysses said to the men on the porch. The armed men reluctantly obeyed. Graves looked angry, but then his face resolved into an impassive mask. He whispered to his oldest wife, who looked at Katya with undisguised hatred.

A young man exited the basement door and called, "Father, your call has come from Texas."

"I'm coming," Graves said and entered the house. His oldest wife and the older children followed him. The other women and children came docilely down the steps. Ulysses led them down the hill to the gate, where they were registered and boarded the bus. He pulled the youngest wife and her two children aside from the others.

"Take them back to headquarters and put her in an interview room. I'll be right there."

When the rest were loaded, the buses pulled out of the gate and headed toward Santa Fe. Two FBI agents stood on the porch of Castleman's house, preparing to execute warrants.

One of the women from the Welcome Center came out to where Ulysses and Angela were standing near the cruiser. "Mr. Castleman wanted you to have this," the woman said, handing Ulysses an envelope.

Ulysses opened it. The note inside said. *Don't think we don't know what you have planned. You may be surprised at what you find.*

Ulysses got in the cruiser, feeling relieved. *Whatever happens next, the children will be safe.* Angela sat in the back with Kaylee, holding her hand. Rosie sat in the front seat, humming and looking at her phone. The other two deputies took Katya and her children and headed back to Taos.

"Something is going on, guys," Rosie said. "Social media says a civil war has started!"

As they left the compound, Ulysses saw a line of cars and trucks coming up the road from Peñasco and turning in at the gate.

"What is all this?" Angela asked.

"Militia from Santa Fe," Ulysses said. "They missed round one, but they'll be here for round two. Count how many there are." He tried to call LizBeth but got her voicemail.

Nick Boyar was furious. He'd returned to his office after posting his wife's bail to find the man who had been blackmailing him for more than twenty years sitting in his Eames chair, drinking his expensive whiskey.

Boyar both hated and feared Max Castleman. Since his wife's arrest early this morning, he had been contemplating how to rebel against the powerful control Castleman had exerted over him since childhood. With Castleman unable to protect Elena from murder charges, one of his grips on Boyar weakened. Elena's expensive lawyer was already negotiating a plea deal in which Elena would testify that the real murderer was Maksim Spak, as Castleman had been known then, and that she was merely an accomplice. Regarding Castleman's knowledge of Boyar's past as a child abuser, Boyar believed he could convincingly argue that Castleman himself was a known pedophile and, therefore, not a reliable witness. The main person he had to fear was Serena, but Boyar was confident he would find a way to neutralize the threat she posed.

"Good evening, Kolya," Castleman said, using the Russian diminutive for Nicolai, Nick's birth name. "Won't you join me? Your Japanese whiskey is delicious. Have a glass. We have a lot to discuss."

Nick poured himself a glass of whiskey and sat opposite his adversary. From the huge windows facing east, he watched the setting sun cast a pink hue over the Sangre de Cristo Mountains. Darkness rapidly enveloped the spacious office.

"What is it you want to talk about, Max?" Boyar asked. He noticed familiar feelings of loathing and anxiety arising in him.

"We're on the brink of victory here in New Mexico. You can make a difference, Kolya. Which side are you on?"

"Do you think the Nationalists will win against the might of the United States?"

"Control over LANL is a powerful step in that direction," Castleman said. "Wouldn't you agree?"

"You need much more than LANL to fight the whole United States," Boyar answered.

"True," Castleman said, swirling the whiskey in his highball glass. "But our allies are watching the instability unfold. The United States is no longer 'whole,' as you say. Many states are on the verge of secession. Who knows what could happen?" He took another sip and set his glass on the Persian carpet at his feet. "This is a time of great opportunity."

"You've always loved chaos, Max. Setting fires, hanging cats, torturing little girls—what is the opportunity for you here?" Boyar asked.

"You also enjoyed the little girls, as I recall," Castleman said, smiling. "Remember when I introduced you to the fun? What is the saying about those who live in glass houses? But never mind that. My opportunity is simple. We will be rich. And powerful..."

"I'm already rich enough," Nick said. "I just want to get away from all this and take Elena with me."

"Ah, Elena," Max said. "Your precious wife. She is very vulnerable, isn't she? Do you want me to take care of her problem?"

"Take care of it how?"

"I can get both of you citizenship in a country where there is no extradition. Poof! The murder charges go away. And once we rule this country, you can come back and run our nuclear arsenal. I can also eliminate Serena as a problem for you."

"And what do you want from me in return?"

"It's simple, Kolya. The Texas militias will be in Albuquerque soon. We should be fully in charge before the new year. Don't you want to serve as director? You can lead us toward nuclear dominance!

"Do you want to see nukes used, Maksim?"

"No, no, of course not! Though the Leader would love to eradicate California," he chuckled. "As always, the nuclear arsenal is about deterrence and the appearance of strength. We want as little bloodshed as possible."

"The Leader? Do you mean The Servant?"

"No, of course not. President Hadest, Duke. His plan is magnificent! He'll control this entire continent within a year. He has promised us."

"What about the Servant?" Nick asked. "I thought he was your master?"

Castleman took his glass and drained it. "He was my tool," he said. "I just didn't realize it until the past year."

"You used to worship him," Boyar said.

"He has been useful. The President was captivated by Danya for a long time. He believed in all his prophesies and curses. Now, he is starting to question him. Last week, he said, 'Daniel is a fraud.' Duke places his trust in me instead. Still, Danya thinks everyone will obey him. He is in for a surprise. I plan to be rid of him and those who pay him fealty." Castleman stood up and stretched. "So, are you with me or not? If not, I'll have to call in the Rook," Castleman laughed. He pulled the chess piece that was his talisman from his pocket. "Oh, there he is!"

"Fuck you, Max," Boyar said. "Don't try to scare me."

"You should be afraid of me, Nicky, my boy. But hear me out; I want you by my side. Think it over. I'll return in the morning. I have some business to take care of tonight."

"What kind of business?" Nick asked.

"That is for me to know and for you to find out. You may hear about it. And when you do, you'll know it was my handiwork."

Serena and Russell Hurley were reunited with their daughter at Taos Sheriff's Headquarters. They wanted to get in the car, drive away from Taos, and leave behind the pain they'd endured.

"You can't leave town yet," Angela said. We have questions for you. You should change motels but stay around."

Ulysses went into his office and called LizBeth Tallichet again, failing to reach her.

Daniel Graves' third 'wife,' Katya Sokolova, was breastfeeding her baby when Angela entered the interview room.

"Where is my other little one?" Sokolova asked in a thick Russian accent. "She needs her medicine." She took out a prescription bottle and put it on the table. "She has ear infection."

"Your older child is in the waiting area, being watched by Deputy Bischoff. We need to ask you some questions, and then we'll send you to the CYFD intake center in Santa Fe."

"No, no, not go there! Dangerous for me!" She snatched off her kerchief to reveal a bald head. "See what they did to me? They hate me."

"Has someone been abusing you?"

Katya looked at Angela sullenly. "What do you think?"

"If you are being abused, we can place you in safe housing."

Katya pushed up her sleeves on both arms to reveal dark bruises.

"Who did this to you?"

"The Servant and his wives. I had little romance. No sex, just loving feelings toward a soldier my age. Now they call me an adulterer." Her baby finished nursing. Katya rearranged her blouse and put the baby on her shoulder to burp. They could hear her toddler screaming in the other room.

"How old are you, Katya?"

"Nineteen."

"How long have you been in the United States?"

"Five years. I became third wife before Julia was born."

"Okay, we will get you a room at the women's shelter here in Taos. For you and the children."

"Will I be safe there?"

"Safe enough. Tell me what you know about the material stored in the bunker below the Servant's house?"

"They plan to move it to Santa Fe," she said.

"Are you sure?" Angela asked.

Katya shrugged her shoulders. "Why does no one believe me?"

"Did you hear where they want to take it?"

"An abandoned school in Santa Fe. St. Catherine's. Can I have cigarette?"

"I don't have one, sorry. You shouldn't smoke with these children."

Katya said something disdainful in Russian.

"What do you know about Max Castleman?" Angela asked.

"I want cigarettes and Coca-Cola," she said. "I had hard day."

Angela went into the dispatch room and asked the lead deputy, Dakota, to find her cigarettes and a Coke.

Dakota came in and set a pack of cigarettes and a glass with ice on the table. She poured the soda and smiled at Katya, who smiled back. "Thank you," Katya said and lit a cigarette. "Could you give Julia a dropper of medicine?"

"Of course," Dakota said. She picked up the medicine and went out. *How can Dakota be so kind?* Angela wondered. "Dakota," Angela called after her. "Would you call the Shelter in town and see if there are beds for Katya and her children?"

"Yes, boss," Dakota said.

Katya took a drink of her soda and drew on her cigarette. "You want to know about Max Castleman?"

"Yes, anything you can tell me."

"He is assassin. He killed many in Chicago before coming here. Here he has killed priest, Roman Catholic, and a man who was anti-nuclear activist."

"How do you know this?" Angela asked.

"My sweetheart told me. He worked for him as apprentice."

"Who is your sweetheart?"

"Lev Kalinin. He was killed two days ago in convenience store."

"What else do you know about Castleman?" Angela asked.

"He runs gang. He used to worship Daniel but not anymore. Daniel is afraid of him. They know all about your plans for tonight. Militias are coming to fight you."

Jesus, Mary, Joseph, Angela thought, feeling a frisson of fear.

"Let's get you to the shelter so you and your toddler can get something to eat."

Ulysses called LizBeth again, and she picked up. "I'm sorry I missed two of your calls. How did it go removing the children?" she asked.

"We took away two school buses full, including the mothers of the children under six. We found Kaylee Hurley, and she's back with her parents. The rest of the wives and children are at the CYFD center in Santa Fe. I have one of Graves' wives here, Katya Sokolova, and Angela just interviewed her. She implicated Max Castleman in the murders of Father Timothy Flynn and Jesse Porter. She also said militias are coming to the compound tonight."

"Villalobos told us about militias coming. Santa Fe Knights and a batch from Rio Arriba County."

"Before we left the compound, we saw more than thirty militiamen already there."

"The Santa Fe Knights are just a bunch of cosplay idiots. They won't stand a chance against Jack Riggs' crew." LizBeth said.

"Did your agents arrest Castleman?" Ulysses asked.

"Castleman seems to have flown the coop. The agents seized evidence from his house during their search. If he ever had a family, it appears they have been gone for a long time—there are no signs of women or children at his home. But listen, there's something I need to tell you," LizBeth said.

"Go ahead."

"The Texas rebels have taken Hobbs and are now skirmishing with the New Mexico National Guard around Portales."

"We could be going to war," Ulysses said. "We're going to need help."

"I was talking with Governor Garcia when you called earlier. She has given the final approval to send the Army Rangers into the Elect compound tonight. Plus, she just got fifty more Rangers flown in from the 75th Regiment. Sheriff Villalobos and State Police Chief Santiago will provide additional coverage.

"What do you need from me?" Ulysses asked.

"Get to Picuris as soon as you can," LizBeth said. "The assault starts after full dark. Oh, just to keep you updated, we arrested Elena Boyar for the murder of her first husband. Eli did an incredible job gathering the evidence."

"What was her motive?" Ulysses asked.

"Cadiz, her first husband, had separated from her. He was onto the fact that Elena was using her connections in Colombia and Venezuela to help the Kutznets gang smuggle drugs. Cadiz was representing the man they framed for Elena's crimes. He was going to expose her."

"Why is this coming out now?" Ulysses asked.

"Because of some detective work by an immigration lawyer named Paloma Walker."

"My sister, Paloma?"

"The very one."

"You are on a roll, Liz," Ulysses said.

"See you soon for the big event," LizBeth said.

Chapter 13

When Ulysses arrived in the cruiser just after sunset, Picuris Pueblo looked deserted. A nearly full moon had risen in the clear sky, and the wind was calm. In the plaza, the homes and San Lorenzo Church remained in darkness. A few dogs ran together across the empty plaza, sniffing at the armored vehicles parked on the far side.

Inside the tribal offices, the newly commissioned command center buzzed with activity. LizBeth welcomed Ulysses and introduced him to the various teams, including several army engineers, computer technicians, drone operators, emergency medical technicians, and logistics support. LizBeth was aware of everyone's skill set and appeared confident and in charge.

Ray, wearing a headset with a microphone, sat in front of monitors for surveillance drones, looking both focused and anxious. Ulysses placed his hand on his old friend's shoulder. Ray didn't turn around but patted his hand. "See those bulldozers?" he said. "Matt's team will knock down that fence as soon as the signal is given."

Ulysses spotted Sheriff Villalobos of Santa Fe and several of his deputies positioned against the back wall of the crowded room. Angela and the other Taos deputies, dressed in tactical gear, mingled nearby. Ulysses and Angela made brief eye contact. Angela mock saluted and smiled. *She's nervous,* Ulysses thought.

Eli sat beside LizBeth's desk in front of a bank of computers, watching visuals of the Army Rangers taking cover in the hilly terrain not far from the Elect bunker, preparing for the assault.

For Ulysses, who had never been in combat, it all felt real for the first time.

"How many armed combatants do you think they have up there?" Ulysses asked.

"Our best estimate is around a hundred, including militiamen from Santa Fe, Española, and Taos. However, there could be more. The Elect have about fifty regulars, mostly gathered near the bunker. Their fighters are heavily armed and have night vision and some drones, though not military grade ones." Eli pointed to a monitor showing images of Elect soldiers near the overhead door leading into a subterranean room where the nuclear material was stored.

"How do you get these pictures?" Ulysses asked.

"It's a cool little drone called the 'Black Hornet,'" Eli said. "The Rangers have a few of them. They're so small that a soldier can launch one by hand, and that's what this monitor picks up. I hope we can see the fight clearly with these, especially with the full moon. We also have a Predator drone we can launch from the Picuris Plaza, equipped with lethal firepower. We'll start with a barrage of missiles from that, even before the bulldozers take down the fence. Once the fence is down, the Rangers will secure the bunker. A team will head to Graves' residence to apprehend Graves and his top staff. After the engineers secure the nuclear material, the Rangers will neutralize the Elect command and control. Eli smoothed his mustache and looked intently at Ulysses. "It's a lot to accomplish," he said. "Are you going out there with Angela, Sheriff?"

"I'm not sure," Ulysses said. "LizBeth hasn't told me yet where she plans to deploy me."

LizBeth overheard Ulysses' comment and approached him. "I have a mission for you," she said. "I want you and your team at the Welcome Center with Sheriff Villalobos and his deputies."

"Why there?" Ulysses asked.

"Militiamen have gathered at the Welcome Center and around the armory, blocking the main road in case an assault comes from that direction. There may be as many as forty of them. We don't want them involved in the firefight at the bunker; ideally, we'd like them arrested and contained. That's your team's mission. You'll be outnumbered but can call for backup if necessary."

"Okay, let me talk with my team, and we'll get rolling," Ulysses said. He thought about Rosemary. *Should I tell her I might be in combat?* He decided to wait.

LizBeth looked at her watch. "Now that it's fully dark, it's time to begin."

"I'll go to the gate," Ulysses said.

When the Taos team arrived at the closed gate under bright security lights, Sheriff Villalobos was already engaged in what appeared to be a friendly conversation with Maurice Baca on the other side. An officer in the Knights, Baca also served as the Police Chief of Santa Fe. The two men were well acquainted. Behind Baca stood Sheriff Bustos of Rio Arriba County, holding an assault rifle, alongside three men displaying Nationalist flags. Two of the men were dressed in black Elect uniforms. One was Mark Shea; the other was Gideon Strum. Ulysses didn't recognize the third man. Ulysses heard the high-pitched buzz of a Predator drone.

"I'm telling you, Mauricio, this isn't a good idea," Villalobos said. "I'd hate to see you lose your job or get hurt. Who would take care of your family?"

"Gary," Baca said, "I don't think you understand how serious this is."

"Cousin," the older man said, "I know you're a very serious person. I've worked with you for years! But seventy-five special forces are headed your way. Do they have to kill you to prove how serious *they* are?"

"This isn't your fight, Gary," Baca said. "Why are you even here?"

"I'm doing my job," Villalobos said. "It's all about the law, right? So why in hell are you breaking the law? Open this gate and let us in."

"No way, Brother," Baca said. "I'm sorry to have to say no. Why don't you go home before this becomes unpleasant?"

Gideon Strum approached the two men, "You are wasting your time, Baca." he said. "Let me take over now. Sheriff, step away from the gate before I blow you away."

Baca regarded Strum with contempt but took a step back behind him. Ulysses approached the gate to stand next to Villalobos. In the distance, they heard heavy machinery crashing into metal. The assault was beginning.

"Mr. Strum," Ulysses said, "give a listen. Do you hear something that sounds like a huge insect? That is a predator drone coming toward us. How about the bulldozers tearing down the illegal fence on Picuris land? Can you hear them? The next sound you will hear is automatic weapon fire from Army Rangers. I suggest you and your men stand down immediately."

"You are outnumbered, Sheriff Walker," Strum said. "If I give the command, my men will kill you all."

Sheriff Bustos spoke to Baca in Spanish.

"Speak English!" Strum insisted. "This is America, you fucking Mexican!"

Bustos and Baca continued conversing urgently in Spanish.

Villalobos whispered to Ulysses, "They're plotting a mutiny against Strum," he said with a chuckle. "They can't stand that son of a bitch."

"I figured as much," Ulysses said. Steady gunfire from below and the approaching drone provided an ominous background. "Gentlemen, would you like to continue this conversation in the Welcome Center while I call off that drone?"

Bustos and Baca looked at Ulysses with relief. They seemed ready to agree to Ulysses' plan when Strum dropped his flag and fired over Ulysses' head. Angela fired back, wounding him in the shoulder and knocking the gun from Strum's hands. Rosie screamed as Strum fell to the ground.

Then gunfire erupted on both sides. Mark Shea turned and shot at Angela, grazing her head. Zach returned fire, missing Mark but hitting another man standing behind him. Mark dropped his gun and ran as the Predator drone came into view. It fired two missiles, killing Mark and the injured man behind him. Baca,

Bustos, and the remaining militiamen, including Strum, ran into the Welcome Center.

The sounds of gunfire, flash-bang grenades, and explosions grew louder from the area around the bunker. Joseph guided a dazed and bleeding Angela to their vehicle and drove away toward Picuris, where EMTs were waiting.

Ulysses walked up to the Welcome Center door and, speaking into his bullhorn, said, "Put down your weapons and come out now. We can't guarantee your safety if we must take you by force." There was no response from within the Welcome Center.

Ulysses considered the odds. Inside the cinderblock building were more than twenty heavily armed, cornered, frightened men, and outside were about the same number of deputies. *It doesn't look good,* he thought. *A lot of people will die.*

He raised his bullhorn. "This is your final chance to save your life," he said to the men in the Welcome Center. "If you don't drop your weapons and come out with your hands up, I will call in a drone strike. You will not survive."

For a few tense moments, nothing happened. Then the door to the Welcome Center opened, and Baca, Bustos, and the rest of the militiamen walked out with their hands raised. "Arrest them," Ulysses instructed the deputies. Handcuff them. Then, take them back inside the building and stay with them until we can arrange transport."

Ulysses and Villalobos walked over to where the two bodies hit by the drone strike lay. Shea was on his side, his legs shattered, and the gruesome head wound that caused his death surrounded by a pool of dark blood. The other man was nearby, lying face down on the gravel driveway. His black uniform was soaked from a massive wound to his torso; his face was burned beyond recognition. Looking at the two corpses, Ulysses felt a strange numbness he had never experienced: no nausea or sadness, only unreality and emptiness.

"That man there used to be my deputy in Taos," Ulysses said, pointing to Mark Shea. "He worked for me for about ten years. I know his ex-wife and his son. Patrick is my daughter's age."

"This other one is Booth Baca, Mauricio's nephew," Villalobos said. "He can't be more than twenty-five. What a waste of a life. I'm sorry about your deputy."

Booth Baca, Ulysses thought, *the man who broke into Pete's locker.*

"Let's cover their bodies," Ulysses said. "The noncombatants shouldn't see this." Already, people, primarily women, were coming down the hill from their apartments where they had been sheltering during the assault. Ulysses noticed Isaiah's mother, Merrily Patterson among the women. They were silent, but a few were weeping. As they came closer, some glanced toward where the sheriffs had spread tarps over the corpses. Scattered gunfire could be heard coming from the direction of the Elect command and control.

"Are we going to evacuate these civilians?" Villalobos asked.

"We should," Ulysses said. "I'll radio Agent Tallichet. I think she'll let us know if there is any imminent danger. Let's get these people into their chapel for now. Can you check on who is handling the removal of the dead?"

Ulysses directed the civilians into the chapel. The women quietly took their places at the back, a few kneeling to pray. No one resisted or attempted to leave; they didn't even inquire about their family members. Once everyone was inside, he instructed them to wait for further information. "We will evacuate you to a shelter," he said, "but we don't know where yet. For now, this chapel is the safest place for you." Ulysses stepped outside and radioed LizBeth.

"Make it quick," LizBeth said. "It's pretty wild over here." People were yelling at her even as she spoke into the radio.

"Was a dirty bomb dispersed?" Ulysses asked.

"No. It appears they didn't have enough dynamite. I'll tell you more later."

"Should we evacuate civilians? I have a chapel full of women."

"I can't tell you right now. Post a guard and make sure they stay safe. Don't let anyone leave. There is a battle raging at Elect command and control."

"How many fatalities on our side?"

"Two, possibly three. I must go. Out."

Villalobos agreed to monitor the women. Five armored vehicles drove into the compound as Ulysses stepped out of the chapel. He noticed the Corps of Engineers logo on the trucks. The driver of the first vehicle lowered her window. "Sheriff," she asked, "Do you know if this road is clear?"

"I don't know about the armory up there," Ulysses said, pointing to the Quonset hut on the hill. "There could be combatants in there. Once you pass it, there is a fork in the road. The left fork leads up to the Graves House; a fight is underway there. The right fork descends to the bunker."

"Thank you, Sheriff," the soldier said. "We'll send troops to clear the armory. We've come to remove the nuclear material from the bunker. The Rangers have cleared it." She gave a thumbs up and drove on.

Soldiers disembarked from the second and third vehicles to secure the armory. Ulysses watched them run up the hill toward a possible firefight. The armory remained silent, and before long, he saw the remaining few militiamen surrender to the soldiers who arrived at their door.

At the Picuris command center, LizBeth turned to Bill Samuelson of the ATF and asked, "What is going on at the bunker?"

"The engineers are working on removal inside the facility," Samuelson said. "With the road open, they can transport the stuff off-site. We expected more dynamite, but there was none in the armory and only a small amount in the bunker. Where did it go?"

LizBeth looked at the monitors on the Graves house where the Rangers were closing in. "Are those flames?" she asked, pointing to the upstairs windows.

"Most definitely," Eli said. "The entire second floor is blazing."

LizBeth's radio crackled, and a Ranger said, "Ma'am, permission to fall back. The fucking house is on fire. It could be boobytrapped."

"Fall back, Soldier. Do you need—"

Just then, a mighty explosion rocked the ground. The house became a fireball, and the trees around it lit up like Roman candles. LizBeth lost radio contact.

"My God," Bill Samuelson said, "How many people were in that building?"

Eli answered, "Probably more than thirty. The Servant, two of his wives, two of his children, his staff, and all the command and control. Do you think it was intentional self-destruction?"

"Could be. They did it in Waco before I was born." She radioed the Army Ranger second in command, Major Donaldson. "What is your situation?"

After a few moments, Donaldson responded. "Thank God we never got inside the building. Still, we have three injured, two seriously," he said. "Medevac is coming."

"Is anyone is left alive inside the building?"

"Unlikely, ma'am."

"Are any combatants left in the area?" LizBeth asked.

"Negative. Some may have run into the building before it blew up. Or they may be hiding in some of the undamaged buildings. We'll do a mop up."

When LizBeth got off the radio, Eli said, "The death toll is going to be a lot higher than we thought."

Ulysses sent Zach, Joseph, and Rosie home, but he stayed at Picuris, sleeping on Ray's couch. LizBeth and Eli took turns running the command center until the Rangers completed searching and securing the compound. At dawn, the Picuris War Council, led by Matt Pando, collected the remains of tribal member Frank Suazo, who had been shot while bulldozing the fence at the start of the assault. Later that morning, Army Mortuary Affairs officers arrived from White Sands to retrieve the body of Colonel Jack Riggs, who had died while leading the assault on the bunker. The civilian Elect were evacuated from the chapel and taken to a shelter by the State Police. Medical examiners removed the bodies of militiamen and other combatants from the grounds. Simultaneously, technicians from the ATF began sorting through the smoking ruins, now the funeral pyre of the Servant, much of his family and staff, and uncounted combatants who were inside. Meanwhile, Picuris residents began returning to their homes.

Ulysses slept profoundly and awoke well after sunrise. Just before awakening, he'd dreamt of sitting by a stream that ran through an open stand of shining ponderosa pines. He was watching brightly colored birds bathe in the shallow water when Pete Dowd came up and stood beside him, placing his hand on Ulysses' shoulder. "It isn't what you think, my friend. It is much better." Then Ulysses woke up. *Pete has died*, he realized. As he drank his coffee on Ray's portal, he began to feel his emotions again. Then LizBeth walked across the Plaza, looking exhausted and anxious. "Ulysses, I need your help with one more thing," she said. Ulysses felt a new sense of dread.

"My informant at LANL tells me she slept on a cot in her office last night. Early this morning, she saw Max Castleman on the second floor of the Executive offices. She heard gunshots, and when things got quiet, she fled. Now, I have no eyes or ears on the situation. The normal order has completely broken down, and we're unsure who is in charge. I need you to check it out and report back to me."

"What am I looking for?" Ulysses asked.

"Castleman. Philip Devin. The toolbox. Signs of a Nationalist incursion. I don't know! But if chaos takes LANL, all bets are off for New Mexico and it's not good for the rest of the country."

"What do I do if I see anything?"

"Report to me on whatever you find. The Governor says I can call units of the National Guard. President McDade is aware of the situation, so we have federal forces available if we need them."

In the hour before dawn, Philip Devin and Charlotte Foster had all but finished implementing their master plan and were enjoying coffee in his office at the pit facility.

"We're doing a great service to humanity," Foster said, stirring her cup. "After today, no one can safely work here for a hundred years. The land can return to nature!"

"Just imagine," Devin said. "All these buildings will crumble. The most powerful nuclear weapons program in the world will be effectively destroyed." He smiled broadly and took a sip of coffee.

"We should be proud of ourselves," Foster said. "I've been working for this since my earliest days in the movement. It will change the trajectory of America. We could become a nation of peace."

Devin laughed. "Char, you crack me up. A nation of peace? You are such an idealist. We'll be cut down to size! Russia will feed on the American carcass. But I'm not staying around for act two. I can't wait to get out of this country. I'm escaping as soon as the timer is set. Are all the disabling protocols in place?"

Foster shook her head at her comrade's nihilism. *He couldn't do anything without me,* she thought. Aloud, she said, "Of course. After the timer is set, staff will receive an evacuation order, and power and communications will be cut. At the appointed time, the alarm sounds for ten minutes. Then the detonation. We will be in the air to our separate destinations by then. Where are you going?"

"It's better if I don't tell," Devin said. "And I don't want to know where you and Monica are going either. Once she drops us off at our rendezvous points, it's goodbye, right?"

"If you say so."

Devin finished his coffee. "Set the timer now," he said. "The day shift is about to arrive. It won't take me long to execute the final computer wipe."

Charlotte left the room to prepare the timer for the detonation. When she returned, her face was ashen. "We need to get out of here right now," she said. I heard gunshots."

"Where is Monica?" Devin asked, grabbing his backpack.

"She's not out there yet. Hurry!"

As they exited the facility gate, Devin saw Castleman running along the fence, his gun raised. When Castleman saw the two of them, he began to fire with deadly accuracy. Foster was struck in the back and collapsed beside the empty guard station. Devin glanced back but couldn't determine if she was dead or alive. Pursued by Castleman, he ducked into a nook where he had hidden his mountain bike in case he needed to escape alone and took off downhill, rapidly gaining speed as bullets whizzed by him. He pedaled furiously, dodging and weaving, and slowly realized he'd been hit just above the ankle of his right leg.

Chapter 14

After Monty and Amelia left for school, Rosemary finished her chores and came into the house carrying her largest pumpkin. She'd had her eye on it for the children to carve a jack-o-lantern, so she needed to cut it open and clean out the insides to carve it that evening after Monty and Amelia came home.

Rosemary turned on the radio. Instead of her favorite news program, Rita Wainwright Reports, she heard mariachi music mixed with an announcement that the Governor would address the public at 8 am Mountain Time. She checked the local KUNM affiliate, and it was the same, although the music there was soft jazz. On the few television stations the Walkers received through a roof-top antenna, a photographic background displayed with a scroll of information about the governor's address to the state. Rosemary went to her computer, but the internet was down.

When a car pulled up, Rosemary heard Ulysses' voice. He had not come home the previous night, but when he called her before daylight, he had said nothing about when he would be home. She wiped her hands on a dishtowel and went outside.

Frances had run out from the goat shed and talked excitedly to her father.

"How's everything at Picuris?" Rosemary asked, aware that her precocious five-year-old was listening.

"It's quiet," Ulysses said. "People are starting to come home."

"Would you like some breakfast? I have a new batch of granola and goat yogurt."

"Yeah, but I need to talk with you. Frances, would you like to listen to a book on tape?"

"Okay," Frances said, looking first at her mother and then at her father. "If you want me to."

"We do, Pook," Ulysses said. "We have some grown-up things to discuss."

After Rosemary helped Frances turn on her headset and start listening to *Ramona and Beezus* for the fourth time, she returned to the kitchen.

"What is with the mariachi music?" Ulysses asked. He plugged his phone into its charger.

"The regular media is off, and the internet is down," Rosemary said. "The governor is going to talk in fifteen minutes."

"Where did you hear that?"

"An announcer says so every few minutes. Do you think it's about the skirmishes on the border with Texas?" Rosemary asked. "Rita Wainwright has been talking about that for days."

"It could be," Ulysses said. "I don't know the latest news. When I last heard there was heavy fighting in Portales."

"Should we leave?" Rosemary asked. "We could go to Utah, and my parents would take us in."

"It is safest for us here for now. I want you to pick up Amelia and Monty from school. Lock the gate at the end of the driveway and stay in the house. Make sure the rifle is loaded and fill up both bathtubs in case the electricity goes out. If that happens, turn off the gas at the meter. Do you know how to do that?"

Rosemary nodded.

"Do you have a full tank of gas in your van?" Ulysses asked. "And is the go-bag handy?"

"Yes, of course," Rosemary said. Her eyes filled up with tears.

"You can handle this, Rosemary. You can keep yourself and our children safe."

"I know," Rosemary said, "But what about you? Where are you going?"

"I'm heading out on a little mission."

"What kind of little mission?" Rosemary asked.

"Something is going on at LANL. Communication between LANL and the FBI has broken down. LizBeth wants me to look at the situation."

"What is going on?"

"I don't know, Rosemary. I'm supposed to be her eyes and ears. It's complicated."

"What are you going to do if you see anything?"

"I'm supposed to provide her with intel. I'll know what to do when I see it. At least, I hope I will."

"Oh, Ulys. What has LizBeth gotten you into now?"

"She needs my help, that's all. She needs someone she can trust."

"Ulys, this feels like a bad dream." Rosemary stood up, put some fresh-baked granola in a bowl, and added yogurt and milk. She set it in front of Ulysses.

Then, they both heard the voice of Governor Barbara Garcia. Ulysses ate his breakfast, Rosemary spread newspaper on the table and began to cut into the stem end of the pumpkin.

"My fellow New Mexicans," she began, "our beloved state is under attack by rebel militias allied with the criminal Duke Hadest of Texas. This morning, I spoke with President McDade. He is fully aware of the fighting occurring in and around Portales between these militias and our New Mexico National Guard. He assured me that New Mexico would receive complete support from the federal government to repel this attack. Right now, armored divisions are en route from California, and air support will arrive from…" Frances, who seemed to have picked up on what was happening, emerged from her room. Rosemary abruptly turned off the radio.

"Let me refill your canteen," Rosemary said. "Is there anything you need me to get for you?"

"What is going on, Mommy?" Frances asked.

"Honey," Rosemary said. "That was the Governor telling us that we must be strong and brave and on our best behavior."

"Why?" the little girl asked, looking more curious than afraid.

Ulysses spoke up. "Frances, don't ask a lot of questions, okay? Just do what Mommy tells you to do."

"I will, Daddy," she said. "I always do."

Ulysses embraced his wife and kissed her goodbye. "Come back to me," Rosemary whispered.

"I'll do my very best," Ulysses said. "And remember our rendezvous points. The fish hatchery if we are headed north and Camel Rock if we are headed south."

As she hugged her father goodbye, Frances whispered, "Don't let Bad Rabbit trick you when you find his hole. Don't go in his hole, okay?"

"I won't," Ulysses said, puzzling over what this could mean. "Be a good girl and help your mother."

"I will," Frances said.

Ulysses stopped at Headquarters to pick up Angela. She was wearing a bandage over the bullet graze on her temple.

"Are you sure you are up for this?" Ulysses asked after explaining his plan.

"I'm fine, Sheriff," she said. "This is just a scratch."

"Yeah, but it bled a lot."

"Not that much, and I got a bath and a full night's sleep in my bed."

They climbed into the cruiser and drove along in silence for a few minutes.

"Did you hear the governor?" Angela asked.

"Part of it. You?"

"Same. We were getting a lot of calls from Taoseños."

"Were people anxious?"

"Yes, but they just needed a little reassurance. Ramona, Zach, and Dakota were handling the phones well. Every deputy showed up, too. Even the ones who weren't on the duty roster."

"That's good. Rosie, too?"

"Rosie, too."

"Rosie needs a desk job," Ulysses said.

"Yes, sir. I agree. Where do we start, Sheriff?"

"Let's go to the place where you last saw Monica Lovato," Ulysses said as they left Taos County and entered Rio Arriba

County. He turned off Route 68 onto Route 75 and soon arrived in the village of Dixon.

"Tell me where to turn," Ulysses said.

Angela pointed to the next dirt road on the left, and Ulysses drove until he stopped near the adobe house in a bosque where Angela had last seen Monica Lovato. "Oh, I forgot to tell you, Sheriff. Eli found evidence that Charlotte Foster, the chemist at LANL, is Monica Lovato's biological mother."

"Peace and Justice, Monica? The one who lives here?"

"Yes, that Monica. Though I think this is Foster's property." Ulysses turned off the cruiser and got out. Angela looked around for Monica's black Tesla. "It doesn't look like she's here," Angela said.

"Let's look in back."

They left the Expedition and saw a marmalade cat sitting under a bush beside a bird feeder.

"The cat's still here," Angela said.

Ulysses knocked on the door. No one answered, but it was unlocked. He opened it and stepped inside. The house felt warm, and the food in the cat's bowl looked fresh. A folding map of the plutonium pit facility lay open on the kitchen table next to a cell phone. Ulysses glanced at the map, folded it, and tucked it into his back pocket.

"Somebody recently fed this cat," Ulysses said.

Angela and Ulysses went out back to check the outhouse, which was empty. They walked to the rear of the property, where the Rio Embudo, a lively creek, cascaded over rocks. Overlooking the creek was a treehouse nestled in a large cottonwood. Near the treehouse, hidden by willows, was the black Tesla.

"Ms. Lovato?" Angela called. "We know you're up there. We have more questions for you." After a few moments, they saw Monica's feet and legs descending the ladder of the treehouse.

"Hello, Ms. Lovato. I'm Sheriff Ulysses Walker from Taos County. You've met my undersheriff, Angela Romero. Can we come inside and ask you a few questions?"

"Were you hiding from us?" Angela asked.

218 • C. R. KOONS

"No, ma'am. I'm hiding from my friends." She lied with an engaging smile. "They want me to go to a demonstration. Can I make you some tea?"

"No, we're fine," Ulysses said.

Monica seemed to notice that her map was gone, but she said nothing. The cat came in the cat door, sniffed at the visitors, and went back out.

"What did you want to ask me?"

"What is your relationship with Philip Devin?" Ulysses asked.

"He is my friend," Monica said. "We play bridge together."

"Would you call him a close friend?"

"Pretty close, why?"

"He is the lead engineer at the plutonium pit facility at LANL, correct?"

"We don't agree on everything. We're just friends."

"Is he involved with Nuclear Peace and Justice?" Ulysses asked.

"Not formally, no. But I think he sympathizes with our mission."

"Which is what, exactly?"

"To end the production and use of nuclear weapons. There is more to it, but that is the gist."

"So, he is producing the very weapons he purports to want to end?"

"He is modernizing the arsenal. It's a struggle for him. I've been trying to, you know, bring him along. He wants to leave his job, but he's not ready."

Angela spoke up. "Ms. Lovato, did your group provide safe housing for Serena Hurley and her daughter, Kaylee?"

"We tried to. But she disappeared. Or she was kidnapped."

"Did you report it?"

"I don't know for sure she was kidnapped. She could have left on her own."

"What did Serena Hurley bring with her from Wyoming?"

"I don't know what you mean."

"Let me ask another way," Ulysses interjected. "What did you do with the nuclear material Serena brought from Wyoming?"

"I don't know what you are talking about."

"You haven't heard about the toolbox? Lying to us won't help you, Ms. Lovato. If that toolbox is used to kill people, you could be facing capital federal charges."

Monica looked over her shoulder. "Did you take my map? It was right here on the kitchen table."

"I did," Ulysses said. "I'm confiscating it as evidence. "What is it you are planning at the plutonium pit facility?"

"I'm not planning anything." Monica's voice quavered.

"Where is the toolbox? Tell us now, and we'll consider it when you are charged."

"Charged with what?"

"Conspiracy to steal nuclear material to commit domestic terrorism."

"I don't know where the thing you want is! I never touched it, and I never intended for it to be used to harm anyone. I am a pacifist!"

Ulysses shook his head. "Because of decisions you made, Jesse Porter is dead, Serena Hurley and her daughter were traumatized, and now weapons-grade plutonium is loose in the hands of domestic terrorists. You are no pacifist, and you will spend the rest of your life in federal prison. A nice cozy cell in the women's max in West Virginia."

"I have nothing to do with this."

"Well, who does then? Who is the mastermind of the plan to detonate the toolbox?"

Monica began to cry but said nothing.

"What about the people working and living nearby if they detonate a bomb?" Angela asked. "What happens to them?"

"I don't want anyone to be harmed," she said in a low voice. "I've been trying to stop them," she said. "They won't listen to me. I don't know what to do!"

Angela asked, "Who are you talking about? You'd better tell us!"

The next few minutes passed in tense silence. Monica stood up and began to pace. Then she said. "They took the toolbox from Serena Hurley. But I don't know what they did with it."

"You said 'they,' and that means more than one. Who your co-conspirators?" Ulysses asked.

Monica shook her head and sobbed. "I can't tell you!"

"You don't know, or you won't tell us?" Ulysses said.

"It's people who work at LANL."

"Philip Devin, right?" Ulysses said. "And who else?"

"Tell us what the plan is!" Angela demanded

"I can't give you names. I don't know the plan! I'm not involved!"

"I don't believe you're uninvolved," Ulysses said. "Not for a second. You were having an affair with Philip Devin, and we know that the whistleblower, Charlotte Foster, is your mother. If you tell us your part, you may make things easier for yourself before the court."

"I won't be at LANL or have anything to do with what happens there."

"You have a role," Ulysses said. "That's obvious. Are you their driver?"

Monica took a deep breath and said nothing.

"So, when do you pick them up?"

"I don't know." Monica was weeping now.

"When is this taking place?" Angela asked.

"I don't know. I've dropped out."

Ulysses laughed. "It's far too late for that, Ms. Lovato. You've already committed crime after crime connected to this conspiracy and will face serious consequences. Either give us the information we need to stop this crime or be ready to spend a long time in jail—or worse. It's your choice. Text me when you reach your decision, Monica." He handed her his card.

The marmalade cat came in the cat door with a limp goldfinch in his mouth. He dropped the freshly killed bird on the floor and looked intently at Monica.

"If you are going to have a cat," Angela said, "you shouldn't feed the birds."

Monica's phone rang as Ulysses and Angela drove off. It was Devin.

"Where are you?" he yelled into the phone. "You were supposed to be here an hour ago!"

"The sheriff was just here," Monica said. "They are totally on to us."

"Look, Monica. Now is not the time for second thoughts. I'm supposed to meet my pilot in an hour. You promised to take me there."

"Who says I have to fulfill that promise?" Monica answered.

"What about your mother?" Devin said, picturing her body after Castleman had shot her. "Don't you want her to escape safely and you with her? We don't have time to waver!"

"Is the timer set? When does the bomb go off?"

"Yes, it's all set! Get going now! Your mother needs you!"

"Are we still meeting at the same place?"

"Meet us at the turnoff to the Puyé Cliffs," Devin said, indicating the site of Santa Clara's ancestral cliff dwellings off NM 30.

"Why there? Let me talk to Mom!"

"Don't ask questions, just come. No one is here, and it's very quiet now. They are closed today." Before Monica could reply, Devin hung up.

Monica took her time packing her rucksack with a change of clothes, cash, her Mexican passport bearing her new name, and her loaded Ruger. She shooed the cat outside, locked her mother's house, and got into her car, her mind racing. *Why was Philip at the Puyé Cliffs? Where is Mom? Should I leave them there? I don't want to go to prison!*

Monica tried calling Charlotte, but the phone went directly to voicemail.

She felt apprehensive and angry as she drove slowly from Dixon toward Española to pick up Route 30 to the Puyé Cliffs. Monica couldn't remember exactly when she realized that the handsome, brilliant older man she'd fallen in love with was a narcissist who lied whenever it suited him and never felt remorse.

She realized that his come-on to her wasn't motivated by love or even attraction. Philip used her for her movement connections to help him implement his grandiose plan. She should never have trusted him. *He's duped me so many times. What a fool I am to have believed him. Once I get to Oaxaca, I'll disappear. I'll never have to think of him again.*

Monica turned off Route 30 into the visitor center parking area for the Puyé Cliffs. The center was closed, and the parking lot was empty. Then, from behind a large piñon pine, Philip emerged, holding his expensive bike and smiling his best rakish smile. *That's his lying smile. Something has gone very wrong.*

Monica reached into her bag and retrieved the Ruger. Slowly, she got out of the car just as a massive explosion rocked the ground under her feet. Moments later, a huge fireball bloomed and expanded above Los Alamos.

"See what we did?" Philip said. "What you helped me do?"

Monica walked toward her former lover, sick with dread. "Where is Mom?" she asked, holding the gun by her side.

"We should get out of here," Philip said, unzipping the pannier behind the bicycle saddle. Can I put my bike in your car?" Then he pulled out his pistol, shrugged, and smiled.

Monica lifted her gun and shouted, "Where is Mom?" But before he could answer her question, she shot Philip in the face. Then she jumped into the Tesla and drove off.

Ulysses and Angela sped through the Rio Grande Canyon. In Española, they turned onto New Mexico 30, passed the imposing bulk of Black Mesa at Santa Clara, and continued at high speed toward Los Alamos. The October morning was unseasonably warm under a cloudless turquoise sky. Ulysses noticed more traffic than usual.

"Are you going to pay a courtesy call on Sheriff Blanca?" Angela asked.

"We can't afford the time," Ulysses said. "She's not likely to be an ally, and she could impede us. I want to start at the LANL executive suite." He drove toward the LANL offices. On the other side of the road, cars were streaming downhill from the complex.

"Why is there so much traffic?" Angela asked.

"Maybe some employees have been sent home," Ulysses said.

"I wonder what it means?"

At the LANL gate, a lone security guard waved them through. They parked in a mostly empty lot, and the unnatural quiet was eerie. Ulysses' phone rang, with LizBeth's number displayed, but the call was immediately dropped. Inside the building, the security station was vacant and dark.

"No security? Something is truly wrong," Angela said.

"I think the electricity is off," Ulysses said. They went through the metal detector with their weapons, but no alarms sounded. The elevators were not working, and no staff were in the offices.

"The executive suites are on the second floor," Angela said, looking at the staff directory.

"I have a terrible feeling about this," Ulysses said. He drew his weapon while running up the stairs. Angela followed suit.

They entered a central hall with doors on each side when they reached the second floor.

"Let's go door to door and see if anyone is here," Ulysses said.

The first door was the SCIF, and it was locked. The next door led into an antechamber for the director's office. The phones were dead at the receptionist's station, but everything else looked normal. Ulysses tried the inner door; it was unlocked. He entered the LANL director's large wood-paneled office, furnished with oversized leather couches, several glass cases of exquisite Indian pottery, and a rare Gustave Baumann painting of aspens. The orderly mahogany desk gleamed under the light of an antique brass lamp, which was lit despite the bright daylight. On his blotter lay a half-written letter penned in a man's stylish cursive. Ulysses stepped carefully on a grey and red Navajo rug, perfectly placed atop a white Berber carpet. Then, Ulysses noticed the face-down body of an older man in black slacks and a cashmere sweater slumped in the corner. A bullet had been fired into the back of his head, execution-style. A silver Mont Blanc pen lay by his left hand.

"Someone must have surprised Dr. Shapiro here early and killed him immediately," Ulysses said.

"Would Nick Boyar have done this?" Angela asked.

"I don't think so," Ulysses said. "LizBeth said her informant saw Max Castleman here before dawn and heard gunshots."

"Boyar's office is across from SCIF," Angela said.

"Castleman may still be around. Let's go see."

They entered the empty corridor and passed another hall that led to the public relations suites. Continuing, they arrived at Boyar's offices at the corner of the building. The reception space was empty and undisturbed. Ulysses paused to listen at the door of the inner office. Then he opened the door slowly, his gun ready. Boyar sat in his Eames chair, facing the expansive mountain view to the east. He didn't turn around when they entered. As he approached, Ulysses saw why. Like his boss, Boyar was dead, the back of his head covered with congealed blood and a white marble chess rook in his right hand.

Ulysses sat in the Eames chair opposite Boyar and tried to catch his breath. Even though this man was undoubtedly an adversary, his dead face shook Ulysses. He looked into Boyar's black eyes, fixed and dilated, and wondered how long he'd been dead. *Where are you now?* Ulysses felt the hair rise on the back of his neck and knew Boyar's spirit was still in the room. *Where do you go from here?*

Angela stood listening at the door. "Sir, where is everyone?"

Ulysses looked away from Boyar and tried to clear his mind. He stood up and called LizBeth, but neither calls nor texts went through. He tried Boyar's landline, but it was equally nonfunctional. "Somebody has disabled all communication," Ulysses said.

"What should we do now?"

Ulysses went to the other floor-to-ceiling window overlooking the pit facility where Boyar had placed a Swarovski spotting scope. Ulysses peered into it.

"Come look at this," Ulysses said.

Below them, dozens of armed security personnel were gathered at the gate of the pit facility. Inside the gate stood Max Castleman, speaking into a bullhorn to the guards.

"Here's our security," Ulysses said.

"What is going on?" Angela asked.

"There is a body on the ground by that guard station," Ulysses said. But it's unclear what is happening with the security guards.

"What do you mean, sir?" Angela asked.

"Are the security guards protecting the status quo or aiding the insurgents? Is Castleman trying to sway the guards to his side?"

They caught bits and pieces of Castleman's speech. He was exhorting the guards to kill anyone not wearing an ID badge.

Angela gasped. "Sir, I think the sun caught the lens of that scope. Castleman is looking up at us."

"Crap," Ulysses said. "We need to get out of here!"

An ear-piercing alarm suddenly erupted in the pit facility. Ulysses and Angela dashed out of the office, down the stairs, and into the parking lot. On either side of them were fleeing security personnel. Ulysses was glad he and Angela were in uniform. The guards didn't seem to respond to them as a threat. Rather than pursuing them, they were reacting to the alarm's significance—a warning of an imminent threat. Ulysses and Angela jumped into the cruiser.

"I think what LizBeth most feared is happening," Ulysses said again as he started the engine. "The Nationalists are attempting a take-over of the pit facility." They heard the whoop of a helicopter circling above them.

"Where are they coming from?" Angela asked.

"It's impossible to tell," Ulysses answered.

A silver Tesla Cybertruck sped past on the main road, accelerating dangerously.

"That's Castleman, sir," Angela said.

Ulysses put on his siren and sped after the truck, passing any traffic until they came to the hairpin turns that led down from the mountain.

"He's driving like a maniac," Angela said. "Why is he trying to escape?"

A massive explosion sent a fireball into the sky above the pit production facility.

The shock wave rocked the Expedition and caused rocks to tumble into the road from the cliffs to their right.

"Because he recognized that alarm. It must not have been in his plan."

"Maybe it was the toolbox. Are there gas masks in this vehicle?" Angela asked.

"Only disposables, and they're useless," Ulysses said.

They kept the truck in sight until it reached the bottom of the canyon and turned onto NM 30 toward Española. Ulysses followed. Ahead of them, people were pulling off the road to get out of their way. "One advantage to a siren," Ulysses said as they entered the Santa Clara reservation.

"Sir, I have service here. I'm calling LizBeth now." She put her phone on speaker.

"Ma'am," Angela said, "A bomb has gone off at LANL. Power and communications are off, and many staff have evacuated. Director Shapiro and Deputy Director Boyar are dead. We are now in pursuit of Castleman. He is driving a Tesla Cybertruck with New Mexico plates. We are heading toward Española on NM 30 and have just entered the Santa Clara reservation."

"Good. Continue pursuing. Don't return to LANL. There is radiation risk," LizBeth said. "The National Guard is en route to the area to secure it and supervise evacuations. I'll contact Santa Clara Governor Gutierrez for backup now."

Castleman turned onto the road toward the Puyé Cliffs.

"Why is he going there?" Angela asked. "Is it because we are following him?'

Ulysses, focused on his driving, said nothing. He turned in after the Cybertruck and sped past the visitor's center.

"Sir, there is the body of a man on the ground near a bicycle. It might be Philip Devin."

Again, Ulysses said nothing, though the information penetrated his awareness.

Ulysses lost sight of the Cybertruck as they drove through empty Santa Clara land on a narrow, winding road.

"How many miles is it back to the cliffs, Angela?"

"About seven miles, sir."

They heard a helicopter flying low and coming closer.

"That explains Castleman turning here," Ulysses said. "Maybe that helicopter could land on top of the mesa. I wonder if tribal police are nearby?"

The helicopter was slowly circling the mesa top. Castleman was nowhere in sight, and there was no sign of any backup arriving.

They could still hear the helicopter but could no longer see it. Suddenly, they rounded a blind curve and spotted the sign for the parking lot where tours to the historical site began. Aside from a couple of buses for transporting tourists, no other vehicles or people were around. Ulysses and Angela hurried up the steps to peer into a well-maintained stone building from the 1930s that housed a museum, a store, and restrooms. The building was empty, and the door was locked. They gazed at the cliffs at the back of the building—a pinkish pyroclastic rock rising against the bright blue of the noonday sky.

Castleman was nowhere in sight. The cliffs contained hundreds of holes, rooms that the ancestors of Santa Clara once occupied from around the tenth century until the late sixteenth century. Ulysses remembered visiting the site with his parents as a small boy, climbing up the steep steps worn into the soft rock and the long ladders that connected the various rooms in the vast network of ancient dwellings.

"Sheriff, I see the Cybertruck," Angela said, peering through her binoculars. She pointed to where it was parked on the road for transporting tourists, blocking the way as if to prevent Ulysses from reaching the top.

"Let's get up there before he escapes," Ulysses said. They ran back to the cruiser, located the road to the top, and took it. As soon as they did, Castleman started shooting at them. Ulysses drove on in the blinding sunlight while bullets rained down. "Stay down, Angela," Ulysses said, "I'm going to see if I can get around his truck."

There was no way to get past the boulders on either side of the truck, so they grabbed their rifles and exited their vehicle. They

228 • C. R. KOONS

ran toward the top of the mesa under a blazing sun and a stiff wind that blew dust all around them. They came to a large boulder near where the helicopter had successfully landed on a concrete pad on top, its rotors still spinning. It was a small craft with only one pilot. Castleman began shooting toward them from about fifty feet away, behind the high wall of an ancient stone building.

Angela took cover inside a pueblo ruin and began firing toward Castleman. Ulysses ran toward the helicopter and sheltered behind it, thinking that Castleman was unlikely to shoot at his ride. Castleman was forced to take cover.

He ran into an old stone building with a very low roof. Angela took that moment to move to the far side of an ancient unused kiva, a circular stone religious edifice built underground and open to the sky with a wooden ladder for access. Angela crouched there, close to Castleman's hiding place. Ulysses bolted toward the helicopter's door. The pilot inside appeared to be unarmed and frightened. Ulysses pounded on the glass with the butt of his rifle, yelling for the pilot to cut the engines and come out. Instead of obeying Ulysses, he lifted into the air and flew off. Suddenly, Ulysses was exposed. He shouldered his rifle and scanned the mesa top for his adversary.

Castleman, shouting in Russian, ran from his hiding place. He shot at Ulysses with his automatic pistol but missed him. Ulysses shot at Castleman but also missed. The killer scrambled down the kiva ladder, failing to notice Angela crouching on the other side behind the stone parapet. If Castleman hid in the underground structure, Ulysses thought it would be easy to trap him and force him to drop his weapon. But when he approached the kiva, his rifle lowered, and stared into the darkness below, he didn't see Castleman. For an instant, he remembered Frances's warning not to go into Bad Rabbit's hole. Then, his eyes adjusting to the darkness, he saw Castleman crouched on the ladder. Before Ulysses could react, Castleman fired his pistol. Ulysses felt the bullet enter his left side like a sucker punch. He fell backward under the impact. Castleman climbed up the ladder and began walking toward Ulysses to finish him off. At the last moment,

Angela ran forward and shot Castleman in the back. The assassin lay still under the harsh sun.

Angela ran over to Ulysses, who was bleeding heavily. "Sheriff, please hang on," she said. "We're going to get you to safety. The tribal police are here." Just before Ulysses lost consciousness, he heard men shouting in Tewa.

Chapter 15

On a Saturday afternoon, Ulysses lay on a chaise lounge in a sheltered, sunny corner of his porch. A book he hadn't yet started rested open on his lap as he gazed at the Taos Mountains glistening with fresh snow. Rosemary had gone to deliver a casserole to a sick friend and took Amelia along to practice driving. Frances was at a friend's birthday party, and Monty had gone for a bike ride with a new neighbor. It was rare for Ulysses to be home alone. He cherished the stillness and the warmth of the sun on his face.

Ulysses had no plans for the rest of the day. It had been a good day for him. He felt relative peace and no pain. In the nearly four months since he was nearly killed, he had faced many challenges. The bullet to his torso damaged his spleen, punctured his diaphragm, and nicked his pancreas. However, his lungs, kidneys, and large intestine remained unharmed. He spent five days in intensive care, and by the time he was released from the hospital, he had lost thirty pounds. Since coming home, however, Rosemary has helped him regain his strength through tender care, nourishing food, and home remedies. His kind and relentless physical therapist assisted him in rebuilding his muscle. In the week when Ulysses celebrated his fiftieth birthday, his doctor said he was a miracle of recovery, at least regarding gunshot wounds. A few days later, he was awarded the Purple Heart Medal by the National Sheriffs Association.

Ulysses believed he had healed better physically than mentally. Although his nightmares had diminished, he still struggled with sleep, experienced bouts of depression, and occasionally faced flashbacks. He was seeing a therapist twice a week in Santa Fe, an older psychologist who referred to himself as both a Buddhist and a radical behaviorist, which seemed contradictory to Ulysses. Nonetheless, they had a strong relationship. Dr. Riley made him laugh, encouraged him to give up alcohol, and wasn't afraid to confront his anger. Ulysses felt seen and understood by him.

Some days, Ulysses felt he was progressing in coming to terms with all that had happened the previous October. Other days, he thought he was still on shaky ground. He often wondered if, given how burnt out he felt, he should continue in law enforcement. But how would he support his family if he didn't go back to work as scheduled in late March? His therapist encouraged him to let go of constantly questioning himself and wait for answers to arise on their own. But would they? From Ulysses' perspective, it seemed unlikely.

Ulysses reflected on the events of the previous October and their consequences. Max Castleman, also known as Maksim Spak, which remained his legal name, had killed Father Timothy Flynn and Jesse Porter, as well as LANL Director Dr. Jon Shapiro, Deputy Director Dr. Nick Boyar, and Dr. Charlotte Foster. He was likely also responsible for countless other deaths during his time as an enforcer for the Kutznets criminal enterprise, including the former boss, Ivan Kutznets. Castleman was further implicated as an accomplice in the murder of Rafael Cadiz, Elena Boyar's first husband and Serena Hurley's father. Elena Boyar would face trial for second-degree murder in the spring.

LizBeth visited shortly after Christmas to inform Ulysses about ATF special agent Bill Samuelson's investigation into the explosion that destroyed the Elect command-and-control building. To overthrow the Servant, Max Castleman and his loyal men moved dynamite from the bunker to the basement of the command-and-control building the night before the assault. During the armed conflict, someone, likely Levi Patterson, an Elect member closely aligned with Castleman, used a blasting cap to detonate the dynamite, resulting in the deaths of thirty-six people, including much of the Elect elite, Daniel Graves, and most of his family. Levi Patterson, an explosive expert who was unaccounted for in the aftermath, was believed to have escaped to Texas, leaving behind his pregnant wife and two children. The fire that broke out and was seen just prior to the detonation remained a mystery.

Charges were brought against Serena Hurley for the theft of nuclear material from Warren Air Force Base. She was convicted of transporting nuclear material over state lines and sentenced to three years of home confinement. Even though he was relieved that the young woman didn't face prison time, Ulysses wasn't sure the sentence was proper given all that the theft of the "toolbox" wrought. But at least Kaylee would be able to stay with her parents.

LANL and the towns of Los Alamos and White Rock remained evacuated due to the spew of toxic and radioactive material over a large radius of the county. A costly cleanup was required, but the time, money, and will for such an enterprise hadn't yet been found. It appeared unlikely that LANL would ever be used again for nuclear weapons production, causing a massive loss of revenue and high-paying jobs for New Mexico and the displacement of hundreds of employees. President McDade was considering rebuilding a new LANL to a site north of Taos and changing its mission from weapons research to solving the climate emergency.

For now though, ending the war between the states took precedence. Ulysses felt relieved when the Texas militias, plagued by internal divisions and lacking training, withdrew across their border, leaving territory they'd captured. Johnny "Duke" Hadest had fled to Belarus to escape prosecution for assassinating the First Lady and Supreme Court Chief Justice. While a splinter group in Texas continued to fight despite severe losses, other, poorer states like Wyoming and Louisiana accepted territorial status and a strict process for regaining statehood.

Governor Garcia proved herself to be a decisive and effective governor in New Mexico. She outlawed the Nationalist Party and the Church of the Elect as terrorist groups. The Elect compound was placed off-limits, and legal efforts were underway to seize the property as recompense for the group's seditious activity. Noncombatant Elect members were allowed to go free if they had committed no crimes.

In the wake of trials for their leaders, militias were ordered to disband and relinquish their arms. Making use of a newly respected 14th amendment, Nationalist and Elect sympathizers were prevented from running for elected office and removed from employment in most government jobs, including the police. Churches with paramilitary associations faced the loss of their tax-exempt status.

Angela, who had recently been awarded the Medal of Merit for her work as Undersheriff, was now Interim Sheriff while Ulysses was on sick leave. She was managing well in a job made increasingly difficult by the instability plaguing the country. Eli had accepted a job in Albuquerque and moved back to New Mexico permanently so he and Angela could be together. Mr. T seemed pleased with the arrangement.

Nancy Levine was appointed Director of the FBI and moved to Washington shortly after Christmas. LizBeth was acting Special Agent in Charge in Albuquerque and had recently been awarded the Congressional Gold Medal for her work during what was being referred to as the "October Crisis." Dawa had returned to work, and Pema was slowly adjusting to being in daycare.

Picuris and Santa Clara Pueblos returned to their quiet way of life on their ancestral lands. At Frank Suazo's funeral, Ray revealed to Ulysses that he and Matt had known about Sarah's work as an FBI informant ever since she informed him that she was the anonymous tipster who alerted the FBI about her husband's raid. Recently, Ulysses heard that Sarah was no longer involved with the FBI or LANL. She was pregnant and expecting a girl in June. Ray and his new wife, Billie, were thrilled at the prospect of another grandchild.

Monica Lovato had not been found. Eli believed she had escaped to Mexico and then to Cuba after the murder of Philip Devin. In January, it was revealed that Philip Devin had been a high-level Russian spy. He was born to embedded spies during the Cold War era and was recruited by the Putin regime in the early 1990s. Some questioned whether Charlotte Foster and Monica Lovato were also Russian agents, but there was no

234 · C. R. KOONS

evidence to support this. Monica's name was added to the FBI's most wanted list.

Ulysses often returned to the moment when he lay on the ground waiting for the bullet that would kill him. He could hear Castleman's footsteps crunching toward him and recall how acceptance overtook terror before Angela saved his life. Ulysses wondered what could have brought him to a peaceful stillness when he was just about to die at the hands of an evil man. He doubted he would ever know the answer to that question, but it filled him with gratitude that such a peace existed inside him.

As the sun descended, it began to grow chilly. Ulysses went inside and lay on the couch by the woodstove, falling peacefully asleep. When Rosemary came home, having picked up Frances from her party, she covered her husband with a quilt and began cooking dinner. Amelia went upstairs to prepare for an evening out with her friends, and Monty arrived home on his bike just at dark. Ulysses awoke when Rosemary called the children to dinner. He lay still for a moment, breathing deeply and grateful to be alive.

THE END

Glossary

Black Hornet Drone—a hand-launched nano-drone which has thermal imaging and photographic capabilities.

Chicoma—or Tschicoma, at 11,561 feet is the highest mountain in the Jemez Mountains. It is sacred to Puebloan people who consider it to be the center of the world. Chicoma means "place of much rock."

Dosimeter—a device which measures the amount of ionizing radiation to which someone wearing or holding the device is exposed.

Gadsden Flag—an historical flag with a yellow background picturing a rattlesnake coiled and ready to strike. It is often carried by militant groups on the right.

Kiva—a round stone underground chamber used by Native Americans, especially the Puebloan tribes, for ceremonial activities and meetings.

Juan de Oñate—a Spanish conquistador (1550 to 1630) who established the colony of New Mexico. He was removed as governor in 1607 for cruelty, especially to Indians, and for dishonesty.

Ohkay Owingeh Pueblo—Formerly San Juan, it is one of the eight northern pueblos of New Mexico. The tribe is believed to have lived on their lands on the Rio Grande River near Española for at least seven hundred years and are believed to have come from the Chaco Canyon area during the time of its dissolution due to drought and internal strife. The language of Ohkay Owingeh is Tewa. Ohkay Owingeh means "Place of the Strong People."

Predator Drone—a medium-sized remotely powered offensive drone.

Plutonium pit—the trigger for a nuclear bomb.

Radioactive Dispersion Device, (RDD)—a device that spreads radioactive material into the air by means of explosives.

Roshi—means "old teacher" in Zen. A Zen master.

Santa Fe Ring—a group of wealthy land speculators, politicians and lawyers who constituted a criminal ring from 1865 to 1912, defrauding and harming primarily New Mexico's Hispanic and indigenous populations.

San Ildefonso Pueblo—One of the eight northern pueblos of New Mexico, San Ildefonso has occupied their current land on the Rio Grande River near Los Alamos since 1300 when they came from the Mesa Verde region during a period of extensive drought. The language of San Ildefonso is Tewa. The pueblo name in Tewa is Po-woh-Geh-Owingeh and means "Place Where the Waters Cut Through."

Santa Clara Pueblo—One of the Eight Northern Pueblos on the Rio Grande River. The ancestors of the Santa Clara pueblo lived on the Puyé Cliffs until drought forced them to their current location near Española around 1400. Their language is Tewa. The Indian name for Santa Clara is Kha p-eo Owingeh which means "Singing Water Village."

SCIF—Sensitive Compartmental Information Facility. It is a secure location where classified information can be discussed.

Taizé—Meditative singing in the Christian tradition.

Tewa—a Tanoan language spoken by some tribes in the Rio Grande Valley.

Tierra Amarilla Courthouse—During a movement to raise awareness in New Mexico about injustices that deprived Hispano people of their land grant rights originally made by the King of Spain and delineated in the Treaty of Guadalupe Hidalgo (1848), militants of the Alianza Federal de Mercedes, led by Reies Lopez Tijerina stormed the Tierra Amarilla courthouse, detained District Attorney Alfonso Sanchez and freed members of the Alianza who were being held before trial. The event brought the issue of land grants to the forefront in New Mexico and increased awareness in the rest of the country of the claims of descendants of original grantees to vast tracts of New Mexico.

Tsankawi—a portion of Bandelier National Monument four miles from the main entrance that features an ancient Puebloan village and cliff dwellings separate from the larger village at Bandelier.

WIPP—Waste Isolation Pilot Program, a deep repository near Carlsbad, New Mexico, built to house radioactive waste including dangerous transuranic waste from numerous sites and the Los Alamos National Laboratory. It is managed by the Department of Energy.

About the Author

C. R. Koons is the author of the Sheriff Ulysses Walker mystery series, three novels set in northern New Mexico where she has lived for twenty-five years. Koons has published a popular work of nonfiction, *The Mindfulness Solution for Intense Emotions,* and a book of poetry, *Bourbon and Branch Water.* She lives on the Embudo River in Dixon, New Mexico with her husband and cat. C.R. Koons is the pen name for Cedar Koons. You can find her blog and her books at cedarkoons.com.

www.ingramcontent.com/pod-product-compliance
Lightning Source LLC
Chambersburg PA
CBHW011513100726
47899CB00010BD/3345